CW00970252

INVISIBLE SOFT RETURN:\

Roberta Degnore

KENMORE
BOOKS

Chicago

2017

Published by Kenmore Books
Edited by Orville Rose
Cover design by Marshall Thornton
Photographic image via 123rf.com
www.robertadegnore.com

ISBN-13: 978-1542324960
ISBN-10: 1542324963

Second Edition

Also by Roberta Degnore

books

Invisible Soft Return:

The Assistance of Vice

The Real Connection (as Rachel Desmond)

Gold Digger!

Stuck Up

screenplays

F*STOP

Do Not Deliver

Burning Women

The Hollywood Fly

ONE

Entering At The Curve, Banking

She made love to her remembering what it was like to be watched by glances that slowly slide away. And when she moved her hands it was not skin that flowed under her fingertips but something more luxurious. There was that gentle and musty smell she remembered from when she would take her in her arms, playful and loving, burying her nose into dense blackness on her neck just behind her front legs where they met her body.

She would say to her, "I love you so much I'm going to squeeze you until your little guts come out." But of course she would never do that.

The aroma of her, the sound of her heart again and the feel of her. It couldn't be. Yet there she was. Black fur, eyes of yellow that are enormous. Alive again. Evet holds something in her arms that is not the woman next to her in bed. An edge moves through her, a great silence after some boundary vibrates past. The other animal she loved and who was dead is there with her in some other world and she is making love to her in a way that is chaste and perfect.

1

"What have you taken?" the woman says.

Evet peels off the magnetic dot from her right eye thinking it was worth it. Custom Sensation Dot programs are better than the Gib/Disney Readymades. She wrings sweat from her hair and sees the thick light falling on her nakedness. It reveals all of her, hides the other woman who is already walking away. Now the noise from somewhere above gets louder. It's like a siren pinging off the windows. And she calculates three floors above and two buildings east something must be happening.

~

She has never been good at accepting reality. Neither am I. Not gracious. That's why I'm so good at designing these EroSims, Erotic Sensation Simulations. I'm good at ignoring boundaries, have to be. So when she found no life in that body there in her living room, Mary Sevenforty was loud with grief as if it were some oldfashion bayonet pushed though her slowly, leaving ragged edges of her. I found out about it. Her dead daughter's body there on the carpeted floor was neater than her grief. I remembered thinking this while I looked out the window away from it all at the soiled blond sun they say used to be brighter.

"Who killed her? Who killed my baby?" she wanted to know.

"It looks like suicide, but we're not certain."

"Never. Not from me."

What did she mean by that? That never would the girl, who had always been mostly mean and self-absorbed, never would she want to get away from her mother? I don't know, or didn't want to know. I looked out of the window there from the thirteenth floor. It was the dead cat next to her who hurt me more, made me unable to answer any questions from the

2

Emergency Patrol. In fact the tears had come to my eyes so freely when the Patrol arrived they thought I was the mother.

It's odd. As if a program I wrote for some SensSim played in me now, I felt the ache of hollowness in my stomach. When the efficient doe-eyed Empathy Patrol got there they embraced me first. They are skilled like ancient samurai or extinct professors whose eyes used to dart above students' heads when they were carefully weighing an answer to a question. Eons ago in these Patrols the sadistic ones and the criminal ones, the old male-ists, were weeded out. It's much better now.

Murder or suicide. It makes a difference although dead is still dead, mostly. Bruce Atman from the cult of Travelers argues on public Holo frequencies against that, but Travelers are never taken seriously and they never get elected because they say it doesn't matter to hold power here in this system of realism. They say it's only constructed by a consensus of consciousness. No need for that kind of popularity, or info-media control power is what Travelers call it. Instead they say they have something else that's better so they disdain sanctioned actions and states of being.

Travelers say they have power but no one believes them. So it matters whether it was murder or suicide because the rest of us, we all think so. Those who don't believe it don't matter to everyone else. And no one can figure out, or stomach, that Travelers seem so content. Like Bruce Atman's easy voice that surrounds the waterfall hologram they use in advertisements where the spray you feel and every sensation and experience is right there in your body. When you buy their Holo you are there, really you are, there. Lounge under the rainforest waterfall with the sweet and pungent fragrance of flowers gone mad with size like nodding Godzillas billowing ever larger with the rush of the spray. It all depends on how

3

many credits you have to spend and the precise transparency of your holographic reproduction.

When you see Travelers on the street they're just like they are in the ads. Always smiling in that benign way and acting like they have a secret, looking superior. They seem non-induced imperturbable, calm without drugs. Or else they're secretly blissed on StimTranqs or LSD23. They seem to be in some other consciousness like they say they are, but because they're always together it seems their reality is only as consensual as the one they disdain that we call Truth.

Murder or suicide is important. She was only nineteen. She was killed, or why did she do it herself? Slit open her neck like that so the flesh curled back from itself, from each side of the artificial gash? The crystal wire blade is on the floor, sticky with blood.

These things happen so rarely I wanted to see it. Any sensation is something I can use when I design simulations. Everyone wants feelings fed right into their neural network to feel pleasures without ever getting dirty. This murder will be on all the frequencies within two minutes. There was a Universal News person running a knuckle prism camera just visible under her skin, recording everything and simultaneously waving everything back to the orbiting newsroom.

Mary Sevenforty's grief was horrible in a kind of shrill moaning. I went over and stroked the cat, stiff, limbs straight out. But its fur is still soft and covers my fingers it's so long. Poor, poor thing. I turned my back on Mary Sevenforty rocking there over her daughter and walked out.

~

The woman had walked for a very long distance. But she herself was not certain. There was dust on the edge of her long dress, dirt on her feet. She was barefoot. On the city streets, the cement and asphalt, she was barefoot and

4

laughing in a strange way. People saw her and others said they had seen her as well, walking in the country before this. All the time in her naked feet, long dress...

~

My bed was wet when I woke up, the input pad I was tapping on still in my hand. But what are these tears for? Really I didn't like the daughter and, after all, she made a choice. But the cat, I will miss the cat.

When I go out I'm still crying for the loss of her warmth, that deep fur I felt, although it was the first time I stroked her. Why am I crying? Because it's like what I designed for the SensSim contract my agent got me. I wrote it for a packager but it hasn't sold to any sector of the various Nets. It's a good thing I'm in New Gargan-York so the sidewalks are quiet. The few people who are out can still writhe with private experience acted out in these public places. None of them notices my tears and I can get emotional help if I want by touching any of the pink shining nerve disks under the Blue Cross symbols at almost any corner. But I don't want to do that.

It's only the waiting. I'm strained with waiting for the Experience Translators to issue the nanochip I programmed, my big break in the diversion business that will lift me out the EroSim cycle.

~

But she's too old for this, she, Evet, thinks. She wipes the tear trails off her cheeks. She stops to look into a store window and dabs at the makeup under the tear tracks with a pocket tazer even though it's impossible for her look to be disturbed once it's etched on like this. And there's something she wants to remember about all this, about herself, but she can't. She feels such a loss for that animal. People make their own choices.

She was taught to respect the other beasts and to get the love from them you can't expect from the human animals who have no time for it these days. When she was a child, Red and Obert, her fathers, took her on many nature outings to the Jersey Wild where they hovered in transparent capsules in the woods to watch the deer, the raccoons. But although they cooed over those natural tableaux her fathers were always anxious to return to the lodges, preened and luxurious in their period safari costumes with matching boots and hats turned up on one side like oldfashion jaunty Aussies.

They would prepare for this for days because after all everyone goes out so rarely. But at the lodges raised on beams high above the forest floor there were always other couples, usually men, with their engineered sons and daughters. Evet remembered the prim joy tightly smiled by each couple or single parent for their artificial offspring. Red and Obert traded stories with the other *faux* parents about gene composition, cell samples that had been cryogenized, and the limits of education implants interacting with DNA cloning. Techno-families, but still trapped by human lust.

They would say, "Our Evet's marvelous, don't you think? But we should have named her Isis for the old myth."

"She's beautiful enough and mostly takes care of herself so that she's no trouble at all. It's mature in an attractive way. And she's smart enough to have fun just outside of the limits, experienced like us. But if we really wanted her to be like Isis we'd have to get her a brother, wouldn't we? You've seen the Holo recreation of the story with Marilyn 100 and Old Blue Thighs? The story about those two, Isis and Osiris? What an interesting couple. Maybe even more than we are."

"What? I never plugged that story," someone would say.

"Isis was gorgeous. Powerful."

"So what was her brother like?"

Her fathers boasted but Evet, their doll dressed and played with, was only perfect in an average way because they wouldn't spend the credits it would take to correct the genetic dispositions that changing trends turned into imperfections. She was now a bit short at two and a half meters, her face was too round without the latest angled lasering-off of skin. Worse, her skin that was the color of sable with amethyst highlights was too light and not as smooth as it could be with new LiquidBlack Grafts.

Still, she has talents in cognitive abilities. She can read, add, and program the Sensation Simulation dots that go on or under the skin, or are swallowed. They engulf the mind with total entertainment. So because she can do those things, and the majority of people are not designed or implanted to know how to even read, Red and Obert decided they didn't need to spend extra credits on the latest skin color changes for her. She could always refine her looks to fit hourly fashions at any time she wants, they thought, and at her own cost from her own earnings.

In those early years at the pretend safari lodges in the Jersey Wild, Red bragged while Obert watched for the look from other fathers' thick lashed eyes that might grow dangerous. Splotches of green would spread under rouge-tattooed, plaxan-molded cheeks in an ugly way. When Obert saw that happening he would quickly pretend to be solicitous and interested in the others fathers' children. But he would hold a delicate hand to his lips to hide the smirk that traced the sculpted lines he had etched on just the year before.

"It's all a game, dear. We love the game," he would say when they were alone afterward.

"Well, Obert, what else is there?"

"Yes."

Evet always asked for credit specks from them to go upstairs in the dome-covered lodge to neuron-in to the Gib/Dis HoloPoint to play in the beginner's level at the VirtReal Wildlife game. She wanted to leave the fathers behind to flirt with the others. They would record enough encounters to replay for a week in their bedroom. Leaving them to it, she went to link into a world of damp, sweet-smelling jungles where she ran after capuchin monkeys, dodged noisy butterflies with their two meter wings and coaxed zebras to eat from her hand. Their velvet nuzzles tickled the insides of her palms and left spit in warm lacey trails up the insides of her arms.

That was the beginning of the feelings. Soft wetness on her palms, it started there. It transported her beyond what might have been her youth, but nothing is limited in replica experiences borrowed as if they are your own. The heavy warmth on top of her, thick hide moving on her. She would spread her legs, sometimes for a female lioness or wildebeest, so gentle and infinitely encompassing. Heaviness of fur and her legs spread wide for the female so that the movement of her hips pushed the other animal's round bulb of sex into hers. It felt like it should be this way to her. At peace in this, one with this deepness and security of purest trust, all this in the game in the HoloArcade.

And what is this, she thinks. Is it a dream or is it a Data Dot repeat? Are all sensations nothing but simulations from stimulation to the neurons in her brain? Is that why every minute particle rearrangement looked, felt and tasted and smelled and sounded real?

~

I can't remember if I fell asleep with the Gib/Disney microtrode in my eye while I was walking. ChipDot reality or a dream, there's no difference. I feel everything. These people talking all around me I'm suddenly aware of, and I feel them. Everyone is so earnest and scented with their emotions so that authentic people approaching manufactured workers on the gargan-City's streets will know what to expect. They know precisely how to react or not to react to each other. The real humans have their features corrected by the surgeons on every corner who are engineers for the latest trends. Most have had hormonal balance adjusted for currently acceptable behavior in lust/desire needs. And some of those I think I see are people right out of research I did a long time ago at the duplication of the ancient paper library in VirtReal. It was the one with the preserved stone lions in front, the guardians from Egypt.

"Like you."

"What?"

I have to pay attention to what's going on here, keep my hands from shaking like this. I'll just watch them, keep my hands folded behind all this plastic burlap.

"Am I supposed to be a nun?"

"Alms..."

TWO

Unsafe Speed In Hairpins

I thought that the brushes with disaster, with being overwhelmed, were only chance. But maybe I'm more fortunate than most women, one out of every three, who was forced to succumb then. Not rare chance but the usual, fortunately escaped from. Fortune? There is dust covering my feet...

~

I like waking up in the New gargan-City without filth and garbage piled a meter high until they came to take it, once every whenever. And then you'd have to smile at the altered people with the masks who piloted the trucks. All they had to do was point the nozzles and liquefy it with those screaming metal claws on the front of their mirrored trucks, but sometimes they didn't. That was before. To learn that I plugged history dots into my eye to form the images on the inside of the corneal implants I wear, everyone wears, that transmit the experience.

When the hell is my SensSim going to sell?

It was called "reading" and "video feeds" eons ago, the oldfashion way they all learned things in the hard times of

10

history. Now, like the Emergency Patrols, everything is un-maled and clean, made more rational. I like New GarganYork. Like the old lady in Dean & DeLuca120 last night at the caffeine inject bar, she spotted me. Like a magnet, but what did I give off to attract them? Nut magnet. It must be because I design experiences. I like nuts around me because they give me ideas for the SensSims. Nut genius, at least they have something interesting.

"Been out twice today. Twice, one day."

"Unreal."

"Isn't it? Maybe they'll put me on the Odd Acts freq like those workers on satellites who had body sex instead of VirtReal for a week. Me, I did something worse."

I have to talk to her because there's no one else here. The stacked shelves of holograph images of the edible products available through the store's connections in the Nets reach to the vaulted ceiling where artificial constellations twinkle in fluorescent pastels.

"Really?"

"Sure. Know what?" she smiles over rows of hinged teeth. Their shape is repeated in the geometric designs on her shaved head. "I got into a Sim, you know? Got up from a recline connection and acted in it. Want a jolt?"

"Which?"

"LightSPEED, auto synapse fit."

"I mean, which Sim were you in?"

"Myths. Took the Son of God part, me, and hung myself from my hands on coat hooks until I could see between real and not. Embarrassing if I didn't have the erase credits to take it off the recording part of the main Nets. Now no one knows unless I tell them what I did, that I did things instead of feeling like you're supposed to. Happens all the time."

11

"Maybe it's a genetic problem," I look past her while I think to myself that this is something I can use for a story: somebody who can't tell real from not.

And when the hell is one of my Sims going to sell on the wide bands instead of only the EroSim Freqs?

"My problem? Genetic? Listen, during the savior Sim I recognize people, real ones from now, and they ask me for blessings and sex and when I give it to them then later on they call me on Augment-Real. You know, from now, and they're much nicer than they've ever been although they never mention anything about what happens between us because I think they don't know," she spit and turned away. "My problem."

Survival of the fittest used to mean reproductive success. I linked that from an oldfashion history chip. Reproductive fitness. Relatives used to help each other to ensure their gene dispersal. It's what they used to call sex, Freud and heterosexual behavior when there were only two genders. I don't remember of course, but it seems like I do because I link so many history chips. Nut geniuses don't have to worry about their gene dispersal and there are no real biological relatives anymore. All you have to do to get who you want to be related to is apply. Fill in the form.

"We know ourselves," I linked on an old book chip, "who we are, by what we do to the world, how it reflects our *selves* back to us."

I suppose that's why male-ists, both men and women, used to tear down the forests, to prove they were stronger or meaner than nature. We touch our face but aren't sure of how we look until we see it in a mirror, seeing it in a frame with other things around us. We affect the world and the world affects us. This used to be classical Environmental Social Science in the last quarter of the 20th Cent. It was the field that said places and how we use them could tell us how powerful we are. But those studies died out because people pretty much stopped going out at all.

There used to be places where women weren't allowed to go, and some where they had to be careful not to go so they wouldn't risk attack like in the public spaces where some men decided only they should have freedom. Then there were also some places where women were forced to be by architectural and social design, like what they called the home, or maybe those church places. But outcasts had no places at all or were shut into buildings whose meaning, by the ugly way they were made, was to show them they were meaningless because those places would never respond to them.

I linked to my HoloSet a lot to talk about this over drinks with dead "colleagues" I never knew. I pretended, and the Holo people acted with me. They were all there like they used to be in an age before, sitting across from me at the bar of the Algonquin Hotel made real and completely artificially interactive in VirtReal space. Rich dark wood, real non-existent leather banquettes, the fizz of the street energy of New York spilling in when the door opened; it was a tasteful reminder of the importance of being there. All those people I learned to listen to who had been Environmental Psychologists at the School Space more than, what, a hundred, three hundred years ago? Those professors were all executed for insisting that Real Estate Developers were criminals. The best of those accusatory big mouths were called radical scholars, but they were "pissing in the wind." That's what one of their Holos told me. They were all electrocuted in smoldering spasms. And it was only after those big mouth-accusing scholars were long extinct that any engagement in development of real estate was changed by definition to "eradication of nature and

13

landscape aesthetic." It was finally made a capital crime. But there wasn't really much land left anyway by then.

I like to be in on those executions replayed on real-time freqs in VirtReal. It keeps my mind off my own program designs. In VirtReal you step into this oldfashion prison that still has metal bars, no positron lock fields, and you walk though dim corridors to the execution room. You smell urine and terrified sweat, the emotions of the condemned that crowd onto the air so you can taste it. All those pale men and women are dragged and shoved screaming into the antique death chamber. Those people, all good family values people they called themselves, were efficient developers. Every now and then I link a chip and walk into the VirtReal to feel it all. During the electrocutions you can smell the flesh burning and your mouth waters at the meatiness of it.

"What are you thinking?"

"Nothing."

My answer to the nut genius: It's not bad if it protects my privacy. But what if it's true? There's a horror that waits just behind it and somehow I know what it is.

Wallow in the gifts of science. Moan with the pleasure of experience. "A dream is a wish your heart makes" is reality sung by a cartoon woman. And you come to think "when you wish upon a star, makes no difference who you are" isn't a lie told by the insect in your palm, or crushed—anything at all you choose. Places are obsolete. It's how life is lived now and I help make the experiences. Everyone stays attached to their HoloSets all day every day and thinks nothing but feels everything, temporarily.

Nothing to think about. Quirks of living don't have to be elevated to high drama. Like my obsession over when my new program is going to sell, it's uncomfortable. But there are kits to fix emotions that show if you're going to be hurt. Easy

14

repairs, cures either organically subatomic or programmed for operation through hardware. Success is only available for the highest strata of credits; everyone else has everything they need in VirtReal. People know from SensSims that only if you strive for something then you might have to use things like humiliation or ingratiation. Otherwise there's no necessity to own those bad feelings.

There's no shame and there's no fear when there's no movement in space and no way of meeting people in spaces that are constantly reconstructed or erased in you own personal programming. You leave no blemishes behind. There is no risk. No problems. You never have to feel disappointment or to rethink anything, but then doesn't that mean we never have to evolve like people used to do? I worry that this is a problem of thinking nothing, isn't it? Maybe. I don't know.

"Alms..."

THREE

Switch Documents

Something is touching just at the edge of her memory but Evet can't remember. Think. It's a process she knows she's done before but it eludes her now. Is she really doing it? Is this it? She sits for a moment in the chair padded with tufts of perfect simulated leather but nothing comes to her. Only desire. She needs to go out.

She has evolved like everyone else to meet the gargan-City's demands and also to meet its offerings. Everything anytime, no boundaries. She will go out, become someone else. The sensation belt is always ready and she's decided she'll use it to encounter sex just like they did before, like in the days when they couldn't do anything else but do it, really, with an actual other person. She can construct that time again. She can link to it by any number of chip or dot or magnetic or infrared connections, walk in it, live in it even though she's never really known it. But she needs the experience, historical sex. There's no other way to gather new practical data from people now, for chrissake, no one knows anything about it. She has to go back if she expects to keep producing those erotic SensSims. In her high-glassed cubicle there is a small cabinet that holds everything. The narrow black Sens belt is studded with hundreds of minute nodes, each a multicomputer and a transmitter. She takes it and, naked, presses it around her waist. Smoothes it onto her so the blackness blends with her skin and the belt becomes a transparent tape that's barely visible. Each node is a pattern of hives, minuscule bumps. It won't be noticed or be a hindrance during any act she decides to perform.

She passes her hands over the main control nodule in the front just below her navel to engage the unit. She can feel the changes start in her, the need to be somewhere doing something recklessly again and again. The commotion moves in her almost instantly. It's a feeling of restlessness. One more touch, a double click, and she changes the mode to: ^masculine\.

The rearrangement begins in her brain in the hypothalamus and changes the nerve impulses and the chemical release from there, the origin of change, and then into the endocrine system. It begins to show in the leaner stretch of her facial muscles, the straightness of her shoulders and their new accentuated musculature. It tightens the pectoral muscles to flatten her breasts, flattens her abdomen, pulls her buttocks tight and higher, smoothes and lifts her thighs, elongates her entire body. It makes every muscle stand out in definition from her perfect skin. The chemical balance has changed so that her estrogen content lowers, overwhelmed by the secretion of male hormones. She notices the different taste in her mouth, how different her own scent is in her nostrils, the change in her attitude and bearing.

The potent feelings are transitory; she's done this many times before. But it's always disconcerting because it reminds her that the male hormone really needed to be regulated by the government, how destructive it was when it was allowed to be freely manufactured in the ignorant and others deficient in conscience and self-control. The hierarchy of stupidity has been changed. She knows it all from history chips. And SexSens belts aren't for everyone. Evet got this one from Kvino from the sumptuous Europ black market. You have to be specially connected to somebody who can access the interNets special freqs to get these units. It's the same as being able to buy the oldfashion drugs that only the very rich or the outcasts can still play with.

"I don't remember anything," she says to the mirrored wall.

She turns away to finish although she doesn't really need to add the other device because her consciousness and that of anyone she performs the act with will feel exactly like she is a male. But she's going to wear it anyway for her own benefit and to complement her outfit, really as a fashion accessory. The appendage is long and ponderous, an artificially skinned male piece, it's already warm from her body. The part of it that's fitted inside of her secures into the adaptor she had implanted and it's fed instantly with her own nerve transmissions and blood supply. The length of it covered with the expensive skin heats and blends into her labia and acts exactly like, no, is precisely the male piece. It will be as responsive as the antique eighteen-year-old male prototype it was designed to emulate.

~

"Am I supposed to be a nun? Should I keep my hands from shaking behind this burlap?"

"No, do it all. Live every part of the occurrence. Take your hands from where they are and caress the face of your lover, long and tonguing strokes of love."

"But I think I'm supposed to be a nun."

"All the more reason."

18

~

I have a hard time accepting death, even if there might be a great deal of Traveler philosophy and real science to argue against its finality. I bemoan loss, can't stand it, maybe that's why I create all these Sims. Reruns mean that nothing dies. But there's something that is pushing at me lately, from the side, like tiny paws. It's a memory I can't quite get a grip on.

So I move around in my cubicle above the gargan-City, walking to activate the muscle exercise dot that keeps me slim and constantly thirty-three years old. I try to remember, something. The xmas tree, so loving for the year's end historic holiday my fathers always bought, is trussed finally into huge white polymer bags from top and bottom. It stands ghostly, the outline of its still-living branches visible there, moving. It tears at my heart. I remember the holiday, or maybe it's yet to come and I have only designed an experience like this for some program. Death is so hard for me to accept, its specter of control's loss, lost to me. Pets, animals of which I was or will be one in some Sim, die and leave my control and I ache from the loss.

No it cannot be, moaned from every age and each throat and each being in which I reside or which resides in me because of my experience. I'm not certain. Death is so final, yet it's so repetitive. I can't accept the loss of control because I love. I love each spider and dog, lover, bear and cat, horse, snake, elephant and shark; I love each and can't stand their leaving, worse, their pain. I would keep them, control them. All I possess in my consciousness I want to possess forever, and I do, I do it with my Sims. But death haunts me. I hate the natural flowering of the trees, the loss of leaves, of flowers' dropped petals and final decay. I can't accept what there is left of nature. The ornament evergreen chopped down and put in my houses I loved and mourned, will mourn, each

19

precious one discarded. Death takes from me. I don't see it as only repetition, or I do see it and keep forgetting? Nobody else thinks these things. Kvino doesn't, Mat/leen didn't. Why am I so different? Where is my love?

~

I began seeking power in earnest and the secrets of life known to the alchemists last year. The fire that will burn me is even now being prepared. I hear the dry, thick branches being heaped one on the other in the courtyard outside my cell. I'm glad that my dear cat has escaped. I pray fervently, wildly, that he has. They would torture us both, at least they have only had me. Look at my fingers, broken. My tongue has been pierced with nails, and there were thick needles pressed through my nipples. Crusted blood now covers shapes of breasts I no longer recognize.

"Oh ignorant men, oh frightened simpletons. Small-cock bullies! Who are you to call yourself human? I shit on you, ignorant torturers. I take control, you can't control me. Who are you anyway? Who dares to persecute me, take my possessions away like that? I know things, I have knowledge that you don't. This is precious, don't you know, you morons? Listen to me! Hear what I can tell you! Listen. Hear me!"

Tak. Tak-tak.

Tak...

"Why won't you listen? Is it justice that my cottage was overturned by strangers, burned to the ground? My things, those few things I loved, even a book, yes in the Latin forbidden to me, you even burned that. It's not fair. There in the exquisite wood, that embracing green quiet, the moss on the bark gentle and soft to my lips, there those droolers tore up all I had. My animals ran away, luckily I released them all. Universe protect them! Listen to me! Is it fair?"

"Come here, Gilbert. I knew it wouldn't be easy to talk to this one. She's so radical, even in her own cult."

"I don't listen to her."

"Of course not. But I feel a strange affinity."

"You, Inquisitor?"

"Why not? I've grown fond of the hearings, the burnings, I truly have. Look at these good sandals I've got. I'm able to walk very comfortably when I don't ride. We're bound together, we two, don't you see? Torturer and unfortunate victim. And yet I do wonder if it's fair."

"Listen to me!"

"I wonder if it's fair that I don't have a wagon of some sort of my own, covered of course. Those who call themselves my superiors don't understand, I could even say they're ignorant of what they should know about my work, the daily trials, of the trials! It's not easy to preside over all these deaths all over the countryside."

"You couldn't stop?"

"What else would I do? I have been apprenticed to no one, as nothing. My family sent me to the Church as a young boy. I can't earn my keep with any skill, don't know how to survive on my own. I have to be a priest. And besides, I learn so much. We humans teach each other, and we're all so different, or seem to be."

"Hear me!"

"It's the knowledge I gain. Those screams, sometimes the pleading, but I learn most from the silences. How I wonder at the silences!"

Tak.

Tak-tak...

~

She was never good at accepting reality. Neither am I. I see images of myself walking down the street. The back of a woman carrying a houndstooth check clear-domed cat-carrier. The black cat, very alert, is inside. Evet strains a little from its weight. It is herself she watches. Me. I was carrying the cat to the veterinarian along the filthy streets; the derelict outcasts who had not yet been captured that day peered inside at the cat as she passed. They were appreciative. She sees herself walking. I see images of myself during a different time on New York streets. Every place I have been, I still am. The Sim-chips plug into the space behind my ears, dots magnetize to my eyes. I walk with my cat. How I love her, feel her here with me, although she's gone now.

There are two men singing along the street, Third Avenue at Fifth Street. The old white man walking the other way passes me and suddenly says, "Where they get that energy?"

"Right? Somewhere," I say back to him. In the gargan-City it is raining and serenely still.

I am everywhere for some reason today. Maybe I've got synaptic gap leakage, that would account for the anomalous neural firings in my brain. Maybe it's from a bad chip contact, I should have it checked. I am part of all of all of them and I can feel their skin like mine. The skin on their arms is mine. I touch it with my fingertips, stroke over its lightness, lighter and rougher than mine. The City is in me, part of me. All this is mine. I must meld the two to remain calm. Reality in my mind, our minds, and being part of all of all of it. But do we want to, do I want to?

Evet doesn't know. She is shaking now, and has stopped walking around in her cubicle, my cubicle, with the view of the City far below the walls of windows. Where is her love? The cat with the luxurious fur is lying somewhere down below in another cubicle and I am alone.

"You should come with me," Kvino says this to me from the HoloTransmitter I've given him the code for.

He is projected in the room, smoking actual drugs and smiling. He has looked exactly the same since the day I first me him at Mars Bar, the club where you can walk through everyone's needs in collective VirtReal nonspace where the bar scene is anything and anyone you want it to be. He is a cropped blonde with dusky features showing permanent even-temper from the drugs constantly dispensed in him, or taken naturally when he can get them.

Sometimes he leads tours in the CySpace DataNets but the people from the Gib/Disney Company, they always end up firing him for his sense of humor, for having one. For the way he teases the awesome neon displays of pure data from the mega-national corporations that arch through dark gleaming nothingness, telling the sightseers it's all techno bluff sleight of hand, slight of mind, too. DaimlerCitroen hired him for a while as a curiosity, to have on display an American who could actually read and who had the skill to navigate CySpace on his own. But Kvino's behavior, the way he likes to float off his tours into forbidden info-banks angers and embarrasses the precise pretend Germans so they fired him too. And the Japanese won't even consider him because he's too irreverent of data, all those zeros and ones. In the old days he would have been killed for his attitude just like others who didn't bow to the power of capital. But then there is no capital after the mid 21st Cent; there is only information.

"I know what happened," he's saying to me. "And I think you better come on before they get you."

"What do you mean?"

"They think you killed them, you killed them for experience. It was on the Police emergency freqs, that data cap about you, just like I said."

But I don't remember.

I tell Kvino that. There was nothing to remember, I have only been here. But why?

If I stand still I will remember. I am a woman who has lost a great love. I can remember. My heart is breaking. My love is dead, died today.

~

"Alms," the woman with the dust on the edge of her long dress says it. "We do not seek alms for ourselves, the *femmes seules*, women alone in the world."

~

"Today they will burn me at the stake for being different. HA! How many excuses, you moron, how many excuses can you think of to murder my kind? Not many, you ignoramus, but then you don't need to because you have your brute power, such power! Cretin! Burn me. There are more of me. I'm everywhere!"

"There you have it, she has confessed to witchcraft, to having unnatural powers.

"You idiot, Gil, don't be so literal. That's not what she meant, but of course I'll use it as her confession. Just please, don't insult me by pretending to believe it."

"You're an odd Inquisitor."

"We all do our jobs, that's all. I don't ask anything more of myself. Do you? I don't think so. Look at you, willing to take the low road, making a condemnation out of a woman's philosophy. But we all have to eat.

"That's a fundamental truth, Inquisitor."

No. A primitive desire for survival, that's all. It's those who can't do anything else, who can't aspire to anything better, who elevate it to a truth. But I'm one of those who can't. For me, survival is my truth. I contribute nothing but my self here doing my job. Sandals and a wagon and good food along with some other bodily pleasures. Don't look shocked, at least I know I'm base but other men who lust for the same things proclaim themselves godly."

"Blasphemy."

"Oh shut up and go make sure that the pyre is burning slowly."

~

"Evet, can you hear me?"

Kvino's voice comes through the HoloSpeaker not quite matching the movement of his mouth. I hear it like it comes from very far away, as if it comes from down on the City streets below.

"—'Dinger?" I say, and I don't remember what it means.

"Evet? It's me not her."

"Schrödinger, my love..."

Man at an early age of his consciousness formulated the belief in a soul, that mysterious second self which even the most debased races believe in. The phenomena of sleep, the return of consciousness after slumber, and the strange experiences of life and adventures in dreamland while asleep would force early man to the conclusion that he possessed a double or second self, and it was merely an extension of that idea which made him suppose that this secondary personality would continue to exist after death.

Spence

FOUR

Specify A Path Name

When I went out that night with my new male body everything came to me. Everything I thought I wanted was there, as simple as a finger's reach to the Sens belt or a thought or an image away. Then night changed to the haze of dawn that I have never seen clearly, I think. A dawn fractured with particles too large to be airborne, but are.

Anyway I had sex with her and remembered what it was like to be watched, not voyeuristically, but in a detached way in slow glances on their way to somewhere else. I remember the feeling. And when I moved my hands I felt a weird sensation. It was not skin that flowed under my fingers but something else soft and luxurious. It felt like fur, a warm and generous animal pulsating, caressing me. No, it was a woman, but my senses translated something different. There was the smell of that other animal, musty warmth I remembered from when I would take her in my arms and bury my nose in her thick coat. (Did I program this?) On her neck, just behind her front legs where they met her body. I held her tightly, filled with awe for this companion creature who was so precious I wanted to squeeze her hard but did not.

There was the aroma of her and sound of her heart. I still felt it when I held my hand over the security scan on the door. Leaned hard on it like I would faint right there, still male and fainted in front of my own cube high above the City. Her particular animal stringency was there with me. Not just the warmth of a living being, but hers. There is the image so real I think I might be plugged in at the VirtReal bar: black fur, eyes of yellow that are enormous. 'Dinger. An edge moved through me like a knife over cold marble. A great silence then a difference, some boundary vibrated past. And I will cry again.

But once the door slid shut behind me with the irreversible sound of magnetic locks aligning I didn't cry. I went to the closet across from the mirrored wall and looked at myself, my male self that was reflected back to me, and I remembered what I've done. From the moment I left the hovercab and dropped into the dark, loud club the feeling of power overtook me, the unisex male-ness. The smoky interior was crowded with really freakish people who actually went out in the City at all, each isolated and mutated by their fantasies, altered by chemical tools and electronic/magnetic add-ons or add-ins. Enormous breasts centered with dusky nipples peaked, alert, and invited watching. Perfectly tight asses, heavy male cocks were cool to the touch or hot, depending on your needs, all of them. These decorated sleek muscled bodies whether male, female or in between or neither, all of it was there for you.

Some were already in the midst of their own worlds and were dancing or contorting in phantom beds in the throes of unreal but accurately experienced sex with blue lasered shadows of their simulated partners who were seen and felt in their manufactured flesh only by the people who imagined them, created them and paid for them. But that was in addition to those who paid to watch those encounters as

27

game Sims. The images could be detected by the rest of us only because of the smoke in the club, the way if made their virtual forms in semi-real threads, outlines of light so that you wouldn't blunder into someone else's fantasy unless there was that green cylinder of empty waiting space that welcomed anyone who wanted to enter their Holo world with them. Some did. Most plugged in because of the Sims, the range of experience available from the bar's main chips and connections. Some of them I designed.

I chose to wait instead for something nearer real, although it's mostly difficult to tell. I didn't want to infra-plug into the club jacks for experience, the belt altered me so that I needed no phantasms. I wanted someone genuine with a past of experiences of her or his own, and my cravings with whoever it was wouldn't extend to having to manufacture any kind of unreality where pain and orgasm gashes and bruises were erased with the breaking of an infraHi-red connection to the main panel. S&M is in artificial splendor lately, a trend because retro is hot again. But some others use the VirtReal to have sex with throngs of people without tiring or to have sex with famous people who are long dead, like the copyrighted images of movie stars like Franco BiDent, old kings like Chuck of England or athletes like M"Tina and Nitron12 from ages before could be glimpsed in blue outlines with some open-pupilled, sweating woman or man lunging over them, or forcing them to submit to humiliations, or licking their lasered genitalia while the blue silhouette of some fantasized little boy with pendulous breasts and a free-swinging male piece flogged them with a barbed leash.

I waited for an actual person in the midst of this. Finally someone who held herself with a kindness, or maybe it was an aura of passivity, stood some distance away on the other side of the oval bar. I attracted her with a look I made real with a

28

dim beam from my mechanical irises that cut through the music and movements of the throng thrashing in its individual realities on the dance floor. I gave her that tangible look and she smiled and then left the edge of the bar. She was waiting for me at the top of the vacuum shaft that led to the private rooms in the sub-levels of VirtReal Nets.

Now I stared at my male self in the mirror while I remembered what it was like. And I finally took off the belt. It made a hushed ripping sound when I pulled it off my skin. A red welt was left in its place, a narrow band of my transformation. And then I had to sit down as the reversal to my genetic hormonal balance began, as my skin rearranged over changed muscles that were allowed to relax now, fatigue crumpling me from the chair to the floor. Maybe I shouldn't have taken the drugs the woman offered. I shouldn't have stuck the gel of stimulant over the one of the coc/meth I had already done over the opium dot. But it felt so good. Now I wish I had an antidote so I wouldn't have to live out the brain-pounding comedown. Of course I don't have to feel that, but it makes everything more oldfashion real to suffer a little that way.

And still something is pushing at my memory like tiny paws prodding for my attention. I remember something happened that wasn't the drugs, wasn't the passion of the performance with the woman. Someone else had been there. I tried not to remember but the tears come fast and I think that I fall unconscious on the floor.

~

"Small cocks, small cocks, small cocks, small cocks...!"

"This one truly has something of the Devil in her, she sings while she burns. My God. While she glows there on those wetted branches she sings. Smolders and sings. What an enviable person she might have been, Gilbert, singing without having to be ablaze like that."

"We should have strangled her first, Inquisitor. The witch will blaspheme until she's a cinder."

"Please don't make me laugh, it wouldn't be polite. Insulting the size of our male things doesn't qualify for sacrilege even in the eyes of the Church, although if given some time I'm certain their Holinesses could make up some law she must be breaking."

"How can you allow her to continue?"

"She's dying, for Christ's sake! But you can go and mount the pyre, Gilbert. Go ahead and strangle her if it bothers you so much, but I wonder why you take her accusation about having a small cock so seriously?"

"That's not it! Look over there, those people are laughing behind their hands at us. It's her, the witch makes them laugh at authority."

"They do dare to laugh, don't they? All right then. Have one of the archers shoot through the witch's throat. Silence her without killing her. Then tell them to arm their bows and turn them on the crowd. But, Gilbert, make sure first that our holy lancers have circled around them from behind. They won't be able to escape the spectacle of power that is us, the Most Holy Church. Let them watch the woman burn, they'll learn to like these slow deaths better in time and they'll learn to laugh at her, not us. Power does that."

~

I remember now. Unknown tears have turned to waking sobs and I moan out loud in my cube. It is the one I loved most in my life who is dead. 'Dinger, my Schrödinger. And suddenly I believe my dreams can be true. Not true necessarily, but real. That's it, real. Is there a difference? I design experiences to play on the SensSims so I question reality, always did, and it gets me into trouble. What I see, feel, do is real. But then I'm not certain because so much is Net-generated, synthetic. Is true, real? Real, true? I know I'd like to deny death although that's probably real so I find myself thinking about what's actual and question it even though no one else seems to. There is a small horror in never being asked if what you used to think was smart.

What's in the world? Everything that's detached and discernable, or is it only what we think we see and that perception is shared by all of us together? But there is a tangible reality, things that are here or there, local, in a place. *Yes?* Or is it only that thinking about reality is what makes it real?

That's what the Travelers say in their ads late at night on the Public Net freqs and I suppose I've thought that if something is common to two people then it lives for them both. I see it on the public-wave entertainment programs that interview people about their experiences in VirtReal. Dates they go on there, sex that they have, vacations to Saturn's dust, climbing K2, Everest...it's all real to them no matter what, no matter if it isn't. They cry, they fight, they talk about how they accessorized their outfits and they recall it all like they had done more than sit with chips or dots adhered to their frontal and temporal lobes, or coupled into receptacles behind their ears, or having the designed data transfused into them by infraHI-red. That's why I don't want to think about what happened, don't want to talk about it. Not even with Kvino. Have I designed this? It's possible there could be two groups of people who believe different things: like painful and pleasurable stimuli being reversed. There would be bruises that are mounds of sweet tenderness, or maybe something like the principle of gravity wouldn't be believed and therefore not felt and so those people float through the thick air. They can. Float in this stuff we have to breathe in again.

Dreams or my designs could be ways to counteract all this fragmentedness. What are the ways to deal with this jagged loneliness from each other and from, I don't know, everything in the universe? So I think maybe my dreams are real. Maybe I make them real in programs. Did I dream that my little girl, the one I loved most in my life, had to go to another place yesterday? She is far from me but near, somewhere. She's part of those near lives not seen, essences felt. Are they simulated images? Near and unreachable so that this feeling rips me from the inside of my heart.

Two beings, female, the same and at the same time different. The same at different times, and different beings at the same time. I know this is not chaos, but the evidence of order in strange attractions. It's simple old 20th Cent science. On the border of chaos there is a breaking free, not a breaking down. From the chaos of death emerges an order, an order that comes from these strange attractions, this strange attraction I feel in my life for that other animal. It is my life, but it is a death. And I have these peculiar thoughts, reveries that I write down, transcribe.

~

The other one said "no." I heard it in my head while I brushed at the dust on my feet. The other being said, "no not that, feel better about it, about my death." And I thought how could I? How could I feel better about missing her so much? Because she is not gone. The other one, my love, is still with me.

A mate. A mate in mind. A mate for all time, chosen and accepted. She chose me, I accepted her. We are each alike. I am she, and she's me. A mate that isn't me but part

of me, the same. Breathtaking. A magnificent girl,
sumptuous girl.

~

Evet is sobbing and it's too strenuous, too raw, too loud. I have trouble accepting the natural order. Perhaps because it isn't natural, there's something else. I have looked every day for the rebirth, the new being who is my lost love. I'll write a program for the return of my soul mate, of part of me. My 'Dinger.

By the third day I feel, though, that the glorious little soul has moved on and is feeling better. Soul? I want that to be true but I still miss her terribly with an intensity I now feel will always leave me hollow. But what kind of history is this that pollutes me? Soul? Afterlives and treacherous Churches murdered for power, not even for the experience of it. Murder for end product not even for an interest in the process, that's what really showed it was the age of ignorance.

"But she had a good life," Kvino said. "She was good, she was an excellent little being."

Yes she was a sublime being. But he couldn't tell me if the choice I made for her was correct. What was right anyway? He wouldn't tell me. To him it was a joke, to be right meant standards existed and that was always a joke to him. But our life is nothing but standards and rules, isn't it?

How I miss her! Child of mine, little being to protect. Oh my heart, my heart is gone. I can't stop crying for her.

How I miss her. But she's gone on to good things, yes good, Evet has to try to believe it. I know it's good. The black feather I found is a sign from her that she soars, she soars. I saw her doing somersaults in the air right after she died. Right after I had her murdered, I think. I can't hold her back. The Travelers say in advertisements I've read on vacuum tube lasered walls that you hold a dead person back from being reborn if you mourn them too much. You can't hold onto them because you keep them, selfishly, in a place from which they can't evolve. They float, hearing your grief, feeling your loss. I can't hold her back. The flasher ads say they hurt, feeling your grief, your anguish, seven times more potently than you do. In case they're even partway right I've got to believe she is good this way, like this. I don't want her to be afraid.

Be strong, my girl. Courage! You're strong, you will win.

"I don't know if what you did was right or what," Kvino says. "But why did you do it? Why kill her? You loved her."

"I didn't kill her."

"It's an experience crime. They have agencies for that. They'll tell you she had to be evaluated, if you thought something needed to change. There would have been a hearing and then they could've probably fixed her, figured out a story line with DNA. You know they don't want this kind of violence to get around, not real violence that people can try to commit outside of games. What if you waved over what's in you one night at some club, spread it through the system and the realness came through? They don't want that to get stuck in data banks that someone else can link into later on. You write programs, Evet, you can't live them."

I stare at him because he's acting like he hasn't heard me deny the murder. I look straight into his eyes. The soft brown spots, nearly pupil-less, smile back from behind the curved lenses lasered onto them. His plain handsomeness unlined by worry or bad thoughts show what his oldfashion drugs gave him. He took my hand in his, smooth and firm-skinned without a trace of his eighty or thirty or who knows how many years alive. He took my hand and he held it over the zippered jacket at his heart. Intimate friendship, a touch of transference: *I am alive with and understand the things of living in this bedlam of*

34

information and science where we all hunger for touch. Touch and warmth. That's why animals are so crucial, vital for us. The give us primal warmth we so easily forget, or never even know about.

Kvino's primitive intimacy, my hand taken to his heart, its beating felt beyond the synthetic leather jacket with its electrodes and infrared outlets and magno-sealed compartments. That was why my crime is the most heinous: animals are strictly protected. No animals are eaten, used, or abused because their utility alive is far greater than any of their oldfashion misuses were. They teach, they're not commodities. Warmth and love. Primal tenderness unmanufactured in the infoNets, the CySpace of glowing data matrices. The human animal suffers from the artificiality in this world; the other animals are our salvation.

"They'll probably want to re-matrix your limbic system for what you've done," he says. "Maybe not let you write programs for a while. Want to smoke?"

"I didn't do anything. But there should be punishment for her, Mary Sevenforty's daughter."

"I forgot that. Damn it, why did you do that, kill her too?"

Nothing is worth it anymore, I think to myself but don't say it to him. And I think to myself that I would kill that woman in an instant if I had the opportunity now, and if she weren't already dead. I don't know why.

I say instead, "I don't care about Sevenforty's daughter, but I'd rather die than live without her, my love. She slept in my arms every night for decades, ages or something, Kvino. My littlest one, the smell of her and how sweet it was will never leave me. I caress it, breathe it into me. There's nothing else to live for without her. I want to die."

"Smoke some dope with me," he looks worried as much as he can through his permanently pleasant features. "Don't

35

think that way, just tell me you're ready to leave. I can hide you in a databank in CySpace where they won't look, not for a while."

"I want to die, to be with her because there's nothing left here for me."

"You're just bored."

"That too."

"Listen to me." He adjusted a panel on his wrist to make his voice sound serious. "She was a cat, a pet, not anything else. And she's dead, programmed out. You know we outlive them usually, that's just the way it is from the input data, it's one of the natural progressions they left in. We outlive them, if we want."

"I don't want to do that. And you know I didn't expect that, can't accept it. I thought she would be with me forever, there was the gene-splicing, we wrote that into the script a long time ago. It's not fair."

This wasn't supposed to happen. I wasn't supposed to lose my best friend to death last year either. And I thought that she would be with me forever too.

He sees that Evet is genuinely surprised like she really didn't think that something could go wrong and the Nets would recognize her proposed program and she would outlive the cat. Maybe she had only designed a fantasy, a draft, and *wham* suddenly they put it online. He sees the small creases in her forehead that lighten her skin to its original whiteness where they appear. Her eyes have closed from their inside implanted irises, nothing but black-shut swirls, pupils like a stereo camera's lenses. She sees only in negative now, black on white while she concentrates to examine the emotion that has surprised her. Kvino takes the replicated cigarette from her fingers and pulls a long drag on it. His thin legs prop against the table and he motions for a Waitron Unit to bring two more fake alcohol drinks.

There aren't many others in this café in the historic section of the City. Only the Marginals come to these places because they are so outdated, them and the places. No VirtReal jacks or infrared connectors, nothing with magnetic control, no HoloSets, no Sim Chip vendors. There are drugs but they are the oldfashion ones, the ones you have to smoke or swallow or inject instead of the new ones that are microdots you press on your skin for chromosome-adjusted time releases.

"I don't want to go on," I say when my eye locks swivel open.

"Come on, I'll hide you until we can get some kind of defense. It was only for experience, right? For practice that you wrote the program that killed her. It's a good motive. Besides you know, for yourself, you've got recorded data on her. She can live in VirtReal with you forever. You can plug it anytime. 'Dinger will be around like before and you won't even notice the difference."

"There's something else," I grab his tight jacket with my hands and surprise us both. "I need to be with her, what's really her, I want to go to her, be with her right now. You see this feather? I found it, it's just like her and it's a sign that she's alive and off to somewhere, I've got to go to her."

His face is incapable of expressing fear but he takes my hands in his. I twist away the one that holds the small black feather and I carefully replace the oddly natural thing in the inside laminated jacket pocket over my heart from where I took it.

He tries to tell her that she sounds crazy without alarming her, but he has to say it.

"You sound crazy."

Dead is dead, so far. Kvino doesn't believe in anything else and he never thought that she did either. Evet, out for a good time with him so many times, looking for girls or men together, taking the oldfashion drugs, she wasn't a bliss-eyed Traveler searching for some asinine simultaneous reality. Not her, it would be too stale, too stupid. Kvino looked around to see if anyone might be listening. The two of them were too advanced to risk being labeled with any Traveler irrationalities someone might mistake.

"I'll take you a D-bank to hide you out," he says. "You've got to get a grip. Don't cry. Can you cry? Anyway, don't do it here."

"It's something else, I can feel it. She was more than that, more than what you said."

"Cat, Evet, she was a cat. She was a cat that you killed."

"No."

He took her by the arm as strongly as his DNA settings allowed and tried to pull her to her feet but he couldn't move her. It was only when she saw others start to notice her that she knew she had to leave. She followed him to his scuffed magnoVehicle and they took off slowly. He looked around to make sure they weren't being followed. He thought about making a run through to CySpace's silent whirls and vibrant data arches to hide her in safety but he needed help before her could break the latest Gibs code locks. He needed to take some precautions because they might put him in data-jail for helping her get away, at least until her fathers could buy out a punishment for her. He knew he had to contact them now, unless their credits had already been program restricted by the courts.

FIVE

**These Supple Variations
And Contradictions So
Manifest In Us Have Given
Occasion To Some To
Believe That Man Has Two
Souls**...
Montaigne

"Alms. Alms for the grace of God."

"Stop saying that. You can't say that. You know we don't believe it."

"Alms—"

"Shut up and listen."

Tak. Tak-tak-tak. Tak.

"Should we go there?"

~

Evet touches the smooth plastic that isn't cool or warm. She hears the voices around her and waits for them to finish whatever it is they're saying about her. The image holograms change colors and shapes with her fathers' excited words streaming toward Kvino who reclines next to her in the magnoV seat. The drab wall beyond the transparent cover of the car is what I'm staring at while they decide my fate, how to hide me. The building's polymers' absolute uniformity outside the car absorbs me and I think that it's exactly like my life has been, or like living is here in this ultra-even world. Like dear Kvino with his constancy, his balanced genetic composition that is sustained and probably even enhanced by the mellowing drugs he lives on. There's no one I trust more, not now that my heart is gone, my dear littlest one.

But the sudden sound of her hands slapping hard against the plastic of the car makes Kvino sit up straight. He sees that she's upset but he can't know what she has just said to herself in such a peculiar voice in her mind.

"Why does she feel like my daughter?"

"Who?"

"Kvino, she was my daughter."

"You were close to her that's all," he pats me awkwardly at the base of my neck.

He puts his other hand over a transmitting node so that Red's anxiety barks facelessly in colorful waves around them. Both he and Obert demand to know what's happening. They want to know if the authorities have seized me, their daughter, am I all right?

I'm crying again and I push away his hand. The smooth fake wall outside, beige and indistinct, calls to me with its repulsive nothingness, gruesome flatness of the newest construction. The feel of soft fur, of a beating heart and that sweet aroma overwhelms me. *Daughter.* And I believe all at once that I must be insane, that I must be ignorant of true reality, any reality, to feel this. The pain racks me. Like a madwoman known only from images I've linked into in Sims, I begin to slam my head into the dome of the hovering vehicle. I am wailing, sobbing and pulling at my hair and face. Certainly I'm mad, no one acts this way. And I see that Kvino has leapt from his seat and barely catches himself on the support step just in time before he plummets to the floor of the subterranean garage twenty stories below where we've been silently suspended at the 'H' level span. I must get away. But I feel heavy. My head lolls against the gouged seat back as if I'm going to sleep.

"Hey! We've got to get you out of here. They're coming for you," Kvino says from very far away.

~

"That one is finally silenced, Inquisitor."

"Have the soldiers scatter the bones."

"They'll be dispersed with the larger logs and such that did not burn completely. We'll take care of it."

"I said, Gilbert, have the soldiers take the bones especially, take them and scatter them throughout the countryside, however far they can take them. See there? Over there near the cathedral are a group of merchants gathering to leave for the low country, send some of the bones with them. And over there's a group of clergy going back to Rome by way of the sea, send some of her bones with them too. I'll take some myself to leave for carrion and to rot."

~

I think of how they used to joke with me and call me their little Isis, my two fathers exaggerating in front of their friends. They always have a lot of friends, men who are quick with their wit and bitter tongued. They flocked to parties at our home where there was always fresh fruit and real bread, never anything that had gone beyond a fifty year limit that was packaged and irradiated and cryogenized for a storage life of more than two hundred years if it was necessary. It was a good upbringing, dispassionate but filled with commodities because of Red's position teaching the gifted children how to count, add, multiply, and Obert's data sorting position that

41

had been bought for him by his genetic distributing group long before.

"Mat/leen, you should take this chip, I don't want it anymore," I remember telling my best friend.

We spent hours in my apartment in my fathers' house where we had access to plugging into VirtReal, using chips in the HoloSets to play in total environments, use Feel Phones, have food flecks, everything in a smooth whiteness that was broken only by looking out the window to see the untouchable trees and grass outside, some of them real, some projected to make a disorder of the most orderly nature so unlike the crisp edges of the placid polymers that was our real world, inside.

"I can't," Mat/leen would say. "You know my Parent Units won't let me have real history that isn't on factory SensSims. But you can tell me about them, you know I like that better anyway."

"What's the difference? If you know the stories you know the stories, why does it matter how you learned them?"

"If I hear them from you I'm not breaking any laws and I won't be lying to my PUs. They won't scan me and find out I've been lying when they ask me if I've been good and stayed in VirtReal and all that, and out of the streets. Besides, you tell the stories differently."

S/he always smiled when we were together, a sign of gentleness that was not only the artifact of genetic design of some program, it was real. S/he was at ease with it, lounged with it while she smoked the imitation cigarettes I bought for him from oldfashion vendors across the river in the City and far downtown.

"But you break all their rules," I would tell her. "You smoke more than anyone, and you always do it without an ion converter so you're really an environment criminal, too."

"I know. But at least I don't have to lie."

We matured together and grew lonelier. Mat/leen concealed something in her/his heart while I kept pace with the acrid gossip of my fathers, acting the daughter instead of feeling the bond. The daughter they wanted to call Isis really didn't love. I learned to value other things, friends, the few who could still converse like Kvino and who lived outside of VirtReal for more than a few moments a day. Those few still create things and are so different from everyone else, odd but respected too. My fathers, unlike Mat/leen's mixed gender Parent Units, encouraged me to learn from the illicit real world instead of living in the sanitized representations in VirtReal and the not much better HipperSpace.

When I went to school every morning we'd login from home and get hooked by infra/magno from our cranial implants to the mainframe. It's the same now, maybe faster. Attention locks you in and you sit in motionless rows of translucent virtual bubbles and stare: seeing, feeling, hearing, smelling, tasting the world projected onto lasered corneas and transmitted through the nervous system. All of it is under the control of the teacher who sits at a finger-sized main deck somewhere and customizes each child's learning to each one's designed interests, ability, body chemistry settings, genetics and menu choices made by their parents.

Reading has long been oldfashion. Understanding is instantaneous in graphic representations, or neural stimulation and re-arrangement directly. Very few bother to continue to advanced learning where knowledge of reading and writing in alphanumeric instead of iconic symbols is required. Programmers and designers of information and info-graphics and teachers are a minute percentage of the population, the rest are Mechanical Slotters, the people who still fill the manual tasks and watch the robots build and then go buy the VirtReal systems, the fingernail computer terminals, the nanodot sub-chips...all the simulators of every experience anyone could ever think to experience. It's real guile, this virtual boosted-up reality that's the world of fabulous encounters in the solitude of your own home and head. I ought to know because I'm one of those who make it, not at all as successful as I'd like to be but I keep trying. I keep getting passed over for mega status although I try. Nothing happens. Nothing happens although I can change thoughts into experience better than a lot of the other designers who are already famous. Transmutation? I can do it, virtually.

I want to find the intersection of spaces that have been forgotten, designed out from memory by a world of information displays that are surrogates for genuine encounters. The intersection of social spaces, the physical space where people actually did things to give places significance have no meaning anymore except to a few people who still move around in the corporeal environment instead of staying rooted, plugged into a world made real on those lasered neural implants everyone acquires at birth.

Space moves around us. We don't move through it. Worlds are created in VirtReal or you can link into the shared hyperspace of entertainment networks. Athletic competitions become contests you really feel and play in. You take the ball and run, feel winded from the exertion and feel the pain of being caught, slammed from behind by colossal enemies from the other team who would have broken your bones if the reality had been anything but counterfeit. Competition linkers sit in their cubicles staring at nothing apparent but they see behind their shuttered irises full playing fields, smell the sweat of four hundred pound opponents, hear the screaming of two hundred thousand fans in their ears and feel their muscles strain with the play, the trying, the total sensations. You can see them in their niches, straining and writhing just a bit, their legs in controlled spasms from the modulated firing of impulses from their midbrain reticular formations. Overt movement is controlled as they run on the perfectly lush green playing field that stretches before them in their minds.

"You're a snob in the sea of techno-equality," Mat/leen would say to me.

"A pebble on some beach where cyber-waves of wasted time wear away at me until I'm gone, you mean? I think you're right, and poetic, which means you're subversive too. But why should I spend the rest of my life like them, never leaving my cube and living through fake life, even if it's fun? Besides, genetically I'm a designer, I create new SensSims, remember? So legally I've got to be given access to real knowledge."

"Go ahead, keep doing it. You can do whatever you want, everyone does, artificially, and that's the good part. Why are you so gloomy about it?"

"How can you not be? Look at you, you've got to come here to hide the drawings you make because genetically you're a dot-chip acid painter, you have to hide the pens I got for you because nobody uses those kinds of things. You draw at night and hide your drawings here, and all day you use the same crystal wire as everyone else in your unit to paint insulators on micro-nanos."

"At least I don't get punished by the Squads like you do for unnatural behavior," s/he would tell me. "You don't hide that you know people who are outcasts, Marginals, for gods sake. I hide, and it's easier. So?"

"So that's no way to live."

Sooner or later we would end our pretend argument that was fun and go on to something else. That was before. It's only a memory now. But I think I believe that my dreams may be real. I think, or try to remember, something else. There's

45

something that pushes at my memory, soft paws pressing against me very gently. There is a dream I can't quite remember but I feel it, that there's something I ought to remember. It's difficult to recall many things though with all the cerebral re-sectioning they've done on me. Still I can't shake the feeling that there's something I want to know.

Mat/leen likes to tell me that I wasn't compassionate because I felt superior to them, and that's why they punished me, for not enjoying the baser experiences of VirtReal as opposed to my own self-evaluated loftier trips into a virtual nature or into virtual classics of literature from ancient history, and because I used simulated entertainments that test data in adventurous competitive survival games. We were friends despite what I called Mat/leen's existential cowardice, living through me was satisfying for her without the risk and he always admitted it. Her steadfastness gave me a feeling of security that allowed me to look for people who can create, who have experience off the data hubs and without stimulation through our universally implanted irises, and I would tell her about it later. Sometimes s/he would venture with me into the gargan-City across the river searching for haunts of the Marginals with me to buy oldfashion drugs and smoke the replicated cigarettes she loved so much.

I remember Mat/leen against a color-peeling wall, sitting quietly in a chair, staring in his benign way at people with a drink in hand and smoking, always smoking. This is how I will always see her, as unobtrusive as some fabricated old aunt, as watchful as a spy, and smoking, always, and smiling at me.

Now s/he is dead, and there's something I'm trying to remember. Is it how she died? Or when? Why s/he died is something I can't begin to ask, s/he was simply too young, I think. Still I dream of her with little remorse because s/he seemed to want it even though death was too severe for him.

46

S/he had become bio-chemically imbalanced and knew it. Her wrist implant panel must have warned her but s/he waited until fixing was impossible. That took courage. I think of her and wish I had told her s/he wasn't like a timid aunt caricature from stories, but that she was as ardent as an outlaw. And what? And as kind as, I don't know what.

But death took her. Death takes from me. I can't see it as only a repetition of necessity, or I have seen it was that and have forgotten. I think my experience of my own consciousness is so unique that I believe each time I become aware of it that it's all under my control. And it is, it was under my control all those times that came before and after and that I've linked into to see and feel. But then who is doing this watching when I am watching me? I feel I'm everywhere, like death. What I live is the entire world. But I mourn the control death has even though it's only reruns, not finality—it's my control. Am I god? Why do I think this?

Where is the pelting, relentless current of time entered, where does she enter it? Where will it enter time, this thing, this creature who burdens itself with consciousness and with love? Who is it who is doing the watching when she is watching herself, when she is watching my *self*?

I believe my dreams can be true. Real. I question reality, always did. From the 1960s I linked a history chip that some of them would try to question authority, but I question reality. What I see, feel, do is the only realness. Maybe.

She is God, Evet is. But she's not certain.

And I'd like to deny death by changing it with my stories.

At an early period in their history the Egyptians had attained considerable skill in the working of metals, and according to certain Greek writers they employed quicksilver in the separation of gold and silver from the

47

native ore. The detritus which resulted from these processes formed a black powder, which was supposed to contain within itself the individualities of the various metals which had contributed to its composition. In some manner this powder was identified with the body which the god Osiris was known to possess in the underworld, and to both were attributed magical qualities, and both were thought to be sources of light and power."

Spence

SIX

Delete To End Of File

"So another one of them has been taught that only God or his agents can make something out of nothing. Knowledge is divine, that's why it has to be controlled. If knowledge were not controlled then divinity would have no meaning, and even worse than that, would have no power. That's why this one and so may others of them had to be taught our hierarchy. And as methods go, burning is a good one. It teaches the lesson with effectiveness, Gil, remember that. Very few of them attempt to take back any of the power they had once, not after seeing a few years of these incinerations."

"But these women only dabble in healing and they never had the secrets of alchemy, did they, Inquisitor?"

"Of course some of them did, just like some of ours. Do you really believe history started with us, with the one we say was hung up on a cross? Why do you think we persecute so vastly with all the trouble it is, really? It's to cleanse, to scrub away any strength from those other than ourselves now that we have seized power. Of course those woman had power once, before us, that's why we see its vestiges in some of them, and we have to terrorize them into never practicing it again. Haven't you been watching?"

"Yes I know about the healings and their communing with nature and all that, but the secrets of alchemy...isn't that worse than blasphemy?"

"Idiot, it's the greatest power. Something out of nothing, can you imagine being able to create, really create gold from dirt, lead, whatever? Think of it! At least try to think at all. Now let go of my horse, boy, let my wagon pass. You have no idea how you annoy me sometimes."

~

Through the nightmares and the images I can't control I feel another place and some other presence when the primeval dream ends. There is a tall Police Agent, radiant in a magenta skin coating that is the uniform of her profession. From a wide silver belt colored nano-lasers blink through a series of infinitesimal toggles, controls that link her to the omnipresent databases with links to every ultra max security sector, even back to archaic Gibs CySpace. She smiles tenderly from an elegantly broad Asian fashion face and now and then touches the ergonomically curved tazer spokes that come from black weapon wristlets and extend to her fingertips. Motionless, she almost looks demure in her gleaming weaponry. The smudged blue of the sky outlines her from behind as she stands in front of the transparent side of the building and looks into the center of the room. Her hands are very white, sculpted, and her fingers look like they are sensitive and artistic. She is fulsome in her splendor crested with thick black hair, stunning. I find it difficult to be afraid of her although I know I should be.

"I'm Bear B.," she says in a sweet voice. "You know you've told me everything."

"Do your friends call you Bear?"

She laughs as if it's natural and her blackened eyes seem to brighten. Her squared posture relaxes and she laughs with enough length to be genuine. I find that I'm watching everything about her, searching for falseness, the difference in something about her that will allow me to see she's not really a genetic woman but a male transformed with a SexSens belt, probably more advanced than the one I own.

"Everyone calls me Bear B., no heritability numbers. Not like Mary Sevenforty or her daughter."

Her eyes have caught mine while she's still smiling and she traps me. But the damning knowledge she shows about me could not hold me like this; it's her smile that does it. Or else it's her intelligence or her scent that does it. Maybe it's just the uniform.

I'm still thirsty from running. The running wasn't physical of course, it's only the psychological component of the expression of my fear, as if I would have run if I were able and if the hiding were truly physical instead of complexly neurological, being wrenched from my hiding place in CySpace like that. Kvino made all the arrangements, transported me with my fathers' credits that are now confiscated, encrypted by the infoNet. But how do I know this? Their little girl, caught and held in the high towers of the Police, a murderer. I committed the crime. I've taken a life, or lives, with my mind but I don't care. And this makes me feel defensive because I know I'm supposed to care very deeply.

But I don't think I committed this particular wrong. After all, I'm no Marginal who has to do things physically. I'm not one of those illegal immigrants who come from the empty tropics seeking asylum and food here in this, hardly the best sector, but solidly mediocre and not broiling to death like ninety percent of the earth is. There's not nearly the standard of living here that there is in Asia or in Europe but it's still

51

better than the famine-beset, dustbowl southern places from where millions flee. No one expects morality from those people. They breed and spread new diseases that lockup imaging computer models in repeated simulations before antidotes are manufactured. So many die because of these immigrants that they are collected on sight into huge magnoCrafts. After that, few of us know or care what happens to them. They're supposed to be deported to their own scorching hot countries but HoloComics make jokes on the diversion freqs that they are terminated and the byproducts of that process are used in various chemical preparations.

It's these outcasts who regularly engage in violence, knowing that their fate, no matter what, is appalling. But I'm not one of them, I'm from the mid-elite and so I have no excuse for what I've done to Mary Sevenforty's daughter. But what have I done to her?

"You told me everything and I'm still not sure you've told me everything." Bear B. walks toward where I sit in a straight chair. "It's atypical, but there's experience in you, thoughts, really, that I think are still unexposed. Thought and experience are our world, information. It's all we have to we share together, that's the law, information. You're hiding them, aren't you? Even through the drugs and realignment we gave you."

"I haven't told you any lies."

"That's been impossible since we implanted that parietal lobe dot for your last crime. But there's something else. Your thoughts are unreal. Your thoughts don't reflect the world, not any world of VirtReal games or HoloSet mass entertainment Sims."

"Ontogeny recapitulates phylogeny," I blurt out.

Bear B.'s black eyes spin open and surprise her with their surprised reaction to me. I feel proud that I've done it and I'm puffed up with my own conceit. I'm showing off for her, trying to amaze her beyond her own estimable competence and fashionable weaponry, and I can hardly believe I've succeeded. It makes the adolescent bravado that overtakes me swell to unmanageable proportions. Although I know all of this, all these emotions transcribed to electro-chemical outputs and valences of my thoughts and even the thoughts themselves are being recorded through sensors I feel subtly humming around me, I want to impress her anyway. I want her to like me, this Police Agent who is armed with horrifying accessories of pain and with mind and body altering nanobeams and lasers at her fingertips. Why do I fall asleep with her here? I have no control.

~

"Am I supposed to be doing this? Maybe I should hide my hands behind this, what it this, burlap?"

"Hide your hands underneath this piece that hangs from your neck in front of you."

"Why, what am I supposed to be? Some kind of nun?"

"Just do what you want, touch your lover's face with tonguing strokes."

"But if I'm a nun I can't do that."

"Of course you can, there is no hierarchy. Take your hand from behind the cloth, away from the beads that are imitation security and won't hide the marks of what you've done and stroke the face you love. There are no straight lines."

~

"Too much history," Bear B. says softly. "You've probably linked too much history. Your thoughts, those thoughts are outside of the Agreed Reality."

"You mean they're not real?"

"Your thoughts don't come from anything we can trace in dataSpaces. It's highly atypical. We can't trace back from where you're constructing these images you have and it's causing you to perform unacceptable acts, like murder. Why does a woman, you, who virtreals normal acceptable sexual commingling with women, men and other animals also have images of unreal, disgusting things in her image banks?"

An accusation I can't answer. She scares me and I want to escape. Then I think that I do escape, but maybe I only dream it.

SEVEN

We Read In Xenophon A Law Forbidding Any One Who Was Master Of A Horse To Travel On Foot.
Montaigne

Tak. Tak, tak, tak-tak.
"Alms, for the sake of—"
"Shut up, you know we can't ask for alms."
"Sometimes I forget."
Tak-tak. Tak.
"Hear it? We have to find who makes that sound."
"Do you think it's the right one?"
"How should I know? We've got to see if it really comes from one of us. We've gone this far to find someone who's capable of the job, don't you see?"
"But we can't be sure it's the one we're looking for."
"That's why we have to find who's making the sound, idiot. And brush that dust off your cape!"

~

I'm groggy but I know there are undetectable prism cameras focused on me. There have been surveillance nanobeams on each of my joints to monitor my movements since they found me in that neon cave of data in CySpace. It was only a few hours ago I think, although sometimes it changes and it feels more like a month. I'm beginning to think maybe my dreams can be real so it might be a month, a year, or another epoch for all I know. Do I know? Somehow I seem to have been forced into the idea that there's no center of me or any margins that separate me from the so-called world. It seems there's no hierarchies and therefore no linearity of existence, top to bottom, end to end. I've awakened from what I imagine was an induced coma to feeling, as if it's always been the way I feared in a vast web, that there are only nodes and linkages and networks. There is no center to me, and there is no hierarchy in space or in time.

What?

It means I'm here with this woman but I feel I'm doing other things in other places now, right now, but it's really different times. So I've got to be insane just like Kvino thinks. They have punished me so often for being, what was it Bear B. said? –different, that's it. They've punished me too often for being different.

You're not like the rest of the girls, the nun who is six feet and two inches tall says this to me, her white habit swirling in a tornado of hatred that swathes her.

What do you mean? What did I do?

You know. You're different.

No I'm not. Please believe me. Don't make me go, I don't want to be different. Just tell me what it is and I'll change. I'll be like everybody else, just tell me how to do it.

The other girls are in their blue serge uniforms and they look at me. Silent veiled eyes and emotions. Silent. Glances hum at the sides of eyes.

Who is this person, this I who experiences this humiliation? The shame that is a force pressing in on me makes me small, shoulders hunch inward, head bows. Bow my head. But why? Who am I to feel this? I must be designing this. I've never been in this cleaning-solution-smelling corridor before, the corridor with the shadows of statues with uplifted hands, bowed heads.

I wake up feeling I must be mad. Now I'm truly terrified of this woman, the beautiful Bear B.

"You will tell me the rest, all of it," she says.

"Like what?"

The humming sound in the room gets louder and the light changes. No longer indistinct ruined clouds beyond transparent buildings, it's a new room that forms and blocks out the clouds, replaces them. An image of a new place.

Hot, bright sun beats down on Evet who is now standing, walking. Clear light undistorted by colloidal particles reveals desert mounds, palm trees. In the distance there is a grove of scraggly fig trees. She shields her eyes from the bright light. The smell of human sweat and body odor unmasked by cosmetic hormonal engineering assails her to near vomiting. A Holo of an oldfashion Middle Eastern state is what this is. She sees three large timber crosses up on a rise to her right. A crowd of people, mostly women, is applauding and laughing at something going on near a multicolored open packing trunk but she can't see because their backs are toward her and so she tries to walk around them to catch a glimpse of it. There's a carnival mood.

"Is this a new diversion SensSim release?" I say for Bear B.'s benefit because I know she must be nearby although I can't see her through the reality projected around me.

The heat is more than oppressive, the smells are disgusting. I sit down on a boulder and wait for this to end. It must be a test of my reactions to this reality, although I can't figure out what this has to do with anything. A thin weed growing next to the boulder brushes against my arm and I pluck it out of the hot sand and start to suck on one end. At least this is something to experience while I wait for the images to change; no one is allowed to destroy plants anymore. I can use the feeling when I design. So I suck on its neurologically simulated sweet juice and I'm bored. I waste time investigating the crude strap on the sandal that hangs from my right foot, on the leg I've crossed over the other and am swinging impatiently. The uneven leather strap has frayed edges and is attached sloppily to a stiff, thin sole that is hot to my touch, evidently from walking in this rocky desert that suddenly darkens.

Now an acrid dampness comes with the shadows. The cold inside of a cave opens around me and I shiver from it, clasp myself for warmth in a reflex of self-comfort. Fear makes the hairs on my neck stand up and by breath catches in my throat. They are manipulating my sympathetic nervous system arousal, the primitive preparations to fight an enemy or to run from one. My teeth chatter more from the induced neurological transitions than from the cold and I must remind myself that none of this is real, it's only a TransInteractive Holograph, virtual reality of good quality, that's all. There's acrid smells like toxic chemicals, and someone in a long robe bending over a crude workbench. I turn away and look for the path that leads away from this place, this scene that means nothing to me.

"This means nothing to me, Bear B.," I say it so she'll hear.

The sound of thick cloth rustling makes me look back. I see the person at the workbench is turning around, probably

58

programmed to see who has spoken. I don't know why I should suddenly feel so much more afraid. It must be designed into the Holo. That's it, it's part of the imagery, this feeling of dread.

"Look at your hands."

Bear B.'s voice surrounds me and I'm on a rough dirt road lined with trees, *wham*, like that. The sunlight dapples through heavy gnarled branches.

"Am I supposed to be doing this? I have to hide my hands behind this, what is this? Burlap?"

"Hide you hands underneath that cloak."

"Why? What am I supposed to be, some kind of nun?"

"Just do what you want, touch your lover's face with tonguing kisses."

"If I'm a nun I shouldn't do that."

"You're not that kind of nun. There's no order. Take you hands from under the cloth, away from the beads that are only artificial security. You can't hide the marks of what you've done, of your crime, or your ability. You're still with us because there is no hierarchy."

Look at my hands.

I fumble from behind this too big, scratchy material and look down. My hands are dirty, stained and cut with small gouges, gashes. All of a sudden I fall on my knees because someone has pushed me hard, thrown me down into the dirt. Stinging tears and sweat burst out of me. Roll into a fetal ball of defense. Moans of primal terror, such whimpers of plaintiveness, so vulgar.

"Too much history," Bear B. says in a soft voice.

The real light, the light I know from the indistinct sky with its floating particles is less bright, easier on my eyes. Bear B. is holding a hand out to help me up from where I'm crouched on my knees in front of the chair where I was sitting. I wave her away, brush at the vomit that is crusted on my black jacket. None of this has anything to do with me. None of those images has any relevance.

I'll admit to murder if they want, so kill me. Send me along with my dear girl, my sweet child who is gone. I think this when I'm sitting in the chair again so they'll know it, they'll get it from the readouts. But I feel my head drooping, lolling on my neck.

~

"It's getting louder, from over there."
Tak-tak-tak. Tak. Tak.
"Can you see who it is?
"There are two of them I think."
Tak. Tak. Tak-tak...

~

"Give me something," Bear B. is saying to Evet as she touches her.

The rays of the weapon controls have retracted from her fingers back into the silver wristbands. Evet feels the velvet skin of Bear B.'s fingertips stroking lightly at the back of her neck. It's calming but very sensual. It seems to transport her, soothes the fear, moves her into an emotional hollow where there's a silken veil that is soundproof and entwines her, protecting her. She hears nothing. Not even the hum of the recording devices, their subtle vibration, nothing can be detected at all. She's protected by Bear B.'s touch. The metallic tapping, that *tak-tak* she thought she heard before in those Sims has vanished like she never heard them at all. She hasn't heard the sound and she can't hear her own soft moans at the woman's continued touch, her caress. Nothing. There is complete absence of sound, no subliminal buzz, no deep hum barely perceptible as room tone. Nothing.

She can't see her hands. Evet leans back in the chair, yearning now, and doesn't want to think about her hands. Were they hers? Her dreams can be real, she's starting to believe that. She won't admit what she has seen, not now, not when she's being stroked this way. The woman is here now, kneeling in front of her in this absolute noiseless brightness.

I remember the feeling. And when Bear B. moved her hands on me she felt a strange sensation too. It wasn't skin flowing under her fingers but something else softer, more luxurious. It felt like it was fur. Thick fur beneath her, a warm animal being caressed. No, a woman. But the touch transmitted something different. There was that smell of another animal, a warmth I remember from some time when I took someone else in my arms. There was the aroma, the sound of her heart beating next to mine. And I feel glorious under her movement now even though it's from a different place.

Nearly twelve chapters of the Book of the Dead are occupied with spells which provide the deceased with formulae to enable him to transform himself into any shape from a bird, a serpent, or a crocodile to a god in another world. He was able to assume practically any form, and to swim or fly to any distance in any direction. Strangely enough, no animal is alluded to in the texts as a type of his [the animal's] possible transformation.

Spence

EIGHT

Change Default Directory

I think I have heard it before. Somewhere in the silence that is pure motionlessness there is a similarity, a resemblance of something yet to come. They will think I am mad or dead if I tell them about this silence, but I won't say anything about what this woman is doing to me. It's something I remember of something that hasn't happened yet. I am dead. And what is the rough cloth this animal kneeling before me wears? This animal?

There is static and a whirling that stings so much I feel nauseous. What's she doing to me?

"Evet?"

"Kvino?"

"If you can hear me there's a way out. Travelers broke the code, waved it to me. Evet? I'm at the panel. You there?"

"Barely getting you. What're you doing with me and—"

"Go with it. Hear me? Audio freq is breaking up. Travelers say don't fight it, it's real. Don't be scared. Evet? Hear m—... Don't..."

What's real? I'm thinking this in motionless silence. What a question. What's tangible is real, what you can see and touch. But I see and feel everything, anything, here at my programming pad, here, where I'm making SensSims. I can design anything. All of this must be coming from me. Even Kvino, the Travelers he mentioned, and all those other things.

~

Tak-tak. Tak-tak.

"Alms! For the sake of—"

"Would you be quiet! I told you we can't do that. You're going to ruin our chances if there's one of us over there."

"Sorry, I forget. It's just that I'm so hungry, it's so sunny today."

"See, the sound stopped."

The woman says this as she runs her hands over the long dress that is rough. It reminds her of the fine wovens from Flanders she gave up.

"You with your open mouth," she says. "You've probably already ruined everything."

"But I need to eat to work, sooner or later."

"You're always too damned hungry. We've been out of the house for one day and you can't tolerate being without a meal. Get out of my sight and let me try to make a friend here, would you?"

"I said I was sorry," the woman holds her hands up to her ears and listens to the grimy fingers she has been sucking on.

There are dusty chickens that run away when the women walk through their pack, moving in a single file toward the shed with the wide opened door. The ground is uneven, dried clods of earth make irregular mounds over which they stumble now and then. The pathetic fowls run after them, hoping something edible might be turned up in their path. But there's no reward, another year of drought has made this yard, the entire grey countryside of rolling hills and erratic woods, barren.

Tak. Tak. Tak-tak. Tak-tak.

The work continues. Rhythmic sounds of metal hitting cleanly, precisely on metal ring out again and again. The figures in the shed that are in shadow because of the bright sunlight outside don't pay attention to the women who approach. One of them is bent over a workbench and swings the hammer up and down to make the sounds. Skilled hands turn silver wire on each upstroke and practiced fingers rotate the small circles it forms with each measured blow. Tak, tak. The movements are deft and rhythmic so that the sound of work is steady. Repetitious.

The sun has traveled since the smith's work began. Where once only weak rays edged through the uneven eastern window now brilliance bathes the place. The smith has changed position to take advantage of the light and to avoid reflections to see the silver clearly. Tak-tak. Each circle is flattened to a precise oval. Tak. Each silver oval is added to a wooden box that has no top. Now the small pieces make a mound that shines in the sun. The smith's work hasn't been disturbed. The involvement of the task, the love for doing it, striking the measured blows over and over again, closes the artist's senses to everything except the work. Repetitious like death.

Even when the chickens scrambled around and made noise, upset by the strangers, and the black cat sitting on a shelf deep in the shadows growled loudly, the smith didn't falter. Hands did not lose their cadence and eyes did not lift from the silver ringlets. Repetition like death.

"We are the Beguines, half-nuns, from Strasbourg. I'm Agnes Tetzger," the tall woman who hasn't forgotten about fine cloth says.

"Your reputation isn't very good, you know."

A figure who is watching the smith and who is also tall speaks from the shadows. Then this person whose voice Agnes perceives as a woman's or a young man's asks the Beguine women in their long robes to not come any closer.

"Give the smith respect."

~

I don't know if I dream or if I do these things. I think I've heard the silence that is pure motionlessness, and there's a similarity, a resemblance. They will think I'm mad or dead if I tell them about the silence. I have been later, and I will be before. I am dead. And what is this kneeling animal to me?

"There's no one who's alone without the others, and everything else. Braided."

This is what I thought I heard her saying to me after she got up from where she was kneeling. Although it didn't sound like Bear B.'s voice but like something artificial. Like I had coupled on some oldfashion computer and its archaic voice chips. Like that, robotic, before they were called Alternates and became just like us. I was still thirsty from all the running I had done to hide in CySpace. Not real running of course but the reflection of it, trying to get away by flying past the undulating walls of undiluted information. Kvino had laser-strapped me to a console that was a magnetic frequency tied to his own in CySpace. He was the one who did the actual maneuvering from his control bracelet, plotting data points that made me soar through the Nets and clip the edges of info walls with g6-force speed that flattened my eyelids back against the mechanical irises that are laser-sutured over my real ones.

Running in a grand virtual getaway that made me sick from gravity's escape, my body stayed stationary in a vibrating hologram behind Kvino's HoloSet. My enhanced retinas beamed all sorts of dizzy colors and shapes to my brain so I did in fact get sick to my stomach a couple of times, or was made to recall I did.

"There's no one who's without others and everything else?"

This has to be a trick. Even after feeling the intimacy with her I wasn't so disoriented that I would fall into the trap of admitting any allegiance to what sounded like sappy Traveler philosophy. Braided? Oneness and equality? This bliss-ninny embarrassment wouldn't become one of my listed offenses. That would be like, what? Like admitting to wanting to virtreal as a 20th century gameshow host, or aspiring to be a rep to sell advertising time on HoloSectors to funeral laser cosmeticians. They can dehydrate my cerebral cortex and half-speed my axon/dendrite synaptic impulses but they won't turn me into a sweetness and life reincarnation believer freak with a smile. I decided to tell this to Bear B. although I could no longer see her and I'm phasing out of this blue-hazed room where two of the walls are transparent, high above the gargan-City.

~

"We need to meet the master," Agnes shields her eyes from the sun that targets her through one tiny window. "We've heard the sounds of working from far off. In fact, the sounds led us here."

It's a secret code, this declaration of being led to the sounds of work. Only these peculiar Beguines can expect to succeed with this kind of deception. Agnes, who is in a way the smartest of them, is one of those renegade women who are excluded from the restricting rules of nunneries and the stupidity of the new Church's repression of women as part of their doctrine. These women have sought as a kind of hallmark of their existence that they are separate from the Church but still closely enough allied so they won't be persecuted for being too distant, or too stylish.

No burning or hanging for them, not now. Even the simple one who listens to her fingers, Sybelle, even she understands this benefit and shows it in her unusual way. She is fourteen years old but looks much older because she already carries the marks and misshapings of countless beatings. This is in addition to the invisible welts of ridicule for her obvious oddness of mind, and for the stump of a sixth finger on her left hand. She understands. The apparent simpleton sees as well as the other one, Mary, who is considered to be the holiest of them all in the eyes of the Church, and that's the way she wants it.

Mary is the one who has visions, mutters, maybe even flagellates herself although no one has witnessed it, rends her hair with her hands, although not so wildly that the effects aren't unbecoming. She considered the idea of coming on this excursion into the countryside, a day's walk from their Beguinehouse in Strasbourg, naked. She contemplated the effects of renouncing all possessions of the world because they're meaningless, and that includes clothing. But she's such an attractive woman that the faithful find her penchant for nudity distracting when she walks through the streets that way. As Agnes always reminds her, there aren't so many who are loyal to the new Church and its violent ways that they can stifle the curiosity of the majority of the unfaithful who stand along the streets to ogle her naked piety. Some even reach out to knead the smooth flesh of the one they call almost a saint on earth while they attempt to insert their fingers into her holy orifices.

Agnes prevents these excursions whenever she can, but Mary from Oignies in the low country is a wily saint-in-training and many times leaves quietly from their Beguinehouse before dawn so that she can be seen kneeling at the fountain in the square, the first rays of dawn imitating a halo over her head of full black hair. Her fame has spread and it makes it difficult for Agnes to keep away the Churchmen who are trying to become associated with her, who are already putting in their bids for relics of parts of her body once she's dead. But she's at least thirty years old and evidently not one of those to take the quick martyr's way out by flinging herself off a town parapet in order to achieve quick stardom.

Mary appreciates attention and she readily says that she has no desire to experience its end. She has plans to advertise her philosophy, which Agnes shares, and which is different from the Church's. She has confided to Sybelle that she and Agnes would like to lead the house of Beguines into fabulous renown so someday they can command an endowment to employ any craftsperson she wants. The need for artisans is one of the reasons they've sought out this young smith, supposedly a potential master, who can be hired cheaper because of having apprentice status to an impoverished father who will sell the talented youngster to any patron.

So Agnes says to the father, "I've never seen a crucifix so inviting to be touched. And so gruesome too."

The gash in the side, the thorns jammed deep into the forehead, the look of agony are all executed with minute precision, concentrated effect. A startling lifelikeness of torture.

"It's like the metal is really flesh," she says. "The softness of it strikes the eye but also calls out to the hand to touch it. It really must be held."

Now the young smith stands with a polishing cloth behind the Beguines who sit at the table in her father's cottage. She watches her work being passed from one to the other, inspected with exceptional curiosity and audacious fingers.

Only the last Beguine, the one who is cleaner and more memorable in her pleasantness and the broadness of her gestures than the others, the one they call Blessed Mary, will not touch the crucifix. Her somehow accentuated blue eyes turn upward when it's put in front of her and she starts to mutter in a honeyed, singsong voice.

"She's doing it again. I think she wants us to pay attention," Sybelle yawns.

With the fingers she has been listening to, Sybelle takes a piece from the bread loaf that's been ravaged to a ruined mess in the center of the table. While she chews she looks from the crucifix to the muttering Mary and back again, bored. She finally grabs up the artful cross with her dirty, crumby hands and tosses it back to the young smith. Mary stops making noises then and everyone relaxes, glad to be able to talk business finally, and about the secret.

"The reliquary definitely contains the ashes, Agnes says.

A crude round receptacle is deposited in the midst of the debris of bread. They all agreed on its genuineness, as best they knew. That was after they made certain of each other's authenticity: smith and Beguines. The Beguines showed the upturned hand sign of the rebels and the young smith, her father and the odd person who stayed in the shadows but who was powerfully felt, returned the completing secret sign with fingers turned down and interlocking.

The Beguines said others who were trustworthy at the time of the burning gathered the ashes. They all agreed to this news that had been carried by messengers from the place of the incineration. The reliquary contains all the ashes the witnesses there could gather of the one who was burned at the stake by the Inquisitor from later on.

Later on?

The Beguines have obtained the dusty remains and have come to this smith, this young woman who is not yet celebrated to have her create a new, fantastic container to house the crisped woman's symbolic body. They fully know that an awe-inspiring storage bin for relics is a way to gain attention, and power, especially before a burning. Mary of Oignies, who has accepted the stage name "Blessed," is the one who has just confirmed and in fact she's the one who always confirms, whether others are trustworthy or not to share the Beguines' secret of the ashes. She seems to know about these things, and she's never wrong. Her muttering over the masterfully grisly cross wasn't caused by any allegiance to that symbol of the new Church but from her feeling that the smith and those here can be trusted. She exhibited the same attention-drawing behavior on their way to this country place just as they were walking through the gates of Strasbourg, which was embarrassing for the rest of them.

NINE

It Is Only Certain That There Is Nothing Certain, And That Nothing Is More Miserable Or More Proud Than Man.
Pliny

Laughing like a darting flame, jumping to and fro without a wind. Is this possible? I must act impossibly to say anything worthwhile. Propose the paradoxical, because it's reality in the end. And the beginning? Why not? I'm not afraid of death anymore, not now that I'm not afraid to live. Before or later, I hated death because I didn't like living. Imagine, to not like living. Now it's all right, I dreamed it. I live and die and live and die again, and still live. It's all the same because the learning continues, eternal knowledge. How do I know this, how did this happen to me? Knowledge of the eternal is eternally knowing that you're learning, eternally. A funny doubling back. It's what living is. For fun, what else? –That's what Sam W wrote in a book he gave me before he died.

Who?

There's something I need to remember to learn. Like paws prodding me from one side.

"Bear B., where are you? Who is this tempting animal kneeling before me? Bear B.? Can you wake me up?"

~

"Is it possible to make metal that looks like moonlight?"

The Beguines were crossing through the gates of Strasbourg when Sybelle asked the question before. Now in the hot and stinking cottage of the father of the smith it's a question as exotic as explosions on a distant star.

"Can you make the metal that looks like moonlight?"

There was silence in answer to the question no one seemed to know who asked. The young smith didn't care. She knew it was possible and she wanted to make that ethereal substance real, but were these women the ones to give her to opportunity? She needed access to the best tools, to gold and silver, to the men who made themselves wizards so they could guard the secrets that were only knowledge. Secrets of the trade transmitted in words for a price, in money or lust or some other kind of control. Secrets conveyed in the actions of procedures that transform those who watch it like the transubstantiation in the Church where the uninitiated don't understand because they aren't taught the trick, the sleight of hand that makes the wine disappear when they always thought the priest drank it. Always a price. Only knowledge. She could do it if she had the education, and the materials. Simple. She tried not to smile at the triumph in the thought.

The hooded figure who stood back against the dirty wall knew what she was thinking, how ravenous she was. Sophia looked over to him, her brother Rudolphe, and didn't smile. The heat of her eyes was like a beam he could feel. It warmed him. He took down the cowl from his head to expose his delicate face to the Beguine women. For as dark and withdrawn as he was before he was suddenly a light in the room, as if a window had been shattered by the sun's brilliance. Sybelle actually showed little enough control to clamp her mouth shut and begin to raise a hand to protect her nose instead of her eyes. The others could inhibit their reflexes and Agnes thought that this was the reason the girl was considered simple and childlike, not a good enough censor of her naturally weird inclinations. She wasn't socialized. Agnes would have to try to remember to give her another training session when they returned to the city.

Sophia was as dark as her brother was light. She was as thick as he was fine. Like two halves they complemented each other, even their breaths seemed to be inhaled in concert, one breathed out as the other breathed in. But they shouldn't be related. Rudolphe was tall and graceful without any frailness while Sophia was short and common but without coarseness. She was attractive with that stance of peasant breeding that accepts no deceit from anyone, and no distraction to whatever she might focus on. When she worked over her metals the earth could quake around her and she wouldn't falter. The village boys had already noticed the gifts in the skill of her hands and in the appeal of her bosomy body. A healthy and apprenticed woman was allure enough for anyone in times of drought and her smooth features would have made her irresistible were it not for the strength of her abrasive personality.

Lately all the work has been Sophia's and her father, ignored by everyone, wanders in the woods or drools silently as he sits on the three-legged stool outside of his daughter's work hut. No one can remember hearing him speak more than a few words. And those were uttered years ago.

~

What's happening to me? They can torture me all they want with Bear B.'s softness, with dreams of wildness and ecstasy. The feeling on my skin of my dear girl's skin, or was it fur? Whatever. They're probing with laser pins now all over my skull and I'm not sure anymore what's me and what isn't. There's someone running toward me as I lie here in this field. I'm not simply reclining, no. I'm tied down.

God damn it, I'm so scared! He's coming for me, that pale man with a sack. I'm trying to get up, to run, to get away from the terror, from the horrific things he will do to me. He's going to do all those things to me again!

Is this true? It doesn't matter, I felt it all. The connection was broken and I realize that this never happened to me, this unspeakable memory. It's only an experiment I connected to that was done by that brain researcher, Penfield, in the 20th Cent. Was he Canadian? Who cares. They're stimulating the part of my brain where they've implanted this foreign memory as my own to see if they've still got control. They do, fuck them, but only for some things. That's why they're torturing me again, there's some freedom left in my thoughts, as bizarre as they are sometimes. I wonder how I can use it. If they can give me odd images and ideas how do I know if what I think or even dream is really from me? How do I sort what is chaos, a messy sprawl of tiny playing cards in my mind and each has a differently designed back, how do I separate and put them in order? Which is from the environment, which is from my own mind, and how do I order those cards in neat stacks of blue or red or translucent curlicued encounters and/or meanings? The world forms me by its great and trivial stimuli for conditioning my responses, thank you Dr. Pavlov. May I call you Ivan? It all shapes me without my consent every day, every advertisement, each bit of manufactured food I've developed a conditioned taste for, what person am I anyway except theirs anyway?

"Too much history, baby."

I hear Bear B. saying this to me as she licks her glistening lips. Shiny with what she did. And I feel myself leaving...

What is this animal to me, the one who knelt here so close in front of me? Do I dare to laugh? They don't want me to remember. They don't want me to remember too much history, but that's what makes it harder for me to control my future if I don't. It makes it harder for me to know what I can create. Where am I going?

~

The workbench shakes with the pounding. Sophia has been working since first light with Rudolphe watching her with the black cat curled across his shoulders. The crucifix the Beguines touched has been sold to them, bartered so that she could trade for more materials, more silver, more copper. She melted the silver and mixed it with the copper and then cooled the mixture in molds shaped for wire. When it cooled enough the thick wire was drawn through smaller and smaller holes that were bored precisely into a thick metal rectangular plate held in a vise.

Little by little and with great effort of pulling the wire became thinner and more pliable with each pull through each smaller hole in the plate. She stretched it through the holes from one side of the work shed to the other. First through the large holes and then the smaller and smaller ones by degrees. And when the sun finally sets she is wet with exertion, aching from the strain.

At the next dawn she is at work again. The long wires are cut. Individual tiny links are formed painstakingly and perfectly. By nightfall, there is a mound of small circles glowing in the wooden box once again.

She was at work by candlelight before the break of dawn on the next morning. Each link is fitted together. With delicate pliers two are folded over each other, then four, then six. She works all day, braiding metal. Two, four, six, over and over again. It lengthens. Her eyes itch from not blinking while she works. Folded and attached, over and over, each link receives the stroke of her hands. She is still at work this way by candlelight after the sun sets.

Another day passes and the chain she is making lengthens. While she works, Rudolphe and the cat watch. He father sits silently outside.

On the next day she makes the clasp for the chain. It is cut from two flat silver circles that are carefully measured and joined in a way that makes the opening impossible to see. The join of the clasps' parts will be imperceptible on the neck of the person who wears the chain, as if there is no lock at all but one continuous chain that is permanently soldered close to the neck. One round moonstone is then set precisely into the place where the clasp appears not to be. Invisible. And the entire necklace, now complete, is polished and closely examined. Sophia finally turns to Rudolphe. He laughs out loud when he sees it and tells her to fasten it around his neck. She does this only somewhat grudgingly.

"It's like the tail of a fox," he says while he looks at his reflection on a polished metal shard Sophia keeps attached to the inside of the shed's door.

"A foxtail," he says. "You can see each strand laced around the others just like hairs in a braid."

He has to take it off so he can feel it, twist it around his fingers. Its smoothness and suppleness are irresistible. Their father has come in and holds out his hand for the chain. It's so pliable that it seems to move of its own accord, alive in his hand. He holds it around Rudolphe's neck again and watches how it hugs the contours of his skin. It's like a rope of liquid silver.

"What about the reliquary?" Rudolphe says to her. "When will you make it for those women?"

"When they bring me to Strasbourg so I can join the guild, the goldsmiths."

"You're a woman, you'll never be allowed in the guild no matter how good you are. You know they only share secrets with each other, and then only master to apprentice, but always man to man."

"I think there's another way with these women," she looks at her father. "I won't give up my love, or my lover."

~

I see the words lasered on my eyes in my dream. All the ancient history chips I ever linked into. Place is important. We know ourselves by how we affect the world, and this changed world affects us in turn. Place is important, but where is it? Place exists in us. Home resides in our images of it; country lives in how we see it in our minds. But if I take my head and ram it into this transparent sheet I think separates me from the clouds outside high above the City, if I do this I will break my skull and bleed, maybe blood will run out of my ears. Is that in my imagery too? Is real outside of us or is real inside of us?

There's something I'm trying to remember about me and being in places. My cat in a foreign country, a dusty place. Do I dream all of this? Place is important. And where am I now, at my handpad designing a Sim, or somewhere else?

~

Sophia feels she wants to go home, or that she needs to find a home. It's something she can't explain, not to Rudolphe or anyone. There's a reason she wants to go to Strasbourg that is beyond wanting to fulfill her art. She is compelled to go because she wants to feel at home. It seems weird and she knows it, she seems to want to go home although she is at home. And she doesn't really want to leave her family. Her father and this Rudolphe are all she knows. She cherishes them, she thinks. Yet she feels like she wants to go to a refuge and doesn't dare talk about this feeling or even admit it to herself.

It is when she dreams in her strawed box, awake in the very early hours before it's light that she sees herself doing things unthinkable for her now. There will be someone, or she wishes there will be someone, who takes her into a lonely workshop and teaches her the perfections of metal. He is as kind as her silent father was when he could still focus his attention on his supple hands to show her how to work the metal. And she will learn. She learns quickly in her dreams. Rudolphe never had any inclination for the work other than to wear what he could out to parties, if there were any. When she dreams of him it's never in the past with her father but it is later on, and she doesn't understand this and so she forgets it.

She dreams of Italy draped in a cloak of joy. Hills of green vines slope to waters of immaculate blue, thick sunlight carried carefully like lips coated with honey. She remembers her mother was her aunt and that it didn't matter. Smiles drenched through the sunlight looking at her, all seeking her to warm her with flagrant love. It's difficult for her to remember through all this solid love, this comforting warmth, if there were really two of them or if there had been only one mother and aunt together. Her father was on a hill all the time while they were at the shore, the craggy sometimes sandy shore, looking up at his silhouette above them in the lush hills.

She feels the cool water on her feet, the sun like a delicate blanket over her. She feels the love that bestows her movement into the water, under water, exploring with sureness. From where she floats she can see the women on the large rocks embracing each other, laughing, waving to her and blowing her kisses. She laughs and dives under the gentle waves knowing she can do anything with mothers there to protect her.

The colors at the bottom of the sea tumble up to her, touch her on the arms and legs and pull her down. She memorizes the hues but can't speak of them, ever.

When dawn comes to interrupt her dreams Sophia wishes she could die. If she were dead she assumes she could live in her dreams forever. Maybe she's right, but she also isn't certain about it. So doesn't pursue it and keeps her reveries, her other life, for the nighttimes when she lives it as fully as life in the light of this new sun that isn't at the mountainous sea but closer to Strasbourg. The city and not the sea. She knows she has to go there to go home.

Sophia, raised in love, feels she can act on her feelings because she has so much to repay. But she wonders sometimes if that can be right. Should she have to repay the love the different mothers gave her? Maybe she'll find out, she thinks, if she goes where it feels more like home, to the place she has never been that already feels like home.

Savage man goes to sleep trusting that his totem will grant him a vision for the regulation of his future affairs. If the ancient Egyptian desired such illumination, he considered it wiser to sleep within a temple famous as the seat of an oracle. A class of professional interpreters existed whose business it was to make clear the enigmatic portions of these dreams. It was thought that diseases might be cures by nostrums communicated by the gods during sleep.

Spence

TEN

Case Conversion

"The cat is the same."

"The same as what?" I whisper it.

"Everywhere. When they picked up the ashes and before that when they searched for the bones and even when you worked and it watched, and also when they made love."

"Then too? It's a very old thing I suppose."

"Sometimes it is and sometimes it isn't, don't you see? It's both alive and it's dead. Fifty-fifty. We burned to a crisp hags who know this kind of thing."

~

It wasn't time, not yet. Evet could feel the humming move through her. Bear B. was the cat. Absurd, she knew this wasn't true.

I knew it too. There were still the laser pins in my skull but I wasn't seeing anything, not feeling the terror like before. I wondered if anyone else was aware of it then, although I don't care because they've done too much to me. Images and memories are in me that aren't mine. And this woman has done unbelievable things to my body with hers. At least I think so or I only think so because a voice has been silenced, a great bravado and a challenging scream is no more. Anyway not right now, but it will return, it came back before and it was beating a wingspan of more than two meters. Am I dreaming again? Whose thought is this? Or did I SimCopy it from a Travelers ad? Wait a minute, I design Sims, whatever I want to. It's me, I'm the hero.

~

Sophia is absolutely certain, sure of herself. The colors of the bottom of the sea are in her mind and they are the secret that gives her confidence. Trembling up to her. She's going home to a place she's never been and she's rejoicing, anxious to reacquaint herself with her new life.

Rudolphe can't believe her haste. He acts as if he's jealous and doesn't want to share her with anyone. Their life together has been idyllic, and odd. He doesn't want her to leave him, but he doesn't want to go to Strasbourg. Someone has to care for their father.

"Why can't we both go with you?"

He talks to her while she wraps her tools carefully in a long strip of leather, wrapping them around and around. He sees she's concentrating on taking care that the heads of the hammers of all those various sizes don't touch each other. He wonders if she's listening to him at all.

"Why can't we go with you?"

She says, "Where would you live? Not with me in their place, the Beguinehouse."

"I don't want to see you go. What we share has to continue."

"Why? We won't be together like this anymore, that's all."

Be together like what, in what way does she mean? It's something they know between them, it seems to be something they want to hide. Have they been joined too much? In a later time they will be, or maybe that was before. In the womb of *Nut* there were two unborns seized in sexual union, brother and sister comingling. The story is known but it's not clear anyone knows if it's these two living again, if they are, from that old Egyptian legend. United in the womb through their intimacies is startling enough to not want to think about, to not have the image. Too late.

Sophia and Rudolphe are abnormal, and they never knew their mother. Maybe this is what makes them so oddly related. And now Rudolphe, who is strong enough, shows his unwillingness to be without the sister who has been the proof of his uniqueness since before they were born. She is the stronger because she knows she is alone, and should be. Connected with him for eternity, braided by intimacies, but still alone.

"You'll leave me with nothing," he says as she walks away.

He's holding the cat in his arms. Its yellow eyes shine with rage and it growls loud as a hound. Sophia has never gotten along with this animal. They've tolerated each other because each is somehow related to Rudolphe. He has many times slept with the cat in his arms instead of her, actually, every night he sleeps with the cat instead of anyone else. They only act as if they sleep together, brother and sister, but it's really the other animal who holds his heart in a vast love. Sophia knows it and thinks that probably the two of them will be happier without her. She feels obligated to worry about the care of Rudolphe and her father now that she'll be gone. The cat will have to feed them and clean the cottage and watch out for them because she's leaving, and that's that.

"They're what you always wanted," she says soundlessly and looks back at the cluster of ugly huts that were her home.

Hearing her, the cat jumps from Rudolphe's arms and takes menacing steps toward her to speed her away. Sophia feels freed by that, and a little lonely. She knows the cat will do a better job of attending to her family. She has never felt her father and brother were truly her responsibility anyway and she's really done very little for them, if she's going to be honest about it.

It was always that other animal who brought home food, who watched for intruders and who ran the household with a steady hand. It's true although she doesn't like to remember it. The cat brought freshly killed muskrat, quail, other creatures, and left them on the table, later cleaning and cooking the victims. Her own mouse or bird she would keep apart to eat although she would taste some of the cooked meat to make sure it was good. At no time could anyone approach near the huts without the cat sounding an alarm. And it was the times when she awoke in the morning, and went to hunt, returned from hunting, or sat waiting at the food table, basked in the sun, napped, and finally went to Rudolphe's bed for the night, that signaled the divisions of the day for them all. When Sophia was concentrating hard on her work she only had to look up to see where the other animal was to know what time in the agenda of the day it was, to know whether food was on the table or near to being prepared or not. She wondered if the Beguines would tend to her as well.

"It's what you always wanted, without me," Sophia doesn't say it out loud. "Goodbye mother."

The cat's warning rumble responds.

Sophia turns away. Chaos. On the dirty road toward Strasbourg where she's never been, she's ignorant of dangers and of what lays ahead. Chaos. Breaking free from her past to leap somewhere unknown. But it's happened before. The chaotic phenomenon in her life is regular. She feels a spiral in her. She left the sea of trembling colors this way, without knowing, with a risk, with the turmoil of complete change in her life.

It is a spiral that feels right within her. Around and back again after a journey to another place, somewhere random and back again to the same thing. The pattern in chaos not yet recognized by science is the chaos of her life.

The rutted road is crossed by a stream. It rushes down the slope of a small mountainside. Rocks, boulders stand in its way and force it to careen around them, twist away at the last moment to avoid being splattered onto their unyielding faces. Sometimes it turns away too late and splintered shards of water are hurled into the air. Some small pieces slap onto Sophia and make her jump away. Never has she seen a stream so cruelly torn apart by obstacles that laugh solidly in its way. Bruised and battered it rushes by, screaming, and she can do nothing to help it. She brushes away the dismembered fragments of it that have wet her face, the blood of the stream that, once whole, is vivisected before her. Sophia is horrified and throws up her breakfast all over the dirt at its edge, making certain to lean over to cover a rock with the bile, her revenge on one of the bullying things.

She watches for a time, transfixed by the pain she feels of the rushing water and there's nothing she can think to do to help it. It's so different from streams she has crossed before and from the placid sea of her youth that allowed her to come inside of it, exciting it with her undulations as she reached down slowly to its heart. The water stood still for her, embraced her, swallowed her with lips glistening from what they had done together. She loved that water and would love this foreign torrent as well but she didn't know how never having seen it before.

She thinks that she has stepped in this water before, the same stream relived with the same steps. She is attracted to it as strongly as she was attracted to the sea. She's done this before. She is absolutely certain of this and she sees something in her mind at exactly that moment for which can't account. Why? But she tells herself that she hasn't and prostrates herself on the bank, kisses the virgin rushing water. It leaves part of itself on her lips and face, in her mouth. Wetness comes from her as it did into her lover, the sea. She has come into this stream before, she knows it now.

She walks backwards from it as if she is loathe to relinquish its image in her eyes. Like a lover. A wave almost raised her hand but shouts coming from people made her stop. A rich person on a horse with a few peasants walking beside approached and she bowed her head to keep from looking into their eyes as they muttered things like greetings when she passed. The man on the horse turned to try to see her but she kept her head down, pulled up her cowl and knew she needed the protection of the Beguinehouse. This world is unstable. The dirt beneath her feet seems to move on its own to confirm her apprehension. From now on Sophia listens to strangers on the road and rushes into thick woods alongside whenever she hears anyone approaching. She knows she has to do this although she's never done it before and no one has told her to do it.

Strong steps and furtive retreats comprise her dance to the city. A poem of pilgrimage in a world not to be trusted and that world becomes foggy, indistinct.

~

We know ourselves, who we are and that we are alive, by what we do to the world, how it reflects us back to ourselves. A history chip I linked said that on the inside of my artificial irises. We touch our face but aren't sure of how we look until we see it in a mirror and see it in a context, other things around us. Smooth surfaces, manufactured air that can be seen. Is this all I am, only an altered thing? And the animal I felt kneeling here, or the woman, what about that for christ sake? Are we really always in the intersection of spaces?

"Bear B.," I say so she can hear. "This VirtReal means nothing to me."

And then I hear thick material moving as the person turns and I'm really scared. I want to wake up, or leave this place somehow.

ELEVEN

...He Resolved To Go Out Of This Life And Not To Run Out Of It; Not To Escape From Death, But To Essay It.

Montaigne

They were surprised and not glad to see her in Strasbourg. But she wasn't sure of that because she has little experience in interpreting other people's subtleties even when they aren't subtle. Sybelle rolled her eyes and walked away and Sophia wondered if this was good or bad even though it didn't make any difference because she had no intention of leaving the Beguinehouse despite the absence of an invitation to stay. No matter how strange these women might be she would become one of them here in these wild streets of the city, and in the midst of their working she would work too. Their home was Agnes' modest two-story house *hinder kursener loben*—behind the tanners, in the crafts part of town. Far away on the other side of the square and the commons Sophia saw where the solid Dominican convent loomed within enclosed gardens. The small and untidy Beguinehouse was nothing like that.

The six women ate together that night in the courtyard behind the house shadowed by the second story's overhang. Sophia thought the rodents and fowl the cat at home provided was better food. Here the women fed themselves, and the goats and chickens they kept seemed to help, but the dogs were inept even if they did work to frighten strangers who passed by. Their mistresses were two Beguines who caressed them and patted them like lovers, one for each of them. These creatures snarled at everyone else, though, the curs and the women too, the dog-loving Petrissa and Ellekindis who were soap makers.

"We don't beg," Metza, a dark beautiful woman says to her while they eat. "We live by our skills, our art. We're all artists, workers who produce with our hands. Most of us are among the very best at what we do but we're kept out of the highest ranks by the guilds just because we're women."

"Are any of you smiths? Gold or silver?" Sophia looks around the table.

Sybelle laughed without looking up and no one paid any attention. She saw in her mind a glorious necklace that moved like a snake made of metal links although nothing like it was ever known before. She suddenly had the urge to draw that image, to take a stick immediately and trace it in the dirt at her feet under the table. She started to do it, bent doubled over beneath the uneven wooden table where they all sat, and the others didn't notice. They rarely paid attention to her beyond the interest in her painted icons that were breathtaking and that traded so well. Yesterday, though, they wondered why she had insisted on being called by a curious name, Mat/leen. She still persisted in it today and they were surprised because she never became passionate about anything really. When the others made a commotion now she didn't bother to raise her head from where she was contorted under the table, drawing in the dirt while her buttocks stayed firmly on her stool.

All the women at the table shouted, for a reason that wasn't clear, that Sophia was indeed and would continue to be the only metalsmith the Beguinehouse would allow. She had put her foxtail chain on the table for them to see and it was causing the commotion that Sybelle ignored.

"The work is brilliant."

"Absolutely fabulous."

"Superior to any I've seen except maybe the masters in the guilds."

Agnes Tetzger knew this all along and so did Blessed Mary from Oignies but they wanted to hide her talent for some time longer. Their negotiations with Churchmen hadn't progressed far enough to introduce Sophia to them. They wanted to keep her in the countryside and out of the company of artisans and the waves of appreciation that would come to her in town. They planned to be the agents for her talent and they would negotiate with the powerful Churchmen, contract for her, pay her a portion of what they got for her work. In that way they would use the income to build a new doctrine they knew would change the world. But now she has come here all of a sudden to expose herself as the source of talent too soon.

Perhaps we could kill her.

The thought invaded Agnes while she fingered the thick cloth of her cape. But of course that was stupid, at least before she made the reliquary for the martyr's ashes. And she still had to bargain with the Church to get that incinerated woman declared a saint, preferably backdated to before she was crisped like that. But never mind now, those underground dealings about that with the Church were delicate and involved enormous profit for whoever held the rights and further licensing of that potential saint's debris.

Agnes and Mary made an agreement after they visited Sophia in the country but her arrival in Strasbourg changed the reality they were constructing for the Beguinehouse and, in fact, for the world. These women don't think normally or in routine ways because they share a vision. The world is comprised of naturalized social constructions, nothing but agreements, and they believe they can produce meaning intentionally. They think they can manufacture values as well as value. Gods. *Per omnia saecula saeculorum* is a sacred eternity that can be entered anywhere, there's no end and no beginning to meaning in life. There's always a new view, a new interpretation and Agnes and Mary know they can give birth to meaning anytime they want. Immaculate conceptions. All it takes is manipulation, and power.

~

"Jesus christ, please stop! Please no more!"

Bear B. finds herself smiling at the irony of the situation. Torture, the maiming of body parts, is manifesting oldfashion religiosity, the pleading to a composition, jesus christ. The wristband's crystals *whir* as she touches them absentmindedly and provokes a protective response in the weaponry controls. She has to give a voice command to override the automatic firing position they've taken because in her contemplation she's forgotten that errant movements will be interpreted as an attack. Funny, as if this pleading creature could retaliate.

Ontogeny recapitulates phylogeny, the individual's development mirrors that of the whole society and Bear B. can't resist smiling at what an excellent remark it was. She's having a difficult time reconciling the mediocrity of this bleeding woman before her now with the impact of her earlier observation. Nothing in this Evet's life data storage predicts this amount of insight and danger. How does she evidence such knowledge when she has not had it in any programs? Creativity is no explanation; it's been proven to be no threat in most people because reiteration in recombination of experiences is the only creativity there is, experience is quantifiable. It's accurate to say experience for some time now has been quantified, period. Database coded life events for each person are stored in CySpace's unlimited Nets. Recombinant creativity.

New events, new codes, none of them are really new anyway because anything can be recombined through headings and subheadings of events. So if you find a new sex partner and invent a sensation you have not felt, a tongue in the orifice where it's never been before, new for you, it can be predicted and coded from events in your life already on file. Nothing new. The predictability of unpredictability. There will be a recording of music with that name, won't there, Jerome Cooper?

What? Who?

Data and information have made life events projectable statistics, no surprises. Control is Bear B.'s job. And the woman moaning at her feet is unreal in this world, unreal because her actions have not been predicted.

So they have pierced that woman who is me, there, in agony. Somehow I can see it. They've pierced me with worse than searing lasers because I've committed the crime of novelty. And I don't know how I did it, I wish I did. The crime of novelty is mine and I've got to find it and find how it works in me.

"I'll help you."

Bear B. is holding out her hand to me.

Do they record the thought I have now? The thought that her hand is exquisite and that I wish she would caress me again, even through all this agony. I can't get up. For one thing, my feet have been beaten as I hung upside down in a Turkish prison in one of the fantasies so they are swollen like pictures I've seen of exotic fruits. Awful, but all I can think of is this naked woman. Is she naked now, bending over me? It must be a thought stimulated by the database, I can't tell the difference. Or is this the crime, oh jesus is this the crime? The crime to know that there might be a difference in the origins of things I think. Is the knowledge that some of what I think is from me, whatever is me, and some of is not from this me, that's the crime? Knowledge. Yes, this must be the offense. I think it always was.

"I'll hold you."

They must know through the sensors that are who knows where in me, they must know how much I want her. For all I know they're producing the desire. Like the Mata Hari I linked from before, will they think I'll tell her how I've done this even though I don't know I've committed—am committing—this crime? I'm nobody. If I know so much why haven't I been one of the famous ones, the ones who have mass credits in data banks? My simulation game proposals haven't even sold to the diversion business conglomerates and I remain a mid-level Sim designer, nothing superb ever happens to me. Why should I be tortured for these thoughts that I'm so unsure of unless they actually mean something, do something? They must be real somehow.

"You have to talk to me, baby, before you can touch me. You have to tell me everything," Bear B. is in my ear.

Parts of her are brushing over me. Glowing crimson seems to reach for me. Open my mouth. Sweetness, cool and smooth wetted lips.

"Tell me," she says.

"Yes."

"Go on."

"Anything. Whatever you want. What should I say?"

Electric shocks explode through every synapse everywhere in my body. Burning torment as colors detonate in my eyes and I shriek! She's gone, of course, and I'm left whimpering, quivering with pain.

"You murdered your daughter!" she roars with a hurricane wind.

I try to think through the pain what she can mean by that, why is it so important? I can't remember having a daughter and with all she's doing to me I wish I could remember, or manufacture a daughter if I can. No image comes. No reality, not a Holo of any kind. The anguish peaks in a horrible crescendo, and I'm gone.

~

I'm glad my dear cat has escaped. I pray that he has. They would torture us both, at least they have only had me. Look at my fingers, broken. My tongue has been penetrated with nails, and there are thick needles puncturing my nipples. Crusted blood is on shapes I no longer recognize that were once my breasts. Soon I'll die. I don't mind.

~

Metza has taken Sophia to her room. They will share the garret in which no one can stand upright, even under the gable, and which anyone can span in four steps in any direction. Each woman has a cot on opposite sides of the high uneven window and, like the rest of the house, the room is disorderly and dirty but somehow agreeable. There is something else besides housekeeping duties that goes on in this place, some Thing. Sophia feels at home. As if she is high above the town, high even above the construction on the new cathedral she passed on the way, and high above the stream that meanders along. She can see it all. She is aware of her

94

place, here, a space that is hers in the people-swarmed places of the town. This space, this volume of air is hers. The vastness of Strasbourg and the knowledge that thrives in its cavities and fissures is here to discover. Her space, this bit of air is what she has claimed as if it is her legitimacy to be here. Already she feels part of all of all of it although she has really seen nothing but it feels like her element, a fish breathing water.

"Do you pray?"

"Should I?"

"Not if you don't usually, no one cares," Metza shrugs. "Do you think we spy on whether each other has any piety? We're not like those rich women in the convents. We're workers and we're not evil, we just don't follow the stupid Churchmen like the slaves they want us to be. All most of us do is look like we're religious enough for them so they don't bother us and won't call us witches or heretics. They can't control us because we make our own living with our hands. See? That's what's really important, the economy."

"If you don't pray, don't they care? What I've seen shows no allegiance to anything that's religious. Won't they find out you don't follow any kind of convent rules at all?

"That's Agnes' job, and Mary's too. They deal with the Church. On holy days, though, sometimes we have to march to the new cathedral or to the Dominican convent and look dedicated, sit through a Mass. We lose time from our work, that's the worst, although generally we get a good time out of it because those Dominicans think their shit is more aromatic than ours. I wink at the young ones to scandalize them. It's good for a laugh and some gossip. But it doesn't matter, what's important is that we can keep on working."

"That's all I want."

"So do we all."

"And you?" Sophia realizes she hasn't asked. "What is your art?

"Saddler. I make the best, a seat that embraces the rider and the horse."

Metza passes her hand that is stained and wounded with marks of tanning and the pick over Sophia's arm. Her smile is full and without any subtlety, and with that look she invites her but Sophia has no interest except in success. She came here to learn how to make metal that looks like moonlight, nothing else excites her and Metza sees this and still smiles with the effortlessness that is part of her. With her battered artist's hands she lays Sophia down and like a devoted companion pulls a tattered blanket over her. She remains seated at the end of her cot and begins to hum to her. Soothed, Sophia allows her body to relax. Comforted, watched over and warmed by this woman she allows herself to fall asleep without uneasiness. Metza, humming, curls at the end of the cot with her head tucked by her knees, her rounded back presses against Sophia's legs like a cat.

The inspiring cause of animal-worship was undoubtedly at first nothing more or less than fear, with an admixture of awesome admiration of the creature's excelling power and strength. Later there developed the idea of animals as typifying gods, the actual embodiments of divine and superhuman attributes...

'The generative power in the animal was identical with the force by which life is renewed in nature continually and in man after death.' Again, to the Egyptian mind, incapable of abstract thought, an immaterial and intangible deity was an impossible conception. A god, and more so by reason of his godhead, must manifest and function in an actual body.

The king was believed to be an incarnation of a god, but he was apart and only one, and as the Egyptian everywhere craved the manifestation of and communion with his gods, it thus came about that incarnations of deity and it's many attributes were multiplied. Certain animals could represent these to a greater degree than man...(and) the gods were but little greater than men; they were limited, and might know death. Their immortality was only acquired by the power of transmigration from one body to another, escaping human death by transference to successive forms and a renewal of the life force.

Spence

TWELVE

Border Options

They tried with various excuses to stop her from going out in the city. Blessed Mary even produced a vision that the other Beguines tolerated, waiting while she muttered at something in the air, before they left to start their workday. Fuller, painter, soap makers, saddler and now metalsmith, all of the women walking in the stinking dust of the artisans' street. An odd recollection seized Sophia and she felt a sudden longing for her mother. All at once, engulfed in loneliness. Where was she buried, what happened to her remains? Sophia has really not thought about this before and now she's overcome and suddenly ravenous to know the answers. Knowledge, but only simple things about a mother. Who else would care?

~

I don't deserve this torment. Bear B.'s delicate artillery has mangled me. I carry my love in my heart, how I ache for her. To touch her, to hold her again. With my broken fingers I feel her rich fur. How I miss her! But she is well. I wish her well.

She tells me, *somehow it's all right momma*. And it is. But I miss her.

She is teaching me to be alone. The old lesson, same lesson that drives me to dread and tears every time it confronts me. There's no one to hear this voice inside of me that translates everything I see and feel so much better than I can. I mean, when I try to speak it or write it. Is it possible to be so fragmented from myself that the power and nuance of what is inside me is lost like an invisible theft perpetrated between every feeling and its production? Maybe there's another self who's doing this. I am alone to live this life here in the gargan-City, to be in this universe of singular souls. But aren't we all part of one, the same? The gap that steals from me is filled with us all, a consciousness beyond the "one." Don't I have many facets?

Shut up, bliss traveler senseless sweetness.

Why do I care, what does the answer matter if I'm trapped in and by the knowledge and the limits of this stupid existence in information Networks, this consciousness of data? Is there something else? And how do I get there if this awareness in a vapid world filled with distractions keeps me here? I've got to break through the Nets to find out.

My darling, my black cat. The bird's feather over the Indian-made small box coffin with the Petoskey stone inside. Majestic magic. I walked to the edge of the vast lake for the first time ever and reached down and picked up a small Petoskey stone.

When was that?

I wrote this, designed it for a SensSim, that's where it came from but I remember it, I feel it. The stone with the entrapped fossil image. Great good luck, except for the fossil. So where is it?

Be well, my love.

This is one of my better dreams I think. Or no, is this the secret power of making things real? They think I have it. I've got to find out how it works. Dream again, design again.

~

For five days Sophia has been walking the industrious streets of Strasbourg. The sumptuous foxtail chain in a pouch tied to the belt around her waist is held more tightly because she has lost weight without her family pet's ministrations. The food in the Beguinehouse is bad, meager. In the town vegetables have to be bought because there's not enough room to grow them, and then there's the drought everywhere. Sophia doesn't eat well but she feasts on nourishment without chewing, quenches her thirst without parting her lips.

Odors, noises, flashes of arguments between the city people that broadcast either dull opinions or ideas that skim usefulness, the feel of fine velvets just grazed against her skin on the back of her hand when merchants pass by, the varied looks of people tall and short and crippled and comely that she's never seen before. The world of color is a violent spectrum to her eyes, a universe opened to an eternity of discovering, everything different, everything new. She realizes nothing should be grasped and held immutable forever but seized and prodded and made slippery and lost to spring away to tease sensation all over again. A gargantuan orb of perception, bounding close and then skipping away again, unremittingly. But connected. She glimpses this new life, only just tastes it with limited understanding and a palate that is stunted.

And no one will look at the necklace. The metal smiths' apprentices wave her away. A goldsmith she's seen confined deep in a sun-drenched angle of an alleyway doesn't even raise his head. His assistant silently turns away from her and continues with his duties as if they didn't see her. It's unusual behavior. Sophia has no way of knowing this of course, or knowing that Agnes has sent word through the clergymen saying the young woman is addled, a little light in the head. They shouldn't waste their time on the fresh Beguine who is mostly an embarrassment to her house, and Agnes promises them she will soon keep her at home.

"The young woman spins well although she thinks she's a real smith," she told them.

"Pay no attention. Don't encourage her."

No one thinks to say anything about this because it has no importance when everyone is engrossed in survival. Metza doesn't know because she's absorbed in her own art, pounding, stretching, shaping the leather for her saddles. And Sophia hasn't told her about her disappointing rounds in the streets. She thinks it must be normal or her own fault. During these five nights that Metza has curled against her legs giving her sound sleep she's ventured to say nothing about the days. The intimacy of the night has remained as separate as an acid-etched line on a lead plate from the trudging frustrations of the day. Agnes, knowing all of this, also knows that she has to act in order to keep control of this young woman. She has called the priest to discuss how he can help, and profit, of course.

"If she's the one who made that frightening crucifix you showed me I don't see why you just don't give her a contract," he says. "If you don't bind her to your house she'll be sought out and signed by someone else. I, in fact, would hire her. She could re-set some of my precious relics with gems."

"You still have the finger of one of my own?"

"You mean the thumb of that girl? Yes I do. You want to see it?"

From under the delicate Ghent cloth covering his fleshy chest the priest Jacques DeVitry follows with his fingers along a gold chain around his neck until he pulls it out. The gold box at the end of it has a cloudy purple covering at the top, inside there's the holy relic. Fingernail, skin, bone and tendon are all there, blackened and shrunken. Everyone marvels at this thing and comments on how it looks just like it did in life. The absurdity is not lost on DeVitry and he closes his eyes in disgust at remembering the *non sequitur,* as if death could ever look like life. Dead is dead, so far. But the reliquary is beautiful even if the putrid remains inside of it are obnoxious to him. He worries that the stench trapped behind the metal bezel of the thick glass someday will begin to seep out, a warning of his drifting faith, and overwhelm him, choke him to death before the odor finally dissipates in the wind. Sometimes in the dead of night he thinks he smells it and he must take a drug to help him get back to sleep after that. Now he thinks the girl might replace the jeweled goblet he uses on his night table, replace it with one made fresh and new to contribute to the lengthening of his life.

"I'd give her work re-housing these holy remains," he says. "She wouldn't even have to open the case, I think, just set the whole thing inside a new one, even thicker and heavier to protect it. And with gems."

His eyes look away as he becomes absorbed with designing the new thing in this mind. He likes to think of himself as something of an artist, something more than a collector. Whenever he employs artisans to make Church objects he always likes to participate in their design. Agnes sees he is distracted now, absorbed in his own goals for aggrandizement by being an art busybody. She takes from inside her cape the crucifix Sophia made and polishes it. The gleam from the shaft of the rood, elongated just below the crossed feet that are hammered through, and painfully, it appears from the way the rusted long spike tears agonizingly at the skin that is really metal but looks so much like warm flesh. And a precision-melted alloy runs from the feet, swift rivulets of blood that trail down the cross. Luscious realism.

"I'd make her sign a contract," he takes the cross. "And fast."

"But I have," she lies.

"Then why am I here? Your house will be rich, or at least as rich as you'll allow it to look from the outside."

"Jacques, please."

"Don't worry. In all my reports I say you run an honest Beguinehouse, although just at the edge of Church rule, always. But you know I let you pass."

"And I know why you do. You're here not to help with the girl but to take help from me. It's part of our relationship like fleas sucking on a dog, and only that. I'll let you have whatever it is you want her to make if you provide the materials needed for it, plus the complete materials for another crucifix of precious metals. Agree?"

The negotiating is made from necessity, and more than a little from greed. Each wants from the girl but the Beguine is in a position of power if she is careful to preserve it. She would coil the thread of control like silk around the priest and around Sophia. Reality spun from conviction. Agnes has something to offer the world, a new reality, a better consensus for reality that both she and Mary from Oignies have started. Blessed Mary is the one who has the vision and Agnes has the managerial proficiency, it's impossible for one to succeed without the other. Agnes is flamed by the spirit of emancipation, the desire to live free of the Church's growing power and, in a conceptual conviction that is similar, Mary is driven by the quest for a different order of power in which her own ideas are the most potent and she herself is the power holder. It's a more ambitious desire, does it matter if it's more or less prudent? It's difficult to ascertain whether Mary's plan for her own religion is any more attainable than the continued success of Agnes' dodging the burgeoning Church's encroachment on her freedom to live peacefully with her own chosen companions in her own house.

Now Sophia brings chaos with her. She leaps into the middle of their lives with delectable promise and with the portent of disarray. She can create unknown originality, unpredictable. She communes with inanimate things and treats those things that are not alive as if they breathed and those creatures that live as if they were dumb stones and dirt. The woman is chaos. Horrified when a cooking fire is extinguished because she thinks the dancing flame has lived, appalled by peasants digging into the earth's sides because surely they must be hurting it, afraid to hold breathed air too long inside of her because it might be frightened by the dark... But she is most grieved by taking water into her to survive when she thinks the courageous liquid has been wrenched from its mother, the sea, where it was born. Her thoughts are extraordinarily grievous permutations of the real.

She treats Metza like a pet. In the seven days she has lived in the Beguinehouse she's learned to wait for her in her bed, to await the feel of her warm back murmuring against her legs. But no attention is given to Metza beyond the primal comfort she supplies. No thanks given. It's uncertain whether Metza expects any or if she might expect a reward for her loyalty at some time in the future. Every night she curls at the foot of Sophia's cot, nestles beside her legs. She sleeps but she also keeps watch. She has not done this sort of thing before with her women companions and has always slept hungrily, an equal beside a woman, arms and legs intertwined. Not with

Sophia; they don't even speak. Sometimes Metza will rub her face against Sophia's hand, bared over the rough blanket, in slow and soft movements. Without accepting this with any return gestures of rejecting her with a blow, she receives the warmth and goes to sleep.

On a morning that screams with brightness and wind Agnes calls Sophia to meet with her and Mary. All the other Beguines have gone, begun the work that is their lives.

"We live in this commune because we're artists, women alone in the world, *femmes seules*, and we come together because of our work and because of necessity. There's no other place for us you know. Women who are artists who don't belong to a family or those religious orders with their insufferable rules have no alternative. We live together to work, and we live by the art of our hands.

The guildsmen would like to murder us, but before they do they're stealing our artistry by keeping us from the guilds and appropriating our work as their own. Saddles tooled with Metza's stamp on the side, for instance, are never delivered to the rich patrons by her but by the guildsmen who take credit for it. They say the work was done by some solitary monk somewhere. Liars. But at least they allow us single women to live, as long as we're useful to them."

Agnes knows she has heard it, but tells Sophia all this again. All the while Mary paces silently in front of a small window that looks out over the stinking street.

"Do you absolutely understand the peril?" Agnes says.

"Is there danger in moonlight?"

It seems she does not understand, in fact neither of them understands the other. But Mary does.

"Absolutely," she says. "When you manufacture the natural it's always hazardous. Something of the real always slips away and then it's just there, out there, something that's

105

on the wind and you can't control whether you breathe it in or not."

~

"Dry my blood with your lips, your breasts, the secret places of your body."

I call and no one is there to hear the hag, to answer me. And there is no blood after all. Dried, burned, gone, only the insubstance of what is substance is left, mingled here with all of you.

"You don't see me, you don't know this," I call to you.

Take my ashes. Start the quest. The charred bones will be scattered by fools, the truth will be permuted into legend. I will become a man, that's what the legend will make me although I am a woman. They fear my power. They feared my power.

Incineration is good to those who touched the burning branch to the pyre where I was tied. For them it was good. They wanted it to hurt. They have no idea how excruciatingly it did. But now, what? I learn.

"Oh brilliance!"

I'd like to tell you, to show you, but it's impossible. Try to find my ashes, collect my singed bones. Make me an icon but then do not revere me.

"Learn. Listen to me! You can be me, in fact, you are me. But you don't understand this, do you?"

Power is fire that brings death, always, every time it's used. Whenever you have the desire to ignite another person, then power exists. But this hasn't always been the way to do things between people, this use of the strength that's in us all.

"Understand? I can see that you don't."

But it's too soon and I'm not angry about it but I get tired of trying to explain what people need to learn to be, the quest. To learn you are everything. Just go and collect my ashes together. Make me an idol, and then do not revere me. Try to learn what this means. Try to slip through.

THIRTEEN

Resurrection Of Animals Dead On Glueboards, Vengeance

Sophia watches Sybelle paint on the wood with consistent strokes which put together side by side, one on the other, become a saint. The pious face with eyes uplifted seems to be soaked with light from below. An odd remembering, Sophia thinks, but effective. Light from a source that isn't obvious makes an impression, finesses a greater impact than gross intensity does. She's impressed. She didn't think the peculiar girl was skillful. The truth is that she believes in hierarchy and has perceived the girl to be on the lower rungs of the linear progression from her.

Sophia believes in exponential geometry, each strata of talent is a star's distance away from the next strata, the next ability, the next skill. This is why she believes so desperately in finding a master goldsmith. Only from him will she learn to make metal that looks like moonlight. It has a name she doesn't even know and this makes her feel ignorant but she doesn't feel as ignorant as she thought Sybelle must be and now she has to erase that evaluation and give her more credit.

But to do this she has to bring herself down and this isn't a re-evaluation she can do easily in her linear, exponential scheme. Fame is mutually exclusive, she believes. If someone else is a good artist, her own chances to become famous will be decreased. So she must camouflage herself to herself.

She must create a new reality to explain a friendship with Sybelle. If Sophia isn't superior to her, as she is to the beautiful Metza whose talent is only sculpture between animal flesh and human asses, then what? Sybelle's art can bring her just as much fame as Sophia's, but she has to make sure there's no room for them to occupy the same level of the hierarchy. An artist must be crafty.

"Why don't you make a mark on the piece?"

"What kind?"

"Yours. To show you're the one who made it," Sophia says.

"Would that get me more to eat?"

"Yes."

Damn it, she wishes she had not blurted out the truth. Of course it's the ultimate truth. The celebrity of the artist in the acknowledgement of skill means more to eat, just like his fat belly, clothes and fashionable accessories display the success of the merchant.

She said it again to herself, that *yes* it was really the truth she wished she hadn't passed on. Sybelle grasped instantly the philosophy of it that Sophia was trying to live and to perfect here in Strasbourg. Smart woman. She understands that reputation is the quest's end, a trade item. Stardom. Sophia wants the adulation a saint receives but she wants it for what she makes with her hands. Is that the same as wanting it for herself? Or is it something different because saints, like Blessed Mary in training, take the fame for themselves personally but artists stand apart from their work to allow the product to glean the renown. True, this reflects back on those who stand a bit to the side, a little behind their works. The artist can be a spectator to her own fame instead of only the receptive object, never able to admire what everyone else finds so lovely, as is the case with saints.

"Make a mark that's yours," Sophia whispers. "What will it be? Can't you do it?"

"Where's the food?

"Later. It'll come to you. First, make some kind of mark for yourself."

Sybelle doesn't move from her bench under the thick-leaved linden tree in the courtyard. Her filthy hands have stopped over the sudden radiance of the celestial portrait she's been painting. She doesn't know who it's supposed to be. The priest always tells Agnes and Mary what's been ordered and they repeat to her what the features are like. She feels their words, smells the description of the saints, and she replicates them from that. Somehow the qualities are always exactly what was expected. Everyone swears she must have seen the saints themselves. But she hasn't seen them or any previous likenesses and doesn't even care to. She only cares for painting and eating, and living in this city.

Devise a mark of some kind that is her own? She decides this isn't difficult nor does she think it's important, although she senses that others will. Amused, she draws with a sharp blade on the back of an oval wooden board.

A few lines she can taste on her tongue, a geometrical shape that is almost triangular. But it becomes an animate form, the face of a cat. Sophia recognizes the creature she left behind, her brother's lover. In Sybelle's drawing it's wearing the same intricate necklace that coils heavily in the pouch now hanging below her waist. A few lines, a geometry of economical shape, but she recognizes it as if it were painted

110

with color and detail and stood as large as the growing cathedral in the square. A few lines on wood that is an abstract design to anyone else but she sees it as the portrait Sybelle has mindlessly intended, the tyrannical animal Sophia left behind with her lover.

~

"I miss you. I miss you, oh my heart. Sweet daughter, oh warm presence. I'm so alone. I'll never be the same again. How I ache for you."

"And what about me? You know I can be all that she was to you, you know that."

It's Bear B.'s voice, very clear, although I can't see her. I know she's trying to trick me but I can't dwell on this or my reaction will show up on the readings and she'll know.

The glass from high above the gargan-City is dark. It's light outside but it's dark in here in the vast room with no sides. That's what they'd like me to think, that there are no sides and I can get up, just get up and walk away right off the side of this hundred and fifty stories or so where they're torturing me. Is that real? Is this thought real? There are so many people and places I feel I have either linked from chips or I've designed myself for SensSims. They're all in my head and I've been dreaming them or they're in Sims and I'm living them but I know they're not from before. They're now. I have to get away to find out how I'm doing this, tapping these other frequencies or bands where these images are running. If they're images.

Bear B. has been scanning me, she knows about my daughter although I don't remember having one, I feel that I have one. The agony of knowing she died haunts me worse than what they've done to me. Like images I've had projected on my newest alloy irises from history chips I adhered to my eyelids, the devices that have appeared and disappeared in this room are from ancient times. A rack for wrenching my joints, spikes driven through my breasts, a cage spiny with needles pressed over my face until the points stuck into my eyeballs, all these things that disappeared after I had screamed and screamed and fainted and was covered in blood and vomit.

"Why didn't you just use VirtReal? I'd feel the same pain. Or was that it anyway?"

"Baby, you're not paying attention. You have to tell me."

Arcs of oldfashion electrical voltage stream rainbows steaming with the acrid smell of my singed flesh. And now it's over and Bear B. is on me. No pain. No scars. The pulsation of her beauty is all there is. There's something she wants to know, something else.

"We'll take you home now," she says.

Two Alternates with the smiling good looks that come with their particular model's production specifications enter and help me to my feet. They begin to dress me. Their skin is soft and too flawless. Probably because they're Police Alters no one has bothered to add the perfection of irregular human skin to. I'm surprised they're as good as they are, though, considering I'm no high level criminal who needs to be misled into thinking they're human. But what about Bear B.? I hadn't thought of it before now. I think so, that she must be real because I don't think that Alters can sexually relate so realistically. What am I saying? Of course they can, and do. In VirtReal anything can happen, but in the present world we can still be limited by bodies, no matter how mutated by technological apparatus, and time and space and what there is left of the weather.

We take a vacuum shaft down to the ground floor and Bear B., tall and smiling, leans against me. Laughing for no apparent reason, she's acting like we're lovers, trailing her fingers over my lips breathing in my ear. Does she dare to do something to me again?

Kvino is there in the vast lobby. It towers so high that a cloud hovers in one corner. A few people walk by rapidly, not looking at anything in typical gargan-City behavior. Nothing has changed since I've been interrogated. I have to ask Kvino what time it is, what day.

"Assholes have had you for a week," he says.

Bear B. takes my arm and leads me to a sporty red hoverVehicle that appears all of a sudden. She waves Kvino and me inside, all the while she's smiling impishly at me like a lover. Kvino tries to keep his eyes off her but I can see he's impressed although his features show nothing but his good nature. He shrugs to let me know he has no idea what's going on either. And I wonder how much he's told the Police already. Although, what does he really know?

Once we're all in my cubicle high over the quiet streets Bear B. asks for a drink like this is some kind of social gathering or something. And he agrees when she asks Kvino if he'd like one too and suddenly I'm playing hostess. While I turn my back to press the drink icons on the wall and get the tray with the containers that come out they don't talk together. In a few seconds I turn back around and she is there. Her! Curled up around Kvino's boots my daughter is looking up at me, purring.

"Oh god!"

Bear B. reaches down and the cat bites hard on her finger, draws what looks like real blood. Just as she would have done, did do in life, this Holo VirtReal essence struts toward me. Goddamnit goddamnit, I can't breathe. She's there and I know that she's not. Against my leg, warm, purring, leaving black polymer hairs stuck to me, she's here and I hate it. My sobs ache in my throat. She's gone. This isn't her, this isn't real, damn it. 'Dinger dead and alive at the same time, fifty-fifty.

"Take her away!"

I scream as loud as I can at Bear B. And I make a fist and slam it at her face as hard I can.

The smile on her lips is sad when she grabs my wrist and encircles it with lightning fingers that hook together. She pulls me to her and caresses me. Smothered by her, shattered with grief, I have to get away. I try to pull away. The cat is purring against my leg and I want to die. I'm tormented. Her soft fake presence, my love, is no solace.

"Pick her up," Bear B. whispers in my ear. "She is real because you see her here. Don't fight reality."

Has she read my thoughts? Within my sobs I strangle with hatred for her, this cop, this fucking bitch. This invasion, this terror of my dead love suddenly here with me. Here, after I stroked her stiff limbs, her cold unmoving fur. But I thought I didn't know her then, there in Mary Sevenforty's place. What are they doing to me?

"Kvino!"

I reach for him. He looks embarrassed and smiles awkwardly, indicating with his head that I should stay in Bear B.s arms. And still I feel the image coiling around my legs. The feeling, how I've longed for this, ached with pain real enough to make me sick, but now it's grotesque. I want to bury my face in her fur but I'm afraid, repulsed. Afraid of death? No, afraid of the real. What is my life? What is this other presence that bursts through some other place in my mind that I know and that I know I'm not supposed to know. I've got to get away to find out where all the images come from.

"Please stop this."

"I will if you'll talk to your mother," Bear B. says.

"My mother? I don't have a mother, you know that, I have two fathers."

"But you do and you know it. You erased her from your life nano-banks when you didn't want her anymore, couldn't stand her."

"You can't do this. You can't do this, it was official. It was all done officially."

"Nor\Newton's Utilities, they recapture deleted data, you know that. Every SensSim designer like you uses them when you write programs. Information is neither created nor destroyed, it just changes location. Remember? Your mother was stored somewhere else, in another sector that's all. Go on, sleep on it for a while."

~

Sophia feels the colors trembling around her, the warmth of the sea, the undulation of the woman curled at her feet. It is the wind scoured morning of the next day, early before dawn and not yet luminous. Blessed Mary comes to wake her when she returns from her early rounds through the city streets that have left her tracks ending in odd places. At the edge of the well with no return footprints, at the side of the tower in the corner of the thick wall as if the maker of the tracks walked through that barrier, at the entrance to the stable with no retreating steps nor animal prints to indicate she had mounted a ride. Mary has carefully constructed the artifacts of her reality this morning as she does every morning. These will be noticed and interpreted by the townspeople and a concordance will grow around them. She is constructing her life in consensual images, bolstering her entitlement to be called Saint someday.

"Do you always sleep this way?" Mary says to Metza, not Sophia.

"Does it make you jealous?"

115

"You know."

Sophia doesn't miss the feeling of Metza's warmth when she gets up, nor does she watch while she and Mary say things to each other with their eyes. She only wonders why this aspiring saint is there and mostly hopes to be told they've found a goldsmith to apprentice her. The work is all there is. She has so easily left the love of her previous life behind, her father and her brother Rudolphe there in the forest with his lover. Another set of things and times and daylight and darkness divided into activities and feelings that no longer exist. The objects are no more, the routine is no more. Because Sophia can no longer see them, no longer taste the days and nights on her lips she presumes they're gone. When she doesn't look at them the cease to live for her. Or, she wonders, do they continue to exist at all? Only one of them, she thinks, has the strength to persist without her attention, that one, the animal with the smirk. The same one that Sybelle has so perfectly imaged. That one.

"It's time for you to start to work," Mary says to her. "You have to fulfill your part of our agreement, if you live in this house to have to make the reliquary, the ashes of the one who will be an icon to all of us and who is like us, she must be housed. They've tried to scatter her ashes and her bones but we've collected them. She's revered by us, a great woman. I'm here to tell you about her, how she was born what they'd call a saint already. In the womb of her mother she united with her brother..."

The symbolism of the Egyptian religion is mostly expressed by means of animals. Thus a god of the dead is spoken of as a jackal, the water-god as a crocodile... Because of this exaltation of certain animals whole species were held as sacred, and this led to the many strange ideas and customs amongst the Egyptians mentioned so often by classic writers, as, for instance, considering a man fortunate who was eaten by a crocodile...

The cat was regarded both as an incarnation of Bast, the goddess of Bubastis, and therefore sacred to her, and as a personification of the sun. Throughout Egyptian mythology the cat is to be found, and generally in a beneficent aspect. In the Book of the Dead it is a cat who cuts off the head of the serpent of darkness and who assists in the destruction of the foes of Osiris... Diodorus relates that the cats were fed on bread and milk and slices of Nile fish, and that the animals came to their meals at certain calls. After death their bodies were carefully embalmed and, with spices and drugs, swathed in linen sheets. The penalty of death was meted out to anyone who killed a cat, be it by accident or of intent, and a case is given in which a Roman who had killed a cat was set upon by the enraged populace and made to pay for the outrage with his life. A passage from Herodotus further illustrates the esteem in which these animals were held: 'When a conflagration takes place a supernatural impulse seizes on the cats. For the Egyptians, standing at a distance, take care of the cats and neglect to put out the fire; but the cats, making their escape, and leaping over the men, throw themselves into the fire; and when this happens great lamentations are made among the Egyptians. In whatsoever house a cat dies a natural death all the family shave their eyebrows...'

Spence

117

FOURTEEN

Restore Deleted Text

I have an exotic desire to date things. A penchant to be able to accurately assign a year and epoch of social history to objects and events. To put them in their place. Child labor and soot-rained European and New England cities, 1860s. The beginning of motor transport for individuals, 1900. Body transforms, 2030.

Too much history, maybe Bear B. was right. Tangible Holograph body imaging, 2024. It makes my skin pinch in needles of panic, sweat runs in streams I can feel down my back even though there's none from my armpits because of the alterations; nobody sweats there anymore because of fashion decisions. The hair on my head is wet, my scalp sweltering. If I could catch a breath in lungs that feel like I've been too long underwater I would do it, greedily eat the air for which I'm panting in shallow gasps. How can I accept this image in front of me? The cat is dead. I held her in my arms. She's dead but now she stands in front of me. I felt her there swooning against my leg and that's what has made me tremble and agonize like this. She's here. Warm and breathing against me, looking with those eyes that are more wise than soft. It's too morbid, this nonreality that is real. Kvino has taken her in his lap, he's smiling and petting her although he never really comingles with other animals as far as I know. They never appealed to him. But now there he is holding her while Bear B. coos at them both, sucking on the finger the other animal has bitten, the weaponry around her wrists glittering in its ready state.

My love is here and they're waiting for me to destroy her, this perverted image that is real. Alive and dead. I turn away from the transparent walls of my cubicle to the vibrating colored lights that separate it from the sleep space. On the solid looking poly-optic wall behind is the panel housing the control micro-nanos. The minuscule lights shine in the same pattern and intensity they always do so the program for the feline Holo isn't coming from there, it must be Bear B. If that's true then when she leaves the image will disappear with her, after a certain distance or time has elapsed. But that's too easy. Now I suddenly know where the program is. It's in me. The implants on my wrist, though, show no signs of additions, my life monitor crystals there look dull but it's no wonder with what I've been through, otherwise there's no change. But in my skull, here, at the base of my neck.

Ranging my fingertips over the grid of pinpoints I feel there's a minute change in the chip pattern that transmits from there into the sensory projection area high at the front of my brain's parietal lobe. They've put it in me. The program nanodot sub-chip that controls the Hologram of my daughter is relaying through the cortex of my brain. I am the enemy. Should I smash out the patch of grid at the back of my skull? I feel with my damp shaking fingers again and recognize a pattern that's clear to me even in my agitation. They have implanted a new cerebral cortex transmitter in tandem with a medulla regulator so if I destroy the images that are projected through my higher association areas then all the basic activities regulated by the brain stem like breathing, heartbeat, blood circulation, all that will stop. To stop seeing this movie I can't just change the frequency, I have to die.

"Phylogeny recapitulates ontogeny, backwards," I whisper it.

My damnation means everything is damned. Everything is damned. If I have to kill myself to stop this artificial reality, to change this lousy existence that's controlled by data instead of by some kind of values then the world has to be destroyed too. Change from the top down, start over with whatever mutant amoebae or planaria might be left to evolve again. I know this, but I've always known this. I've never done anything about it. What can I do?

Evolution begins ontogenously, the effects are reflected in phylogeny. You are the architect of your own personal damnation or progression, and it all makes a difference.

"Who said that?"

I wish it was last year when Kvino and I were taking oldfashion drugs and feeling good. I wish it was still before. I wish I could sell my new game unit to the diversion industry so I could be famous like the MegaCelebs are. I wish the Police would leave me alone because I don't have anything; these voices in my head must come from whatever they're transmitting to test me. Why don't they make me famous first and persecute me after? Then it would be worth it. All I want to do is live my life. Like Mat/leen used to tell me, I'm a virtreal snob. I think I'm better than the masses who live in the networked unrealities, but why am I not famous yet? Where's my break in the diversion business? Who cares about the lousy data control of the world? Just give me my own stuff, my success.

120

"We're going to leave you now," Bear B. says.

"You're taking her with you, right?"

"She's yours. See you."

I look at Kvino and see that his hand is firmly embedded in Bear B.'s magnetic grasp. Whatever plan he's been making to help me can't start now. A neon strand of light from her weapons bracelet hums around his wrist.

"If you don't want the image around you know how to turn it off," Bear B. heads for the door.

"What do you mean?"

"You know."

She takes one long step back into the room to kiss me. My lips sting from it with a taste that's like a sour cream replication. Her tongue is quick and then she's gone. I can only imagine what she'll do with Kvino and I feel jealous at the thought, at the image that comes too easily to visual life because of my additional cerebral implants. I don't want to see him enfolded by her magenta skin, but the movie is vivid, my irises shimmer with them when I try to shut them out. Think of nails hammered through hands and feet. That works. Elementary thought control works.

And fear. I don't want to turn around where the Holo of my beloved must still be, probably lounging on the chair. It will want to curl next to me, purring from its recorded implant. I loved her, my real daughter, but not this one, this duplicate. It only enacts my pain.

> Half alive and half dead at the same time.
> Probabilities that make you real.

"Is that true?" I say to myself or to the voice I think is probably someone else's in my head. Probably.

I might have saved her, my child, had I been watching her instead of exploring something in myself. Some *what*? Some violence. My self? My thoughts, exploring some violent Sim plot killed her, yes. And no I can't live with it, me, that self.

Goodbye world that I never bothered to help, I'll find the answers that aren't anywhere. It's the only way. I'll be with her again and I'll know why it all happened when I'm allowed to die. I will know why it all happened. If there's another way it's only advertised Traveler nonsense, to have questions about the universe, about phylogeny.

LOOKING FOR ANSWERS
VOYAGE TO THEM WITH US
TRAVELERS
wave 23.1.3r

The words streak past leaving a faintly glowing trail of boson specks that lead back to the nanochip that emitted them. Kvino must have dropped it there by the door. What has he been doing with them? Nobody really believes these kinds of ads that flash by when you access Sims. No one has any questions. But Travelers do, it's in every jingle that plays in their ads. The rest of us make fun of it, ignore it, but what if it really means something?

If the police do it to me they're doing it others. Must have. There have got to be people asking the questions. Can I make reality with my mind? Is that what I've done with my violent thoughts, killed my daughter? They've brought back her Hologram to scare me, force me to tell them how I did it. But that's what I've got to find out and maybe Travelers might know something or at least feel the same questions. Anyway Kvino seems to think they have something and that's with considering how much he really can't stand their sticky congeniality.

If I could even begin to believe that there's some good in me, what would I think of all my vile dreams, the pictures, the realities in my mind? How bizarre I am for having questions. How could I be good and the world be good in any way with such ugliness engraved inside of me? All they have to do is cut into me, make a slice with a crystal blade and peel back even a few centimeters of skin. Inside are the pictures of evil. There are my constructions of vulgar people, ignorant lazy creatures I despise in the world. The ones who are stupid, who dress badly, who are bigots and narrow minded, who believe in oldfashion values of grouping genetically similar harvested fetuses together in *faux* family arrangements that exclude others. I hate. They're inside of me. I judge everything. All the loathing of foreigners I never felt, all the abhorrence of rapes I never thought about, all the racist venom that revolted me when I saw it in the history of the world. I hated and judged everything. It's all inside of me, written inside my skin, all the worst of humankind is me.

That was why I killed my mother. Because I'm like that and she made me that way.

Probabilities you choose—

"Shut up!"

At my mother's funeral, the one I designed, as she lay there and then sat up with her eyes rotated open, nodding her head from side to side then lying down again stylishly, I thought all those things. But I was afraid. I was afraid to think any of it because then my mother would be able to hear it. There at the funeral mall were my appointed grandmother and aunt, who were already dead, sitting among the sparse gathering of mourners. I wondered then what time and place it really was. Have I known those women before in other ways, other relationships? Is it true that consequences repeat? Or, consequences repercuss? I can't think anymore and I'll fall asleep here in the miniature hallway so I won't have to be near her, my dead daughter, alive just a few steps away.

~

Agnes, using more exertion with the hammer and small axe than she anticipated would be necessary, breaks the crucifix into two uneven pieces while Blessed Mary tries not to laugh. They are alone in the middle of the night in the shed at the rear of the cluttered yard. A mistake has to be corrected and Mary is taking it better than Agnes. The priest DeVitry has had Sophia followed in the street and yesterday his men brought her to the cathedral where he spoke with her. Obviously not believing Agnes' lie that she was already under contract, he offered Sophia the possibility of a feudal agreement of his own. If she fulfills a commission he has given her to his satisfaction then he will employ her with his other smiths where she will not only learn what she wants but she might even earn land of her own.

"I don't care about that," she told him. "I don't want any land, I only want to work."

"You're young. I'm offering you this standard contract no matter what you say. Later, you'll know I'm being fair with you."

Of course DeVitry was doubly angry when he discovered Agnes lied to him. The smith is a free agent and he was quick to dazzle her. As soon as word of this reached Agnes she made the plan that she's started to engineer in reality. Breaking the crucifix Sophia made is the first step. *Shoddy craftsmanship.* The accusation will inhibit the priest's plans for a time until she can maneuver another scheme into action. Blessed Mary, amused by Agnes' labor, knows this is a crucial time in their reality manipulations. Her solution for their sudden problem is even bolder than her colleague's.

"It's time that I begin to be revered more seriously," she says, retrieving the broken pieces. "Do you know what I mean? It's time we organize for my sainthood on earth, and that's without my being imprisoned or tortured or martyred of course. Although prison might not be intolerable, depending."

"I thought we agreed that we needed a miracle first."

"Then let's have one, for christ's sake, and we'll have it commemorated in a fabulous object of some kind, something to make up for the terrible construction of this crucifix that meant so much to the financial success of this house. That's what we'll tell her."

"As long as we haven't shaken the girl's confidence by doing this and blaming her. Now I'm having second thoughts."

"Stop it," Mary smoothes her hair. "I'll sanctify her, after all I can do that kind of thing. Besides, she needs to believe, to be a little scared, don't you think?"

"Absolutely."

"We need to bind her more to us, you're the one who said it first," Mary sings what she's saying like a church chant. *"The girl is selfish, the girl is focused only on herselffff. The work of her hands she will learn, she will learn, should be for usss, and not for her alone, not for her alonnne."*

"Enough. You made your point, but we have to be careful. Priests are richer than us and can offer her more of everything. Did you hear that Bishop Milo in Beauvais will probably give Magister Ivo a fief just for repairing his mazers, hanaps, all his cups with silver and gold? While Ivo plays around with his own work he's contracted to make three new base bottoms every year for the castle bowls if they're needed, repair the Bishop's *écuelles*, and make six new ones every year, with gems of course. He repairs the basins and makes two of them in a year. They're still negotiating details but the girl will think all of that smithing is easy. She'll be impressed that the Bishop supplies the gold and silver, everything, and you can bet that smith Ivo is keeping some of it for himself."

"She owes us a reliquary for the sacred ashes, and the repair of this cross, of course. I'll make her beholden for something for me, a chalice or precious box of some kind in my honor maybe."

They talk in the darkness because they put out the candles they used when they destroyed the work of art. Words need no light when each speaker knows their intent. When the goal is clear. If these two didn't know each other's desires so well they might need to see a look in an eye, the lift of a lip or a glance away at a moment of lying. Words can be given meaning by sight. But these two need no confirmation because their voracity is equal in intensity. Ravenous women, neither has eaten anything that truly satisfies them. This isn't their world and they know what they will replace it with. Clear motive makes their actions easy to decipher. They talk in the darkness and know precisely the luster in each other's eyes.

Sybelle has smelled them out there through the dark. She can feel what they're saying in her own mouth. Their words are warm and greasy, green like caterpillars behind her teeth. And heavy, pressing down on her tongue like stones, still they feel slippery inside of her. Now she knows every one of them, every word impressed into her. They are a vision of objects, these words, that she can never forget and the tone of their voices beats against her cheeks, her eyes. Each of the objects they speak presses into her. If she wanted to, right now she could paint them in scenes onto the wooden wall next to her straw mat. Sybelle sees, tastes and feels ever word they say. Sometimes, there on her soiled mat, she flinches from the blow of an idea or swallows hard a bitter thought.

She knows everything that has passed between the two women since the time she first met them, since they took her in two years ago. She hasn't forgotten anything, none of the abuses before she came here or any of the intrigue and planning for their new reality since she's been here. But Agnes and Mary have no idea of her sensual proficiency, not outside of knowing she's very odd and they must protect her. But her peculiarities could bring them the recognition they want because they could sell Sybelle's natural talent as a saintly miracle. Tasting the spikes and slipperiness of words, seeing emotions as if they were rocks or clods of earth she holds in her hand, feeling the weight of the colors of cloaks, not the material but the colors of stinging red and slightly bitter blue that winds around her ankles, and even feeling the melody of those colors on her skin, her tongue. These are miracles of twisted sensations. But Agnes and Mary don't know she has these abilities and she won't tell them.

"I could tell you something," Sybelle says to Sophia at dawn, Metza still sleeping at her feet.

"What?"

"It could be about you or about me, I haven't thought about which of us it is. But it's probably both if I tell you, half and half."

Sophia is distracted by the fly that crosses in front of her eyes. It lights on a long strand of straw that sticks out of her mattress. How do those hairy legs feel, she wonders, moving up and down the stalk like that, And what can the straw do about it? She frightens the fly with a furious movement, closed fist, angry punch. *Bastard, bastard!* The fury wells in her and she thinks what if it had touched her lips that way, the way it touched the slender body of the straw? And her fierceness awakens Metza who dares not stretch her arms over her head, arching her back as is her habit before rising.

127

Now she doesn't even blink while she watches the tightening on Sophia's face. She watches, and when there's a flicker of change she rubs her neck softly against Sophia's leg and murmurs from deep in her throat.

Sophia doesn't respond and leaves the bed. Her mind is on what the halfwit told her because she feels instinctively that something about it is important, maybe even more important than that priest's slimy offer. She's sure that Sybelle has more behind her slow eyes than it appears.

FIFTEEN

...We Must Sometimes Lend Ourselves To Our Friends, And When We Would Die For Ourselves Must Break That Resolution For Them.
Montaigne

"Somebody ask me! I understand the quest, and I have something to say. Listen to me!"

~

The workshop is inside a fortress. Thick boards make the sides and roof of an antechamber attached with hardened clay to a rock formation that widens and becomes cave-like because of that architected chamber. The sculptures of saints outside announce its gaping threshold. It would be only an indented side of a hill without this carpentered façade. Oil and wick lamps light the interior. Slabs of wood make shelves that line the walls in an uneven march to the domed top. Chinks of stone make the floor, also uneven, and to stand there to observe all of it is disorienting in the dim disarray of vessels, pots, cauldrons, ewers, flasks and pestles of various sizes and colors, not to mention the smells leaking from them.

Sophia is sweating in excitement. Her aroma lends a human ambience to the earthy and acid scents. Even Agnes and Blessed Mary can smell her from where they stand well behind her in the gloom.

"No," Mary looks around. "This isn't any kind of place for a miracle. "Not open enough for witnesses, not enough room for the hordes of believers later on who will come to revere my memory. Carrying candles, staying to meditate and refresh themselves in my spiritual presence, wanting to see and to kiss a holy reliquary with part of me preserved inside, like maybe a fingernail, piece of skin or some hair but not a lock though. There has to be enough of my body to go around to all the shrines I'll sanctify to dilute the Church's stranglehold on people's dreams."

Agnes says, "Have you decided then that every relic has to be genuine?"

"Don't you think so? Nothing should be simulated, look what's behind the scandal over John the Baptist's supposed head. All those pious crooks say they have clippings of his beard direct from the decapitation, splattered blood and all. But there are so many bristles the man would have to be huge and hairy to supply all the relics of him that are sold in every village and every town square."

"It's annoying."

"Saints have to plan these things, or they should. When there's a new reality to be built for the good of the universe conscious saints have to plan these things. Swindlers sanctified by the Church have already done so much that's rotten. The means will transform only when ends transcend."

"That's a mouthful. 'When ends transcend...'"

"We'll shorten it."

130

This is what they always end up talking about when they plan their strategy. Evolution.

"Minds still have to develop much farther to make and to aspire to transcendent ends."

Sophia hears none of it, blots at the moisture on her face and neck with the coarse material of the cape the Beguines gave her. Feeling her tightened belt's constriction when she moves her arms she's reminded of the bad food at the Beguinehouse. Not one of the women know how to feed the commune and she has the thought now of Rudolphe's lover who must still be providing well for him and her father there in the countryside. But this is her home now. This murky workplace envelops her with ringing promise. She can hear the humming of the jars and their smells, the sound of boiling chemicals. It is success, eventually, and the wonders of learning right now so she's anxious for the master to appear. The priest DeVitry has guaranteed her a limited apprenticeship to Magister Ivo but Sophia has no idea of the machinations and bargains that have been struck between him and Agnes to allow her to work at all. She has no idea because she doesn't care. For her this workplace exists not in the half-cave but beneath a warm and embracing sea that shivers with unmentionable hues.

~

When I wake up I don't know what to do, whether Kvino will contact me or if the cat is gone. I don't look for her. I slip through the door and go out in the gargan-City. I meet someone acting like a man who is emitting a perfect frequency. He hails me on the friendly spectrum that produces a pink gleam in the microcrystals on the receptive sector of my wrist and I hear the soft tone that accompanies it: no aggression found by my scanners. He smiles, assured that my assessment of him is tempered with the feeling of safety that's been transmitted. He won't be hostile. No one with his appearance status' medically architected handsome features could be anymore, what with genetic engineering identifying and destroying violent tendencies in the productive ranks that dress with the kind of trendy accessories he's wearing. Entertainment. A microdot of exhilarant will make me forget who I am and what's happened, what I should be doing now instead of being with him.

Go with him down the neon red blinding tube, down into a dark vacuum where we float together. A matrix of pinpointed tazer lights dazzle around us, rotating slowly. He smiles, presses on the adapters at his wrist.

He made love to me remembering what it was like to be watched in glances on their way to somewhere else. He remembered the feeling. And now when he moved his hands over me it wasn't skin moving under his fingertips but something else. Fur under him, a warm animal caressing him. He knows this, sees me, but the feeling is different. There was that smell of the other animal he remembered from when he would take me in his arms and bury his nose in my thick black coat, just behind my front legs. He would hold me tightly, filled with love, with awe for me. I was so precious to him he wanted to squeeze me hard but didn't.

My warmth, my self is here with him. He sees me. A fifty percent chance of being alive, fifty percent that I'm dead. He didn't think I could be real yet here I am, black fur, yellow eyes that are enormous. Gone now, but still alive in his mind. Some boundary vibrated past us. The animal he loved and who is dead is here with him in his world or some other world and he's making love to me. He will cry again, and he knows it. He will cry when this act is finished with me, with...

132

I've never been good at accepting reality. Not gracious. My dead daughter's body there on the carpeted floor next to him is neater than my grief. I remembered I thought this while I looked out the window away from it all at the dirty yellow sun they say used to be bright.

"Who killed her? Who killed my baby?"

It was the dead cat next to me who hurt me more, made me unable to answer questions. But this is something I have to do, I have to find out why I can do this, how I can.

Every night when all had retired to rest, she would pile great logs on the fire and thrust the child among them, and, changing herself into a swallow, would twitter mournful lamentations for her dead husband. Rumours of these strange practices were brought by the queen's maidens to the ears of their mistress, who...concealed herself in the great hall, and when night came sure enough Isis barred the doors and piled logs on the fire, thrusting the child among the glowing wood. The queen rushed forward with a loud cry and rescued her boy from the flames. The goddess reproved her sternly, declaring...she had deprived the young prince of immortality. Then Isis revealed her identity to the awe-stricken Athenais and told her story, begging that the pillar which supported the roof might be given to her...she cut open the tree, took out the coffin containing the body of Osiris, and mourned so loudly over it that one of the young princes died of terror. Then she took the chest by sea to Egypt...opening [it] and wept long and sorely over the remains of her royal husband. But now she bethought herself of her son...Horus...who she had left in Buto, and leaving the chest in a secret place, she set off to search for him. Meanwhile Set...discovered the coffin and in his rage rent the body in fourteen pieces, which he scattered here and there throughout the country.

Upon learning of this fresh outrage on the body of the god, Isis took a boat of papyrus-reeds and journeyed forth once more in search of her husband's remains. After this crocodiles would not touch a papyrus boat, probably because they thought it contained the goddess, still pursuing her weary search. Whenever Isis found a portion of the corpse she buried it and built a shrine to mark the spot. It is for this reason that there are so many tombs of Osiris in Egypt.

Spence[19]

SIXTEEN

Map Special Characters

"You're shocked at why I do these things but not at the horror of what I do. You only worry about the reasons, isn't that right, Gilbert? That's even odder than my sins."

"Sins, Inquisitor? I never meant to accuse you."

"You didn't, and you wouldn't dare. My position in the Church is too solid now that I'm one of their most successful, most diligent assassins. I could have you on the rack in a minute, snapping those joints of yours, *pop*, like that. You're right to flinch, you've seen enough of it. Hearing it is the worst though, isn't it? Almost worse than watching. That sound, I can hear it like the knees of that last old lady were yanking out of their sockets right in front of me again, right now. See, I've got goose flesh from the thought. And the way she screamed, oh my God. And you, look at you, you're red to the ears and your eyes water at the memory. That last old one was another on the list, another tortured for no good reason."

"Inquisitor!"

"That man, her accuser, the one who couldn't keep his chin cleaned of his own spit, didn't you see him laughing when we burned her? Now he's got her cottage and her land, the livestock too. He got his revenge for her having cursed at him for trying to cheat her."

"But that was exactly the charge we proved, that she cursed him."

"She cursed at him, idiot. She called him a bastard halfwit and a sneaky coward after she caught him trying to steal her cow. She ran him off with a club, remember, they both testified to that. Later when his lousy patch of ill-cared for potatoes rotted in the ground because of his own laziness and ignorance—he never went to town to carry back barrels of water to overcome this drought—it was then he said she had cursed him and caused his bad fortune because she's a witch. And what did I do, and you too? We made her another example of the Church's power. Her problem was that she didn't go to Mass, didn't submit to confession with that fat, ugly priest who runs the town. He was the one who gave her up, and I carried out the Church's will. Absurd how they call it the 'mother' Church and then go around murdering mothers."

"Only when they're guilty, when it's necessary. After all, she confessed."

"Wouldn't you? My God the pain it must be! My stomach turns. And don't be so shocked at why I say I do it, all this. Let the scholars who get paid for their time argue about the connections between methods and outcomes, the ones who ponder whether horrific means justify the 'heavenly' ends. Why aren't there ever any different kinds of ends? I only get paid to follow the edicts and that's why I do it, not to punish the women they call witches but because they tell me to. Is that what shocks you? I think it is."

"Sir, whatever you say to shock me doesn't matter because obedience is what we're taught. That's what you're doing, and I'm doing, and it's glorious in the eyes of the Church."

"Obedience? Unquestioned obedience is just stupid conformity, Gil. And that's indeed what we're taught. You're right, they say it's glorious. But what are the consequences of ignorance?"

"Are you testing me on Church doctrine? Is this a trick?"

"Remember when we tortured that one at the end of last season, the hag with the sense of humor? The one who sang while she roasted, sedition songs or redemption songs—*songs of freedom*. Anyway, she was funny. Skin peeling away in a black sheet from her legs while she laughed at us. You remember. Did we really see it?"

"What do you mean, did we? Who could forget?"

"I mean did we see what was really there, a woman who could burn and sing at the same time or was it a dream we shared that was made by all of us, not by any one of us alone? Gilbert, can you grasp this? Try to listen. I'm saying that maybe we didn't really murder that woman so sadistically in the flames with that arrow through her throat to finally stop her from ridiculing us. Maybe there was nothing there at all, only what we expected."

"What am I supposed to say? We took her ashes, at least we tried. They were so hot. We scattered her bones."

"Or his. There's a myth, but never mind. Maybe we only expected everything to happen that way because we're so used to it, used to it like the stink of a town when you near the wall with the open dung ditch. Maybe what we saw is what we expect or is our own need, to have a martyr like all the others. We sacrificed a woman to the flames because she lived in a different world that we conceived all together where we thought she could fly and her cat could talk, run errands. A different world from this, but we murdered her in this one we call ours and for all we know she might still exist in her own place somewhere else."

"Very funny, Inquisitor. This is a joke you're making. Funny."

"Try to keep up with me. We did what we did because we were ordered to do it. What if we, never mind you, what if I refused? What if I refused to assassinate innocent women?"

"But they're blasphemers, sinners, witches—"

"Now who's joking? Come on, that's what the Church says but have they actually done anything to you? Or to me? Cause, effect? It doesn't matter because we always find them guilty, don't we? Always. We have to because those are the orders we work under to get paid. That's a reality. We murder because we're told to, not because we've been wronged. Get it? No cause, no effect. That's the reason I burn women alive, it's just part of the order of our world and I uphold it. What I do is horrible enough, but it's why I do it that's worse. Unforgiveable. That reason is part of the expectations that make our world real. The world is the gross things we think are true, the consequences we expect that are real, but only for those people who believe it. To them we're murderers. But to those who get away, we don't exist."

~

I came out of my stupor or dream and was aware of the sensuality. It wasn't the same thing I linked from the history chips from the end of the 20th Cent. The sex in CySpace was good with him in a supplanted physical space kind of way. We went beyond our bodies although not beyond our beliefs, what we expected, even though what I guess both of us have learned to anticipate was enhanced beyond what we could have created alone because of the databanks we accessed. The Nets gave us reality and it felt good. Although I could have done the sex by myself with an Alter or something that was completely cognized, completely artificially not there, the addition of his actual body meant a different warmth in the pressed heat of genuine flesh without being processed though the Networks. It was that physical interaction that was sensational and he did it very well.

Do I want to go any further now with, what? Who? With this thing who now looks like he's changed his or her SexSens belt back to the default setting. But I don't need intimacy anymore. The sex was enough. Still he stays and I see him lingering at the entrance to the tube, the one blazing with vermillion neon. But the one where I hover is colors only, ringing, dripping and it too beckons us to that experience again. We rotate slowly in radiated gloominess, more and more closely, spiraling down toward a soft blacked-out bottom. The microdot stimulant has worn off. My wrist implants' access quadrant blinks, crystal clear yellow in my dark skin, asking for a response to its query whether to attach more of the drug onto my endocrine molecular pattern. It will automatically activate my autonomic nervous system with the substance if I agree. Do I want him again with his male-mess, or will he do it this time as a woman? Otherwise, I wonder, do I have to talk to him, or her?

Choose amusement space:\a,b,c

My implanted bracelet is sparkling and there will be sub-menus from this or else I can simply choose *repeat*. Then this man as woman, or the other way around, and I will be replayed in our ecstasy, the replay hooked through our peripheral nervous system will make us feel exactly like we're doing it again and exactly like before. It might be fun to be able to slow down the action or to freeze-frame a few of the good moments. I have to think about this. The Nets give me time, the microcrystals on my wrist continue to blink. Everything waits for me to decide as I feel myself slowly rotating. Me, just another node in the vast infoNets. A reddishly green impossible glowing and humming, turning thing, a quari-dot, a speck in dataspace. That is my *self* for which the part of the Net controlling my sector waits. It waits for me, my designated node in the information cosmos to specify my new coordinates, all my possibilities. My smooth ebony-skinned body self is not consequential now. Try to think. And I try to think of what this thinking means.

Competition. Why does this come into my mind? Because I'm being timed, because I must earn credits for the usage of CySpace and I can by minute increments increase the tiny sectors of information that I can access. Competition. Is this natural? They've always said that it is. Murderers and victims. Ancient history, Darwin—and before he was given credit for Spencer's work already conceptualized—he said it was competition. But he was male then. Competition. But the autocatalytic sets co-evolve in symbiosis, not inequality. Why do I think this?

Because it's true if you understand that we all, all of us, are not outsiders. We are the universes, gods. Each one of us is and has been self-generating, autocatalytic, self-organizing and co-evolving. There is consequently life after life, after life. Afterlife.

"If we evolve in symbiosis instead of competition, then there shouldn't be any of the negative male-ness, no competitive games," I find myself saying. "What would that be like, life after life?"

"We're going to take you again if you keep bringing up these pesky reasons. Nobody cares 'why' anything. We're going to have to take you again if you don't make a decision. How do you want it this time?" Now it's Bear B.'s voice like hot wax bubbling in my ear. "Stay away from reasons and consequences, baby. Too much history. Have sex."

"OK."

I'm a coward, I think to myself. The fear of feeling again what she can do to damage me makes me spineless. She could create sex with me again, that would be all right. But the pain, what she can do with her weapon wrists is something I don't want to experience again, even though it only happens in VirtReal. So I'm a coward. I say *yes* to sex. Let her construct whatever she wants to for me, I'll do it. It's all just Holos anyway, even me. To the extent of inhabiting this certain set of coordinates in data space now, yes, me too. Real is what you feel, and VirtReal makes you feel therefore it's a certain kind of truth, right? Certain? So I feel and know that it's not real or not me, or that the sensations or the bruises and slashes or whatever they program for me will go away after the Nets connections are de-accessed and I've logged off so it's not real. But while it's happening it's real no matter where my body actually is. Am I the only one to think of this? Can't be. I have to find out. I have to get free to find out.

"Kvino?"

"Whatever you're looking for, stop it," Bear B. says. "Just look at him/her, right there in front of you. Feel it, just feel it."

And the woman who was a man a little while ago takes me in her arms and I think all of a sudden as I'm encircled in softness that there's something I'm supposed to be doing, someplace I'm supposed to be. When this satiny flesh was a man I knew then that he would go away, that he'd be taken away and exposed to extreme danger. Sealed away unable to breathe. I don't know why I'm thinking this or how I know this because I seem to know this is going to happen to him. Another Sim plot I've got in mind that I'll design? Call it *Osiris and the Cat Woman*.

But my newest lover is breathing in deep pulls below me. And I try to think what it is that I'm supposed to know, or what it is that I already know. Why do I think he may be my brother? This woman moving under me, siphoning from me. She *is*. I don't have a brother, but she may be my brother because we were united like this, shocking, in the womb before we were born. Disgusting. But why do I not feel disgust instead of this trembling, this rising up to meet her?

It's a myth. I think this through the waves of feeling, I think about the fact that I'm living a myth that I'll learn about later. *So are you.*

Who?

"What about the murder," Bear B. booms from everywhere.

"That's not part of the myth," I say just as loud, damn it, to take control to make my conception real. "That's a reality, murder, a reality that a lot of us know, Bear B."

"Then why did you do it?"

"I didn't murder my daughter.

"You did."

"Didn't! Ask me some other time."

"And what about your old friend?"

"Mat/leen? Yes I killed her," the words rush from me. "But that's what you want me to say, so I'm not saying that at all. Just joking, see?"

"You'll have to be punished," she condenses herself into the woman who is on me. "You need to be disciplined for too many things. Let's start with what happened with your brother before you were born."

"I don't have a brother."

"Liar liar, hair on fire!"

And I feel heat and something like a coma coming on.

~

"When moonlight shines from the earth outward we are witnesses at the rim of a birthing so distinct and so unfathomable that we think we can't see it, that we shouldn't see the lushness of its light. Things change at that edge so monumentally, species go extinct and new ones spring into existence there. Frightening. We therefore say we don't believe it and so our reality doesn't leap from that rim into chaos, the new order. You see it all depends on where you're standing, near the edge or not, and that depends on how much you know, how much you can see. And then on how much you can, or you're willing, to risk to join the chaos. It's a new order of reality, it's living again, another life, a terrifying voyage on the threshold. But you can be a traveler."

"I want to see the moonlight they say can shine in metal, is that what you mean by moonlight shining from the earth? That's all I want from you, to know how to make that. I want to give birth to it," Sophia looks directly into the smith's eyes.

He's not as old as she thought he would be. Maybe he's only a little older than her brother and even his movements are like Rudolphe's. Delicate, graceful and challenging.

"That's all you want? Too bad. It's no small knowledge, but still, is that all? Can you really say that all you need in life is to learn how to make electrum?" he says it politely like he can't believe her but doesn't want to embarrass her.

"Is that what it's called?"

"You mean you've come to me with all this fanfare of connections and bargaining with priests and those crazy nuns for something whose name you didn't know? And for what? You've probably only heard it rumored, you haven't seen it, have you, the metal that looks like moonlight?"

"But I know it's real."

"What faith. Yes, it's electrum."

He watches her leap for the word with her eyes, her muscles tense then quiet again as she leans toward him. It all happens in the blink of an eye he didn't allow. Magister Ivo has another daughter in her to replace the one he sent away. Ravenous, lusting, a new daughter who will bring him honor at the same time she will steal from him. He thinks this as he looks at her, leaning toward him, watching him. A spasm runs up his spine and makes his head shudder on his neck, small attacks he has now and then. They never cause him any bother except if he's working. But Sophia pulls away and leans away from him now. So he knows he can frighten her, but how long will the power last?

Agnes and Blessed Mary seem to want to prolong that time because they sense that the girl will overpower the Magister. They can feel she will gain the potential to overpower them all. They stay near her.

"You'll live in the house in town, you know, and travel out here every day to work with him. Sometimes we'll send Sybelle with you to visit," Agnes finalizes the requirement to commute on foot. "Besides, you're already obligated to us, like repairing the crucifix that broke, for one thing. We've already accepted it as payment for your room and food because you are, after all, living at my Beguinehouse."

Agnes knows the pressures that will fall on Sophia if she loses control of her daily routine. She can't allow Sophia to be distracted by DeVitry or other priests who have the power to instantly elevate her status. Agnes don't trust her to withstand the transition. Little else works as well to nail down power from the Church as having something the Church wants, something they're willing to flatter, pay or kill for. In this case, it's Sophia's skill. This worries Agnes and Mary because the Church always needs some way to turn its booty from the Eastern Crusades into objects they say are holy and which, most importantly, will be transformed to not look like the stolen goods they are. What the Church snatches has to be altered and Agnes and Mary wonder if this is really the true transubstantiation, better than their advertised changing of wine and bread into what's supposed to the blood and body of their christ —how gory. This conversion is less gruesome and more profitable, the sanitizing makeover of golden Islamic treasure into crosses and christian bric-a-brac, holy *tchotchkes* they can tout as treasure of their own.

They've all manipulated reality for this to happen because the nuns take vows of poverty and priests do not. But Agnes and Mary, being Beguines, avoid the rules the Church demands of regular nuns. For as wily and wielding of deadly power as the clergymen are, these women have found a route around their malevolence. And they need Sophia as much as the Churchmen do, probably more, so they can manufacture their own expensively crafted relics and call them holy.

SEVENTEEN

Spinning, The Quest For Mindlessness

Saint Teresa, "Babs" to her friends, is here right now. She's one of the leading proponents of nonlocal causality, you know, like telepathy, psychokinesis and so on. It's cause and effect at a distance, reality from quantum physical forces that work only when we look for them. She's speaking at the rally, defying material realism is her live\s long, eternal, cyclical pursuit and it comprises the forbidden data she makes certain gets to the Travelers.

She visioned a different reality when she was alive that time. The hag they burned was one of her best friends. They were very close, Babs and Mary.

~

Gold, silver, rubies, the sacred symbols of the Church. They are the real documents of the faith. The masses of the ignorant see or are told stories about the relics because there is an entire narrative that goes with each one. The broadcast information is clear, unsullied by the personal interpretations that are necessary when words alone are used whose

146

meaning must be figured out. Words convey innuendo and are manipulated by thought but when concepts are supported by awesome tangible objects—like palaces, sculptures, paintings, cathedrals that make you feel small and so on—their impact requires little else to solidify the reality of who has the power.

These icons that transmit information, visual representations of data that are authoritative and easy to absorb, propagate the Faith. Like Sybelle's representations in paintings, Sophia is the only artist the Beguines can afford who has the talent to tell the stories they want spread by coding information into art works. But hers are costly precious tokens that use gold, lapis, silver, rubies, tourmaline and yes, electrum. The means make the ends valuable. The extravagant objects of religion, they are a corporeal information network. Blessed Mary watches Sophia's eyes unwavering on Magister Ivo's hands as he nimbly hammers the silver leaf over the Maplewood of the Bishop's mazer and knows she has found the technician she's been looking for to encode her data.

Ivo feels Sophia staring and thinks how relieved he is that the strange Beguines won't allow her to stay with him. The girl is not likeable. There is more than enough room inside the Bishop's family fortress where Ivo is rewarded for his work with a permanent living annex. All it would take is a word from him for accommodations to be made for his new apprentice, but he doesn't want that. He doesn't want, what? He thinks of what he's feeling, and figures it's that he doesn't want to have more contact with this driven, precision-eyed girl. He wonders briefly how Sybelle, his own repudiated daughter, is bearing the effects of the scorn he's certain Sophia must heap on her simply by ignoring her. He can see already how the two older Beguines she is supposed to respect are treated like they don't exist for her, this hungry young smith. Only the work, only his hands as they work have any value for her. It's obvious to anyone who watches her, watching him.

"It's time for you to go," he says.

Sophia's eyes lance his. While Agnes and Blessed Mary wrap their cloaks around themselves she continues to stare. It's only when Mary takes her arm and pulls her with strength that surprises Sophia, only then does she move to leave. Surprisingly, the angelic and enticing Mary is undetectably muscular. If she didn't know about her saintliness Sophia would think that the painful lock of fingers on her arm was tightening on purpose.

Sybelle had watched the Beguines walk away like this down the narrow road from the castle years before and she assumed they must be the best of friends. She never spoke always thinking she was peculiar and possessed by bizarre ideas that invade no other woman. She's still careful to be quiet and noncommittal with other people, especially women, because there is always the danger that her calamitous thoughts about them might erupt. And there's her father, so ashamed of her and of the fact that she was more of a daughter of the castle family, the Bishop's family, than his because of his neglect and not caring what they did to her.

She knows the world very well by the proxy of other people, firsthand. She knows the advantages the priests take of her and because of this she finds the romances, *chansons*, hard to believe. The guests who visit the Bishop's castle bring the world with them, in fact they are the world because they are the powers that create and control everything. From their hearsay she knows the indiscretions in sounds of shuffling clothes and the excitement of looks from veiled eyes, touches beneath cloaks, intrigues behind chamber curtains that flow into the power circles at court. She knows which Churchmen keep their own women and which are intimate with other men's wives or their sons. And sometimes there are murders.

In all the gossip there's nothing like what Sybelle has heard and felt with her own senses, tasted and smelled and probably worse, more than what she's done, what she's witnessed. She has seen her best friend murder herself. Not with a blade like happened to the cat. It was murder not suicide because she had become a different person than she was before, unlike herself, and she was forced to do it, that's what Sybelle thinks. Murder, because her friend was so changed when she killed herself. Her friend Matlen was the Bishop's wife, the mother of his two sons and a happy woman of dry wit. But four years ago there was the new edict from the Church that declared priest's wives unholy. Suddenly she was a sin.

That was when Matlen started to act like the outcast she was seen to be all of a sudden. Labeled unholy and unclean, the reality of her life changed and she was eyed both by stinking peasants and by elite Church lovers. Mortified, she finally freed her husband from the reminder of the love that was declared sin rather then to live and perpetrate the new reality.

She returned one day at high noon with her sons. A visit to the castle that was once her home, Sybelle remembers the day very well. She understands now why Matlen didn't speak to her and why she met her eyes only once to smile. She said she was taking the boys for a look around the battlements and went up on the highest parapet. Sybelle can see it. Matlen's blood oozing from her shattered face, and she feels her own face throb from her ear, across her cheek and through her jaw. The rock pierced Matlen's face on the ground. The leap from the parapet with her sons accomplished what she must have planned because she was smiling. Sybelle reached her first. She sees the splintered facial bones and the jagged teeth that protrude through the torn and bloody skin of her cheek. She sees it now, feels the pain now on that side of her face.

Holy Mary mother of idiots, pray for us innocents now and at the hour they kill us, amen.

"Come my child and tell me your impure thoughts. Any thoughts? Dirty thoughts?"

"Just one..."

She wanted to see him dead, the obese town priest with stinking breath. The aching desire to see his head splattered open must be a sin. But who cares? Instead of telling him that she memorized whole sections of the romantic *chansons*, the recounting of love between men and women and, she made up something. Generic sins, they protected her privacy. Later, madness will protect her even better than lies.

Now she wonders again about her privacy outside of the Beguinehouse. Her father, the Magister so respected, has taken a renewed interest in her. He shows it by making sure to keep her away from his new apprentice, as if he's afraid she will reveal something of herself to Sophia. And she wonders if she's so transparent that her father knows what she's been hiding for years.

She tries to inspire jealousy in herself because the newcomer spends time with the father who rejected her, but fails. She only wants to talk to Sophia, not displace her position with her incomprehensible traitor of a parent.

"Father," she calls from the workshop door.

Magister Ivo works by the light of a candle. He's aligning all the hammers, picks, forceps and crucibles in rows according to their increasing size. The scored, stained top of the massive slab that is the table becomes beautiful with the arrangement. The tools are lovely like autumn leaves shimmering on the branches of a tree. For the task Ivo has taken off the heavy concealing robe he wears all day.

"Father?"

"Call me mother," he says.

Of course Sybelle knew that. But then she forgot what she wanted to say and smiled at him.

In the morning she would try again to find some way to share herself with Sophia, to catch her eye. But her eyes focus only on metals, the alloys the Magister sets before her. She concentrates on the metal, warm and supple under her fingers. Like the sea, colors shimmer up from it in rainbows as she heats it. Spellbound, she is beneath the enveloping water again. Her mother is on the shore embracing her aunt, or is it some other woman, much younger?

~

"I've never been younger than now. The flesh of my body is firm, smooth like velvet to the touch. Go on, touch it. Touch me!"

"What for? You say there are only ashes, charred bones? Be a little generous, would you? A little creative, for christ's sake. We are all part of the same intelligence. How many times do I have to tell you? How many times before you finally get the point that every time you crush an insect without thinking of the consequences, you may be smashing your own mother? Or is that what you want to do, coward? Stop whining. Listen to me! I don't know why it's so hard for you to stop being so goddamn self-absorbed. Who do you think you are? Don't you know you're god? Yes, oh intelligence of the universe. But in your present state of mind when I say it to you it sounds like a joke. Hey you, Intelligence of the Universe, stop putting out those glue-boards for mice, that's your family you're torturing, that's you!

But you don't get it, do you? You're part of the myth. When they took advantage of my limited human awareness and lured me into that fancy coffin telling me I could keep all those jewels encrusted on it, it was because I had forgotten who I was. Only love could have saved me, and I forgot it. So I died then and lost my body. They distributed my ashes and bones all over the place so I wouldn't be able to get together as me, that *me*, again. But I did anyway. My sister who was my wife put me together, and I did the same thing all over again. See what happens when you miss the point?"

"Small minds! Small minds!"

"What a pain in the ass. I had to do it over, all that scattering and all that collecting again."

"You don't know my reality yet. The pain of the burning, the *WHOOSH* of my skin igniting, the Buddhist monk sitting in flames in the middle of the street. Call me a hag, he wouldn't care. In a certain place of being it's better than being called a king, better a crone than a coward, we always say. Wake up, would you. Wake me up!"

~

It was asserted by the priests of Denderah that Nut had her origin in their city, and that there she became the mother of Isis. Her five children, Osiris, Horus, Set, Isis, and Nephthys were born on the five epagomenal days of the years—that is, the five days over the hundred and sixty... Nut plays a prominent part in the underworld, and the dead are careful to retain her good offices, probably in order that they may have plenty of air.

Osiris is usually figured as wrapped in mummy bandages and wearing the white cone-shaped crown of the South, yet Dr. Budge says of him: "...he was an indigenous god of North-east Africa, and...his home and origin were possibly Libyan." In any case, we may take it that Osiris was genuinely African in origin, and that he was indigenous to the soil of the Dark Continent.

Isis was perhaps of Libyan origin, and is usually depicted in the form of a woman crowned with her name-symbol and holding in her hand a scepter of papyrus. Her crown is surmounted by a pair of horns holding a disk, which in turn is sometimes crested by her hieroglyph, which represents a seat or throne. Sometimes also she is represented as possessing radiant and many-coloured wings, with which she stirs to life the inanimate body of Osiris... No other deity has probably been worshipped for such an extent of time, for her cult did not perish with that of most other Egyptian gods, but flourished later in Greece and Rome, and is seriously carried on in Paris today."

Spence

EIGHTEEN

Display Attributes

"You are part of the parable as you hear it. Listen to the story in the secrecy of your own thoughts. You are part of the group that has a mother, and somewhere there is a father but I don't remember him at the moment. My sister and my brothers are odd, sometimes murderous, but beautiful at the same time. Listen to me, you can't get along without knowing this. Ageless, I can tell you. Cyclical. Listen for your part in the story.

"The sons and daughters of the woman Nut are a powerful group. Nut, after all, gives air to the dead in the netherworld, they depend on her. And one of us, me, her son Osiris is revered, the patron of mummification. Part of the reason for this is that I was murdered by my brother Set who spread my bones all over and although I was revived by my sister who was my wife, Isis, I died again. I'm therefore as closely connected with death as mother is, by suffocation, burning, plummeting from heights, gunshots, carbon monoxide, electrocution, drowning, yes you could say I'm related to death. We're all related to death, related to each other and related to death. I don't know how to break the bond. Of course as I contemplate it I get closer to an answer, or I get better at it but I still end up dying violently and painfully in order to learn more. Although no matter how much I endure everyone always likes Isis better, even our sister Nephtys liked her best and was intimate with her."

~

For the artist there's always the work. Sacred. There is the work that holds Sophia silent at the bench, squinting over it. This is how Rudolphe will find her when his lover allowed him to go. She works on the supple metal over and over again, working it. Repetitions like death.

Sacred goblet, holy vessel for wine is gold-leaf-formed over the carved wooden mold. Magister Ivo shows her how, his hands modeling the movements she must make. The young smith is one with him and even more than that. She has made a world of metal and no one pierces her loneliness because she won't allow it. Her love involves her completely like a lover who cheats if you're not vigilant every moment in fulfilling his needs. It's enough for her to conquer these metals: Sophia, victor over the inert. It's more than most women can hope to accomplish as wife, widow, secluded or crazy nun, hard laborer; any of the alternatives aren't attractive. Very smart of Beguines to have cloaked themselves in religion to pursue their art. Sophia thinks this while she polishes a fire-blackened silver orb to decorate the goblet.

Sybelle watches her from the doorway of the workshop because she doesn't have the courage to speak to her about the work and about her father, or mother. Sophia is consumed by the quest for eternal recognition, and Sybelle wonders how she can tell her.

~

I'm trembling when I awake in my cell above the gargan-City, sweating. The dreams are lifelike although I can't remember something and this is what I realize I have to do, to get to what I forget because it's important. What I know is I've dreamed of endless failure, a treadmill of running and searching and seeing the same painted scene pulled past me in jerky movements. Buildings lurch by going backwards at the same window, sixty-fifth floor and third from the left, the same motionless figure raises its hand in silhouetted static greeting as it disappears and reappears in endless mockery. Shivering and cold from the dream's reality I'm aroused from it panting with fear. And what about what I forget?

"Where am I?"

Sun, splintered and thick, indistinct with debris diffused through it makes me turn away. Why am I not accustomed to this failure that grips me? I sweat, shiver. All my work swirls into glittering whirlpools of data that disappear into the black vortices of editors' *delete* modes. Why? I've been genetically planned for the diversion business. My VirtReal stories are good, better than the ones programmed by Dorothea Taste\thirty who organizes obvious plots:

The gamer enters a familiar room that's arranged and dressed by an interface nano-probe attached into your own thoughts so it's familiar to you...

Choose path:\ a, b, c, d

...and determine what particular room and day/night or walk/sit, and program your mood, thoughts, memories, everything. Then the subprograms extrude subconscious aromas, temperatures, full sensations and memories for the scene. There's always an auditory or visual stimulus that's just barely perceived fifty percent of the time at each person's absolute threshold for recognition. It spikes sudden fear by artificially induced sympathetic nervous system arousal the gamer can chose with his/her thoughts, then,

path:\ a, b, c, d, e=user interface action.

And there's always submenu choices within *user interface* that give programmed alternatives for real crime experiences or experiencing historical events. It gives you a choice of what character to live in each incident.

Lately *Jean D'Arc* has been popular, as has BlackHole-06 or being the victim of poisonings of various sorts. Then there's the trendy 20th Cent's Nazi death camps—no one really does the Armenian genocides or North American Indian slaughters. Of course nobody understands that all of these things were real, that all history has simply been re-dated onto boson-chips and is on the *divertissement* frequencies, amusements, life VirtReals that are oldfashion true reality. Scanning through them, playing their experience games is what you do all day, every day. Games.

"What about me?"

What's happened my break in this diversion business? Something is very wrong that I've got to outrun Bear B. and her Police Squads to find out.

"Kvino? Hey, Kvino?" I keep hailing him but there's no response.

My EroSims aren't just interactive, they're energizing and give people odd and unique involvements. Better than Taste\thirty's or the recreations of those re-issued de Sade fantasies. They say my work's good, so where's my fame data URL in CySpace? I awake shaking with rage, my breath gasps of brittle anxiety. I can't stay this way with this small amount of allotted data space that falls too far below the amount that constitutes standardized fame. I want to own one of those gleaming dimension-spanning structures you can spot as soon as you access CySpace. A four-dimensional address in the vast

Nets of information arrays given shape, sound, size, depth, texture by their volume in that limitless arc of data. It stretches from every access point implanted in every person in the universes.

That's real fame, data fame. Everyone who plugs in knows you when information about you occupies that kind of nonspace. What you eat, wear, how you sleep, the sound of your laughter, the sound and aroma of you voiding body wastes, the way you climax, your perfect face that smiles and experiences SensSims that are famous through the worlds because they show everyone else how to react, how to behave, what's the infashion and what's the oldfashion. Everyone knows everything about you and can take tours in the Nets to glide past the huge patterns in the informational cosmos you occupy. It's everything the diverse and complete data the universes have stored so that it really knows the MegaCelebrity.

Listen to me! What about me?

I'm one of the few, the gifted, who can read and transfer data codes to format new combinations of icons or words at a pad console. Where's my fame?

It's hard to breathe. Anxiety attack. I learned these from history chips because they don't happen anymore. The Travelers especially say they shouldn't happen because of something they believe about our creating our own reality. Anxiety over success instead of the other way around. If only I could see the efforts of my work, almost tangible in a real nonspace. Like being a sculptor and getting immediate results from working krylo or even synthesized old metal. But I have no reason to be thinking these scary things about myself that make me shake, the fears spinning whirlpools in me whose rush of water I can feel like hands dragging me downward. Yanking like the buildings lurching backwards past me. I have to try to break the code, the barrier they've got in my brain to my own memories. I succeeded in committing murder with my mind. At least I have success in that. I've got to find out how I did it and they're blocking me with this anxiety about stupid career success in entertainment Sims.

I've got to stop this ringing dread. I'll just tune to some freq that will Virt me out of this feeling. Diversion, use what everyone else does? I'm not any better, can't rise above it. Another failure, tune it out. Diversion is what I need, but look at what's on now. It's all Traveler crap, another interactive infomercial, a laughable Mega SensSurround Holo and it's taking over my cubicle.

Wave 1.32\R| T/freq=| "The prayers to me are quite helpful. You must realize how much good thinking about the Dead does. There is brilliant calmness that bathes you as you ready for another go at it in the human realm we recreate. Mighty Osiris that I am, or was, among other things, I'm still touched by people's offerings, so simple and magnificent."

Hot sand, pyramids loom up in an instant world where the sun is crisp and intense. This mammoth sandstone sculpture of an ancient god talks and walks around me.

"What's that?"

He takes a question from some kid in ready-to-swim skin. Another Holo beamed into this Holo.

"How do I feel these things if I've gone on to other experiences in other lives? Easy, time's not a straight line that some of you still insist on believing it is. Imagine a ball made of something dense like oldfashioned alabaster, or zeonized plastic, and that you can see it through a scanning BosonTron microscope so you can see past positrons and quarks and everything right to all the infinitesimal but vast empty space in its denseness. See particles that move so intensely they are really waves. Imagine all things of the universes in that ball..."

Screaming through thick blackness I try to grab onto an immense emptiness that flings past me as I spin out of control. *Stop it!* Blinding specks of light like tiny searchlights sear my eyes and it feels like drops of acid are burning through my lenses. *Stop! Please!* My stomach is pressing up into my throat. It really is, it's not just a feeling. The spongy sac is working through my esophagus, choking me. Bile runs out of my mouth and nose.

"...The ball is spinning with blinding speed and it's not solid of course. If you're at any one place in that ball and start to travel you may end up at another place that exists in a different time. See? Because of the spinning, the constant movement. You can be in a couple of places, really any amount of places, and of times at once. You can move back and forth through them. And you can be aware of it or not depending on how much you're appreciative of your true essence that's not simply human but universal in nature. Universal nature, that's important.

"And it's true the symbolism I'm using is that of the earth, the solar systems as you know them, it's all the same thing, the same idea. Everything's the same stuff and ontogeny really does repeat phylogeny although the reverse can be true too..."

The acid beams of cold white light burn tiny holes into my eyes, my face, my arms. I can feel wind that is searing, hear it whistling through the holes. Alone in blackness the points of light that hurt me are millennia away. I can barely see them through the emptiness that is heavy but I know can't be, and still they hurt me.

"Look out at the oldest Milky Way, it has a shape, but when you travel in the midst of it and it's only empty space. Now you're inside what's really the same thing as a microscopic image—remember ontogeny and phylogeny?

Then imagine, look inward at yourself, really look, and see at that fine-grained level you're only empty space too. And you know it. So who's your awareness? You're thinking all of this right now, you, all that empty space that is you. What does your consciousness consist of? There's no chaos at this level, it's all emptiness. You just have to be sophisticated enough to understand that it all leads to higher orders. All of us are composed of the bits, but mostly of nothingness, but also of the bits that compose everything else. We are everything and everything is us, the same. Do you see? So what we do at any one time on that glob of material, the earth, isn't what it's all about. We're only here at various times to learn, to try to learn that a bigger awareness we're all part of is our real essence.

"You know about this but have mostly rejected it, it's the stuff they teach throughout the ages as mystical transcendence or something, maybe transcendental consciousness but it's really not. It's only reality, just electrochemical impulses of a gigantic connectedness that each of us is an equal participant in along with everything else, living or not, rock or dog. We live only to learn how to experience existence, try to evolve to our higher non-selves. I mean, come on, look at all that empty space you're feeling that is you. And, of course, we have to learn to love..."

I've disappeared somewhere in a black velvet shroud and I can't feel my legs, arms, or even my eyes that hurt so much are gone somehow. *Get me out of here*, I think I say but I don't feel it. Quiet. It's very quiet, very still. That's the feeling, there's no more spinning at a sickening speed. It's not even like floating, it's just peaceful like an exquisite sleep with complete awareness. I think I'm smiling, or something that can smile is feeling that way because there's nothing here that's me. Then who is the 'I' who watches me?

"...It's all just energy that makes up the eternal consciousness, that's why I loved my sister and she loved me and our other sister in such intimate ways. It doesn't matter, all that sex, it's all just a kind of light that's learning energy if your intent is pure. That's the key, love, and doing good for everything in the universes, every person, plant, bear, fish, insect and blade of grass or invisible patch of air. We keep coming back to live to learn how to do this. You'd think it'd be easier to simply be good, but no, we have to come back as terrified lions or poor sharks or spiders and be caged and tortured to death before we learn that treating creatures badly is deadly for our souls, our higher non-selves. I myself, or *selves*, have died so many times I'm beginning to think I'll never get it right. The great Osiris that I am, how did I ever get so greedy to let myself get tricked into that jeweled coffin Set made? We all make mistakes, I guess, the trick is learning to forgive, that's real learning.

"Limited existential things like fame, that's nothing real, only emptiness. Things are nothing if you look closely enough and you feel it for yourself. Everything is empty. Emptiness makes up everything. Everything. Do you understand this at all?"

~

"I'll do anything to get it right, Magister. I'll work all night here by the oil flame, please let me do it. I'll learn it, I have to. I'll finish it by dawn if you let me stay to work tonight."

"You're too hungry," he says. "There's more than being the best smith in the world."

"What else can I do?"

"You have no idea. There's something else after the edge of a chaotic life, something stupendous."

"Let me stay. The container for those ashes can make me famous."

162

Sybelle tasted every word they spoke, heard ever odor of the acids they used, felt the growing animosity between them on her skin. She saw with her eyes the sound of their quickened breathing, and she smelled the movement of Sophia's hand there over the gloom of the workbench. A waft of congealed butter came from the small deft tapping motion of her right hand. The movement was barely smellable so she raised her nose in the air like a dog to pull in the full sensation, the aroma of the fingers that gripped the worn handle of the iron hammer. The narrow movement of it up and down laced the uneasy turned butter odor with the scent of dusty chicken feathers fluttered over droppings on dry earth. She smelled it very clearly and shook her head, snorted out those hand movements from her nostrils. She probably won't forget any of this from her twisted sensory memory. The smell of rancid butter or dry flapping wings will always be the movement of Sophia's hands.

She wants the fame that will let her live beyond her life, she'll stand aside and watch her works being praised. Blessed Mary wants the praise for herself and that's the difference between saints and artists, the final object of adoration. But what force of will each of them demands! Sybelle shudders because she recalls the taste of Mary's and Agnes' words from that night she heard them talking in the shed behind the Beguinehouse. They have such enormous plans for reality. Sybelle remembers and tastes the green caterpillars of their words moving in her mouth again. She spits. The sound of the rustling of heavy material reaches her eyes when the figure at the stone bench turns to see what the noise is. And Sybelle doesn't know why suddenly she should be afraid.

She runs away. Her sandals slap the hard packed dirt and she runs to the castle, past the spot on the ground where Matlen's and her children's blood soaked the ground, and into the damp interior behind the fat doors, and up the uneven stone stairs into a high dark room. Safe in the turret, unsafe in the world that is changing around her and assailing her crossed senses with confusing things she can't order but that will be impossible to forget. Her senses bulge and overflow with them.

NINETEEN

...Tis A Hard Matter To Reduce Divine Things To Our Balance, Without Waste And Losing A Great Deal Of The Weight.
Montaigne

I've got to wake up. I fell asleep again with the VirtReals blaring. I can't stay crumpled where I fell in this corner by the door all day; I've got to work. Work, design Sim stories, get famous. But I'm not willing to go those few steps to the room to get my handpad because I'm afraid I'll see my beloved, that thick silky fur. What? Oh no, she's been sleeping wrapped against my leg!

"GO away!"

I frighten her when I jump up but reach down quickly to comfort her, a reflex of love. This isn't her, though, remember? This isn't real and she isn't real and I can't love her. Why not? Everyone else does this all the time. Nobody dies, nothing has to die because the Holo images of whatever you want go on and on driven by bundled sub-nanos of data that make them act and react precisely as they did in life, whether tree or mother. But I didn't program for this and I've got to find out how they did it to me, to her. Alive and dead at the same time, sweet Schrödinger.

Sometimes funerals are a better solution. Even some of the MegaCelebs are retired in death like that, their data nodes in CySpace erased except for neon memory traces, no transmittable sensory information remains. That kind of mostly permanent departure is usually artificial when it comes too soon after death. It's done to whip up enthusiasm for the dead star's latest VirtReals. Every once in a while they're revived to give an interview, sell more chips. But for average people the Holos of dead relatives fall into disuse because they're not as entertaining as Celebs. People forget the pain of a loved one's loss because their neurotransmitter balance naturally reformulates, or else they get help from ingestible chips like *MEM-AID\Neg Path* or *LoozIt!* Both products are very popular. They stop the desire for the Holo recreations of the dead. This is good because it gets expensive to maintain the conduction of those dead images from databanks in the Nets as they take up info credit space.

I stand aside carefully when the cat stretches like she always did, like animals do to dissipate the lactic acid that builds up in resting muscles. But she's not real, so why do it? Good program design. My leg is hot where she was curled against it and I feel good seeing her, my daughter who I love so much although I know the image is false. Recreated data, just like the HoloSims everyone lives in every day. What's my problem with it? Why do I think I've thought her alive again just like it was me who willed her dead? That would mean there's another dimension, and that's not possible. What's wrong with me? Is Bear B. right? Do I deserve to be tortured, my chaotic mind made more orderly?

"Kvino? Answer, will you. Hello?"

"KVINO THREE/-472 UNAVAIL. START MESS."

The words are there high in the air so I have a lot of room for my message. Why so much room? It's odd, but at least this time there's a response to my hail. Why is he unavailable anyway? Maybe they're holding him for hiding me in CySpace or for the weird message he left me that said something about Travelers helping me out of this mess. Or else he's with Bear B. I can still see the way she looked at him, tied him to her with neon wristlets when they left me here.

"Call me," and my words streak onto the air in verification.

I have to get out. She's purring now the loud motor sound of contentment. I wish I could hold her but I'm afraid of this thing that may be my own creation so I charge my cred-ID dot in my thumb and run out the door. I don't even bother to turn back to see if the auto closing is complete or if the cat stayed inside. Of course it has.

I'm on the streets of the quiet gargan-City and I pull a PedPad from the nearest stand and take off. On a low walking altitude I fly toward the crumbling district that's still called downtown. I wish that Mat/leen was here, still alive, and I wonder why her parents never recreated her in Holo. But of course they probably did and never told me about it. Who knows, she may be sitting with them in their precast living room right now having a fabricated experience with them. It's strange to picture it, and by seeing it in my mind do I make it real? This is what I have to find out because that's what Bear B. has been trying to extract from me, how I do it. But it's like searching to find a memory after it's forgotten, the trace tantalizing but misty and unrecoverable.

That might be why I think I prefer funerals and that's odd considering I hate the loss of control that comes from death. But I realize it's not so peculiar because it's funerals that allow me to retain control, like when I buried my genetic mother. My dead grandmother and dead Aunt were there. That was power, and it was a legal death. Now Bear B. wants me to bring her back? I've been fighting what I inherited from her for too long, I've almost got all of her traits and intolerance erased from me and I've got the electro certification for her death. It's binding, that's what they told me when I bought it. But something's not right about any of this. I have something in my mind that they want and I can't figure out how my dead, or at least data-lost, mother will make any difference in whether things become real from me or because of me.

"Drink 3," I say to the Waitron Unit.

The place on the decayed deserted street where Kvino and I last met is unusually busy. A table of three bliss-idiots, anther with two regular people. I make sure I don't look toward the three. You give them any encouragement and you can't get rid of them, they're always trying to press advertising nanochips into your hand or any dataport they can find.

"Link these, sister, feel the emptiness."

Jerks. I'll just sit here and have my drink and try to figure out what to do. I'm not used to all this free time. I mean, I'm usually working on EroSim designs for the diversion industry or else I'm with Kvino or I'm linked into high-level VirtReals. No one's used to having unplanned, unfilled days except for the Marginals. That's why there's few people on the streets, everyone's working their production jobs from their cubicles and then Simming out on VirtReals everyday, the very newest popular sensation stimulations. Everyone wants to be up on them because there are interactive quizzes and you can win credits by answering questions about the Sims or you can be on game shows or you can talk to people, meet, have sex all over the world, all in VirtReal without leaving your pallet. Nobody needs to go out, nobody frees up any time from their

Gib/Disney HoloSets that keep them hooked into the culture where everyone experiences everything in exactly the same way.

Thy will be done, holy Nets.

"I have something for you, sister."

"Damn," it comes out like a reflex to the bliss Traveler who's come from his table.

"I know how you feel," he smiles.

"Look, I don't want anything to link, unless— Never mind, I'm not interested. I'm waiting for someone."

"I know"

So why doesn't he get away from my table? It's embarrassing to have him standing there. The Waitron's going to record that I'm one of them or that I'm a sappy sympathizer. Why did Kvino say anything about these nuts and put me in a position to be seen with them? This is a mistake. Probably this guy wants a donation, as usual. I wonder if I have any extra credit dots in my thumb.

"I've got a message for you from Mat/leen," he says.

"What the hell?"

"Can I sit?"

I look around as casually as I can, moving just my eyes. How am I going to get out of this, or is it possible he's really been sent by Kvino? It's too coincidental that he mentioned Mat/leen because I was just thinking about her. But I still don't want to be seen with this guy. His smile and tender eyes are weird with no chips perceptible on his face or coloring his wrist sockets to account for it. There's no stimulus for him to be acting in this annoyingly benign way. I can't sit here and talk to a bliss-ninny like this.

"Take a few credits," I say, searching the compartments on my jacket. "I'll send drinks to your table. OK?"

*^we jack secured freqs -K sends help^*

The words flash from a fleeting blip on his wristband to his palm for a quari-instant. He made a nonchalant movement with his arm to flash this as he sits down, still smiling and looking at me directly in the eyes. Startled, I swivel shut my pupils but he raises his eyebrows and shakes his head with the cheeriness of some oldfashion repro of a Santa reminding a kid not to be bad. His long dark hair is shining around his head and I notice that he's beautiful. He has smooth skin of course but his features are attractive in their humanness, as if he's not been modified all that much by cosmetic lasers. He moves confidently, movements like those of a woman who knows she's appealing and knows that you think so too.

"I'll take a drink, thanks," he says. "We have meetings, you know. Why don't you come? We've got Sims that most people find more than entertaining if you let yourself try something new for a change."

"Everything's new. I can get anything I want for my own Sims."

"Not like ours, I think you know that already."

I forgot about it but now the sight of that mammoth sandstone god striding around the pyramids overwhelms me with a blast of heat. And then there's blackness, nothing, complete silence for an instant.

"See? You know."

I don't answer because he changes to an expression that I think means he's giving me a warning. He glances toward the Waitron Unit with quick significance and I avoid her look over at me. My wrist read out tells me that my heart rate is increasing, as if I didn't know, and I want to get out of here before I learn something else that Bear B. can torture me for. Travelers get information from secured frequencies? Is that what he flashed at me? I don't want to know that. I don't want to know but it's information I need if there's data about me on the blocked security Nets that can tell me what the police want from me, what they think is the secret in my head. But breaking secured codes to get it, why would these blessed-out freaks be doing that kind of hazardous radical action? I don't want to know and I wish I didn't need their help, and mostly I wish Kvino hadn't sent me that message to get me involved with them at all.

"My name's Atman. Bruce Atman 7721. And I can tell you about Mat/leen. That's what we do you know, we can show you the other ranges."

"Wait a minute, you're him, the guy from the commercials in the desert. You look different from the Sims."

"Everyone says that."

"You're thinner."

"Can we talk about the other ranges?" "Whatever. Do you follow people's data trails in the Nets, do you copy their magno-mail? Is that you're trick? So you know my friend's gone and now you're trying to hocuspocus me into believing you know something I don't. I suppose anyone can steal Repro Sims. Please leave me alone."

"Come to a meeting," he smiles. "You can laugh at us, show us how wrong we are. But she wants you to know you're a snob."

What? How can he know Mat/leen's words? Has Kvino told them, although he doesn't know. Or have they stolen surveillance tapes her family kept on her, a recorder buried in her basic cranial implant matrix to have a record of everything she did? It's possible. Now I'm perspiring through my hair roots and I feel nauseous.

"Come and see our Repros of her. Don't be scared."

^we can help -agree^

I'm not sure I saw the secret message. The flash was less than a blink.

"Here, this will tell you more about us."

He's still smiling when he gets up and drops a few half-nano prods that link into any HoloSet. I touch them and their titles magnify on the air: PAST NOW and FUTURE NOW. I leave them on the table.

"You won't be able to get in without those, bring them with you," he says. "The directions are in them."

Where the hell's Kvino when I need him now that he seems to have set me up with these nuts? Probably ultra stoned somewhere or else Bear B. is holding him a SexSim captive, and I can't imagine him fighting to get out of that. I watch the Traveler go back to his table and wonder whether she's recording Kvino in the act so she can have him in VirtReal anytime she wants from now on. He wouldn't object to giving her the data. That's right. It comes to me, I remember now that I've done that too. I've been crucial, important to Bear B. because she needed me. I made a difference to her. I made a difference.

We know ourselves, who we are, by what we do to the world, how it reflects our selves back to us.

It was not synthetically vivified data, not cyberSex. She needed me to feel that way. She didn't want a VidText of a re-quantified experience. She didn't want infinite points of view of it, some interactive message with someone's data abstracted from it thousands of miles away. Shared data nodes? No. She needed me, real. Skin like smooth cream moving on her, and something genuine from the depths of intense abandon.

We create our own reality you know. You can't give up reality to game space.

Who said that? Is it coming from where the bliss-ninnies were sitting? They're gone and I've got to follow them to find out why the Police want to control something in me. Some

172

talent? That's funny, as if my talent's not already controlled by lack of recognition.

"But recognition means you've had it before."

"What?"

Who am I talking to like this, saying things and answering myself, posing questions that are spoken out of my heart? No one can be creating the voice, the voices, except me—Creator.

Khepera then wept copiously, and from the tears which he shed sprang men and women. The god then made another eye, which in all probability was the moon. After this he created plants and herbs, reptiles and creeping things, while from Shu and Tefnut came Geb and Nut, Osiris and Isis, Set, Nephtys and Horus at a birth. These make up the company of the great gods at Heliopolis, and this is sufficient to show that the latter part of the story at least was a priestly concoction.

But there was another version, obviously an account of the creation according to the worshippers of Osiris. In the beginning...Khepera tells us at once that he is Osiris, the cause of primeval matter. This account was merely a frank usurpation of the creation legend for the behoof of the Osiran cult... From the inert abyss of Nu he raised a godsoul—that is, he gave the primeval abyss a soul of its own. The myth then proceeds word for word in exactly the same manner as that which deals with the creative work of Khepera... Men are then made by a process similar to that described in the first legend. From these accounts we find that the ancient Egyptians believed that an eternal deity dwelling in a primeval abyss where he could find no foothold endowed the watery mass beneath him with a soul; that he created the earth by placing a charm upon his heart, otherwise from his own consciousness, and that it served him as a place to stand upon... After these acts followed the almost insensible creation of men and women by the process of weeping, and the more sophisticated making of vegetation, reptiles, and stars. In all this we see the survival of a creation myth of a most primitive and barbarous type... But it is from such unpromising material that all religious systems spring, and however strenuous the defence made in order to prove that the Egyptians differed in this respect from other races, that defence is bound in no prolonged time to be battered down by the ruthless artillery of fact.

Spence

174

TWENTY

Reassign Keys

"You have to live with her for a while until you understand why you killed her."

"I didn't kill her and you know it," I watch Bear B.'s imitation smile. "Where's Kvino?"

"Call him," she says. "I authorized it."

"That's why I couldn't reach him before?"

For days I've stayed inside knowing Bear B.'s double would follow me whenever I went out. It's been too risky to go to the Travelers.

"You know everything must come through me. You're accused of a crime and until you admit it I control everything you access in personal data space, CySpace, VirtReal or Augment-Real, HoloSims, everything that goes through the Nets. That's my job, get used to it, baby. And get back to your dead mother and figure something out with her or else."

"That's supposed to be scary?"

"Or else I'll take you to Police Tower for another session of image tracing, and I know you don't want that. So use the cat, use your mother, the things you have murdered, and come up with an explanation for the images you have."

"How am I supposed to do that?"

"Kiss your lover's face, tonguing strokes."

"Christ, what?"

I can feel her heat on my skin, her breath in my ear. It makes me flinch.

"Please don't."

~

Sybelle has been chosen to help Blessed Mary practice her miracle. In fact, Agnes insists on it because she trusts the professed simpleton. She pretends to have no idea of what amalgam the girl is capable of perceiving in the miracle with her weird sensory twistings. But she has some idea, and just doesn't want to deal with it. Too complicated.

"Put the vat with the brain over there."

Sybelle hears its shape and smells the sound of its wrinkled grayness slapping against the sides of the crock. It smells like frogs every time it hits, the shape sounds like a bell. She looks blankly at Mary, not curious at all about what she's going to do with it and not caring whose brain it is. If she were asked to draw it she would like that, she would and could easily do it although she hasn't seen it.

"Watch everything, Sybelle, I want you to be able to describe this to others, to make icons of it," Mary says to her radiantly.

"I can do that now."

"What?"

"Draw it."

"Not just the vat," Mary keeps smiling, talking right into her face. "I want you to draw what I'm going to do with what's inside. It's going to be the start of my sainthood, the start of our new order. So just wait for it, all right?"

176

"All right," she says to appease her and wonders why Mary reminds her of her father.

Agnes and Mary are moving things around under the tree at the back of the Beguinehouse. Ellekindis and Petrissa with their dogs are off in the street making their soap, Metza is in the tanners' street working the leather for her saddles. Sophia is, of course, the farthest away at the Bishop's fortress with Sybelle's father, Magister Ivo. Thinking of him or her, Sybelle waits at the plank table for Agnes and Mary to finish their preparations for the miracle. She wonders why he gave her up to be raised by others and then hid his own identity to become a goldsmith. Is it because of her oddities that this parent rejected her? Probably. After all, she's peculiar in everyone's eyes and they don't even know the half of it.

"The mystery of transubstantiation. A miracle," Agnes says. "Done by Mary."

Mary comes out of the shed wearing robes that Sybelle, who tastes lead in her mouth from Agnes' words, had never known before. There is a white garment underneath a fragile blue one and both are slit up the sides. This allows Mary to move within the garments' narrowness and shows her legs. She is luminous. There is an aura of light around her head like the halos Sybelle paints on icons. It's unmistakably there, a halo, she can smell it. It's like burning metal, like taking two rings and rubbing them together very fast so they get hot. There's that evanescent aroma, metal. The brightness around her intensifies as she smiles at Sybelle and she has to swallow quickly in order not to spit out all the metallic drool that wells up in her mouth.

Mary spreads her arms and begins a haunting wordless chant. But it's not really wordless; Sybelle realizes it when she chews it. First the sound of her voice makes Latin words, and now she's singing them in common language. If this is Church music the priests can have her killed for it, but somehow the melody doesn't seem to be that, even to Sybelle's untrained palate.

"*There is no other... We create form...*
Form is simply emptiness. Emptiness is all form...
There is no other... Ahh-Ahhhh...
We create form, we create allllll..."

The words taste like cold blueness, almost like water that is very heavy on her tongue. But once she makes them out and tries to understand what they mean she becomes uncomfortable in spite of their succulence. This is what they're going to call blasphemy for sure. *We create all?* Is she joking? Sybelle knows very well what this means, that Mary is saying she, or we, are Gods. Who else creates? This is going to get all of them killed, Sybelle has already seen the revenge of the Holy Church and it terrifies her.

"You can't do this," she says. "It's against the rules."

"Quiet, mouse! Wait for the miracle," Agnes says.

Mary is still smiling and dancing under the linden tree where the vat with the brain is on the ground. The halo clings to her, moves with her.

"I am a woman," she says. "Like all women before me who were great souls. Paracelsus, Avicenna, they were women, Gautama Buddha, Jesus too. For every renowned man there are ten powerful women working in secret and they are unknown sometimes even to themselves. I demonstrate... Now I am the power of all of them, even those who are women who become men like Murasashi, Hildegarde, Joan. Watch me."

Sybelle feels sick at the sacrilege. The powerful are never going to let this go unpunished. They'll find out about it even if Mary stops now. But Mary doesn't stop.

"Watch the transmutation. Here's what they consider the heart of a man. I will eat it and become a man."

She takes the brain out of the vat and is holding it in her hand. The wrinkled thing seems to be howling even to normal senses not as bizarre as Sybelle's but she doesn't know how this could be because it has no mouth or any other orifices for that matter. But she knows there's a sound on the air because she tastes it. It's like salty blood.

~

Why is everything black, am I asleep? I've dreamed something and I'm afraid. And what happened to Bear B.? I was feeling good, warm with her. Where is she now? I'm really afraid.

I dreamed that I passed stiff, light, dead bodies over to a nun in a black dinner jacket who burned them in a trash barrel or a large steel vat. I was afraid of her because she became a him.

When he asked me something I said, *I'm dead already.*

And in a doorway to a department store that was windy and blown about with leaves, near what would be a busy corner in daytime, I saw my dear daughter's toys she had brought there.

So cute, I said to whomever was with me and we laughed.

Her black and white checked little catnip pillow and another toy. I wanted to put them in a safer place away from the busy corner but we decided *no* because when she came back for them she'd want to find them there where she left them. When she came back. I felt happy at that. But I didn't see her, my girl. My littlest girl.

We tend to make 'natural' what are really only social constructions—Potemkin villages—in and of the world.

Who said that?

Any time you begin anything it is the first step in producing meaning, and it is intentional no matter what you think. You can begin anywhere, even with dreams, and there is no end. This reality can be added to, anytime, and you can always make a new view, a new interpretation of it because you can be whoever you want to be and live it through that being.

Somehow I know this, it's familiar, not just a description of oldfashion hypertext or living in CySpace. I remember linking an ancient chip about Leibnitz and his monadology, that each monad mirrors the whole world. Each microcosm contains the macrocosm. Having consciousness is like being God, we create everything because we have everything in us. Is that where I got it? –that ontogeny recapitulates phylogeny?

It's like CySpace, it's anything we want it to be as long as it's been programmed somewhere in the Nets. We can do anything in CySpace, that's what's happening to me. But Bear B. arrested me because things I image aren't programmed, that's the problem. Consciousness-created space that isn't programmed? Can't be. I have to get to Bruce Atman, to the Travelers. If they can highjack secured data transmissions they can help me find out why I'm creating. Creating? What's wrong with me? I wish I could remember the rest of my dream.

~

"I'm the reincarnation of everything mystic. Every one of them is here, me," Mary smiles. "Those dead are those not born too."

She puts the brain on the dirt in front of her and throws a burlap sheet over it. Then Agnes hands her a smoldering taper and she lights it so that cover and, presumably, brain begin to burn. Mary spins around, her halo smears a rainbow across her. She stops with her hands over her face.

"What do you think I'll look like?"

"Go on," Agnes pokes Sybelle. "Tell her what you think."

"You mean now? I don't know," Sybelle says, hearing only the clang of empty space in her eyes.

"Hurry up. Just do it. Guess."

"No, leave her alone," Mary says. "If that's what she says, it will do. There's something deeper in her mind she can't articulate, that's all, something subconscious that I can evidence. Watch, I can be what she's thinking even though she doesn't know what it is."

Mary drops her hands from her face and there is nothing. There is nothing but undulating emptiness in the center of the aura whose heavy *clang-clanging* sound defines where facial features out to be.

"What have you done, idiot! Think of something else, fast," Agnes elbows Sybelle in the head. "See her face, for Christ sakes, see her real face again!"

So she pictures Blessed Mary in her mind but instead of an image she feels sounds and smells colors, tastes descriptive words. When Mary spins around again and uncovers her face a cacophony of texture and aroma, sounds and colors, sweetness, bitterness assail the halo that quavers wildly now in an explosion of color that keeps transforming and singing chaotically. She has become a concoction of the girl's ability to image across ordinary sensory barriers, the synesthesia creates a new being and it makes Mary unable to control her own body anymore. If she wants to move her eyes to the right she discovers that she has to blow through her nose, if she wants to speak she has to press the skin of her arm above her elbow."

"Be yourself, Mary! Mary!" Agnes shouts at the apparition. "You are distinct. Create yourself again. You've retreated from your body and your Self. Come back! You are responsible for creating yourself because nothing has changed. Nothing has changed, listen to me! You do it all just like we all do, so you can't give up responsibility now and splinter apart there in her weird place. Get out of her world! The brain doesn't have to burn anymore!"

And the other world that Sybelle created fades away as Mary reconstitutes herself in the usual reality that all of them have agreed on as the normal collective world. Mary's form hardens into the figure they know in this world, different from the one she entered because of Sybelle. That specific interaction they had that came from her peculiar construction of reality is over. And Agnes waits for an explanation while Mary puts the brain back into the vat and tries to neaten herself up, straightens her robes, smoothes her hair. Her aura has faded away.

"You ruined the miracle," Agnes says.

"No she didn't," Mary pipes up. "Maybe she's the miracle."

"Or just crazy."

"One or the other, it all depends on how we talk about it doesn't it? That's the point of our new order, we're the creators."

Blessed Mary fans herself while she speaks. She has hiked up her robes to her knees.

"You've got to stop saying that otherwise they're going to come and burn us all," Sybelle says.

"It wouldn't matter. But what about you? Have you always felt the world the way you felt me just now? It's marvelous, miraculous."

"Or mad," Agnes spits on the ground.

"Or that too, if we all agree to see it that way. But I wonder how we can use it for the new reality or if we should. Do you think, Agnes, we can fit it into my miracle demonstration?"

"Absolutely not. But I do think we should practice with it and kept it secret to use in case we're ever being stoned or attacked some other way. If there's ever a group that holds a singular idea believed strongly enough to threaten to overpower our reality—like the Church—then it can be our weapon."

"Good strategy! When we transubstantiate we want to make sure the change is under our control alone. I can become anyone's fantasy made external by evaporating into their essence and becoming that. I mean, I've learned how to meditate and leave the shadows of this reality and so it looks like I can apply the principles of the other realm to the physical world. Alchemy. Transmutation of substance, that's me."

"Please don't say that," Sybelle says. "It's as bad as what Sophia's trying to learn. The metal that is moonlight or gold from dirt and lead, it's all the same as this."

"Really?" they say together before Agnes goes on. "You know more than I've thought you do. Is Magister Ivo an *Adept* in secret? You were raised at the castle, does he know more than we think? Can he grow gold from seeds and does he know the secret of *aqua vitae*, the elixir of youth? But, if he does, do I really want my life prolonged, this one at least?"

"Agnes, Agnes, don't fall into the trap of believing what we use in our shows. You know we can do all of that, if we truly understand. Lead into gold, death into life, it's the same and it's easy once you know how. It's only mind, it's only belief, this world. We all decided what we would do in this life before we traveled here, when we were ineffable. If we can just remember what it was like to be in that other actuality beyond these shadows we live in then we would understand that to change dimensions all we have to say is, what?" Mary starts to dance. "Here look at the brain in the vat that's laughing at us as we think all this. How to get the brain out of the vat? There! It's out. *Poof.* See, it's so easy when you know you're the godhead."

TWENTY ONE

There Is No Desire More Natural Than That Of Knowledge.
Montaigne

It frightened her and Sybelle ran away through the gate. She knows there will be retribution for this seditious and unholy talk. Only priests can control the change of substances like wine into blood and stale bread into somebody's flesh. They murder people who can do the same trick and the girl is terrified of them. She runs toward her father, or her mother, who she realizes now has kept herself safe all these years by becoming a man.

When she arrives at the workshop in the fortress she finds her father or mother bent over Sophia at the bench. They are in such deep concentration that Sybelle can see their breath in aqua waves of jagged shapes that are so regular they could be symbols rotating slowly in crests and valleys there on the baritone gloom. She watches their breathing this way and sees their diligence, how in concert they are in focus. Weird liquids gurgle and shine in the crucibles before them and they don't even blink away from them for an instant. Without knowing,

Sybelle knows what they are doing. It's against the laws. She moved silently into a dark corner behind wooden shelves overburdened with casks, crocks and tools. When the end that she fears finally comes she hopes no one will find her and she tries to close her ears to what she sees, her eyes to what she hears.

"Verdigris," Ivo says. "You made it like the Egyptians. Good, you took the unjuicy grape skins off the copper pieces when they turned the perfect color. Now you can use it to decorate utensils and you'll get rewards."

"And the silver?"

"*Lapis infernalis*, the queen of the metals. Your tincture of the moon looks excellent. The silver nitrate, enough. Very little copper, just enough for the blue tint. Soon you'll be able to treat the falling sickness and problems with the brain with your silvers, just like the Arabians do."

"And the king?"

"Gold. Your *crocus solis* preparation is well done. The metal into the acid, the solution distilled with water and precipitated with potash. Good. You washed and dried the powder well?"

"Very well."

"You know you can drink the stannate of gold when you make it into solution, just a little, like I do," Ivo whispers. "It's the Elixir of Life.

"But I want to make gold and electrum so the things I make with them will live forever, not me."

"You can't do that. You can't use the metals for objects without using them for cures. They're part of life, stupid girl! It's your life that will infuse your objects naturally when you use your skills to help others. How long will it take you to learn that you're not distinct from everyone else and that you're not separate from what you create, ever."

But she doesn't understand this, and doesn't care. She knows she's separate from what she makes and she's only humoring the Magister by letting him go on about their connectedness. It's as if he thought the world was different from what it is, from what she can see. Ridiculous old man.

The torch he's made for her that flames from the bottle's narrow neck burns skin, her skin, so it's now one with her. If she jabs her hand with one of her tools, she bleeds. Separate things make effects on the others, and she sees the effects. If everything were connected there wouldn't be any causes and effects. And she knows these things very well because she makes effects all the time. Alloys of metal, plate into wire, wires into necklaces, gold leaf onto goblets. Her hands are the causes for it all, her hands and the knowledge of the Magister. This is her world and she will maintain it at any cost. The torch flame is her friend; it dances for her. When she extinguishes it after each work session she does so with tenderness, gently laying a square of heavy material over the narrow opening from which it hisses.

"Goodnight, little flame."

She kisses it. She kisses the air where it danced and feels it hot on her fragile lips. The flame is another lover, like the bench beneath her buttocks, the dirt under her feet in the yard, the air she carefully breathes and exhales without damaging it, the leaves on the trees whose violent movement in the wind she worries about. Everything that does not breathe is her friend, lover, child. And all things that react to her are like inanimate things. The cat who is her brother's lover, maybe her mother, is especially mean and she always treated it as if it didn't exist. She never looked at it directly in the eyes when it wasn't absolutely necessary, like when she left it and Rudolphe and her father behind.

The trembling colors of the sea come back to her on the undulating flame whose trail she kisses. Warm like the sea. She opens her mouth so it will enter her. She misses its intimacy and the feeling of the wetness inside of her, on her. That was not oneness. Or was it oneness because she never really could feel where the warmth ended? And yet it was on her skin. Yes she felt that. Her flesh that was part of her and not the shimmering tropical sea whose temperature was the same as her blood but still was not her. She knows the difference because there is one and her mother and her aunt, or another much younger woman, caress each other on the sun-heated boulder at the edge of the sea that envelopes her. Their skin shimmers like fish scales under the viscous water that buoys her, carries her and caresses her too. They wave to her and she feels safe because of it, because of them.

"Mother?"

What is the unique bond of the cohesion, adhesion, the connection, alliance, the link and the nexus? For Sophia there is no answer, she doesn't remember that woman. She remembers an image on the edge of the tepid, gentle sea but she does not remember the woman. The stone that was the bed for her and the other one is more vivid to her than those people. The stone is humming underneath them and moving so that their bodies undulate with it. The boulder embraces them with arms of small speckled stones that have been pressed together by the weight of the universe on them, now the weight of the women making love within its grainy grasp. It moves against them and gently abrades them and keeps moving, surging over their nakedness while they coil there on top of it and in it.

Shining, moaning, the boulder is swooning beneath their love and Sophia feels privileged to see it and to feel the ecstasy of the stone. She remembers the image at the edge of the sea, but she doesn't remember the woman. She wonders why only for a moment.

"Sophia."

"Who's there?"

She turns and the heavy robes she wears to protect herself while she works make a sound. Sybelle tastes it in her mouth and makes a move to run out of the gloom away from it. The sound of heavy cloth frightens her because she doesn't know this has happened before and was watched by the person who dreamed it then and is dreaming it again now. The vantage point is different because the dreamer dreams it all as another person. It dreams that its soul is everywhere and can adhere in anything or to another person, even to dirt or rocks, beetles or dogs, rats. So Sophia frightens Sybelle and the dreamer sees it all. It felt the same fright before through Sybelle's eyes although now it's not the same.

"I want to talk to you."

"Sybelle, is that you? You sound strange, not like you. Are you afraid of something?"

She almost said, *but I thought you were too stupid to be afraid of anything.* The starkness in the discord between the vague detachment the halfwit usually showed and the fear that is clear in her now make Sophia stop herself even though she doesn't care about Sybelle. The silhouette she sees near the doorway is erect and alert, the posture manifests the state and intention of a mind at its apex. She didn't know the girl was capable of such self-possession.

Why have you been lying about yourself? –she almost said but stopped herself again. She realized now Sybelle was wily enough to lie if she wanted to. She wonders how her clothes feel being worn by such a wizard? No magic could have created the erroneous impression of her better than her dunce act. Sophia begins to feel better about her or about her assessment of her. She can no longer think of her as a dimwit whose talent can rival her own inexplicably, instead she's a normal artist with intellect and skill that are not only estimable but worked on and worked toward with intent. So she can relax, she thinks, because Sybelle isn't some peculiar prodigy but just another lying artist. She likes her better for it, for as much as she can like anything that draws breath.

"I want to tell you something," Sybelle does not move closer.

"What?"

"About you and me."

Sophia wonders what she'll get out of this, how profitable will her confession be? There are no other terms in which she can think of it just like she can have no other relation with Metza than to treat her like a loyal pet who sleeps at her feet every night, or between her legs.

So Sybelle tells her how Agnes and Blessed Mary have used her talent for their own gain, how they have manipulated her career with the priests. She tells her how they destroyed the crucifix that screamed with agony so she would be obligated to make another and so she would be unsure of her work and agree to stay under their control so they could be her scheming mothers. Sophia listens to all of it. She even listens when Sybelle tells her that she can see the wind and feel odors on her skin, smell shapes. Agnes and Mary plan to use this talent of hers the way they will use Sophia's to dazzle people, and from the confusion create their new order of reality.

She laughs. Sophia laughs at all of it and shocks Sybelle because she thought such a serious artist as Sophia would be outraged. She doesn't care. The reliquary for the future martyr's ashes is so important she wants to work, she's learning, she's taking all that the mother in disguise as the

190

Magister has to teach and this is all she cares about. The intrigue of new realities don't concern her because she doesn't believe in them, she only believes in the reality that she creates with her hands. The reality that she creates. Sybelle listens to her and tastes her words and wishes she truly could be the halfwit she has acted so she wouldn't feel so agitated now by Sophia's stupidity.

~

"If I'm Osiris, great arbiter of the underworld, why do I keep making mistakes? It's all learning, I know that, and I know that's why we take on bodies, so we can learn and experience the joys that can only come from living. Still, sometimes I despair. And you?"

Damn, I've fallen asleep again with my Set on Traveler freq. The image of this beautiful woman is floating near my nourishment panel, still talking, although I thought Osiris was a man.

"I know you despair too. It's because we forget. Do you realize how much we've forgotten? It's staggering. Evolution. Think about evolving, we're always doing it and so is everything else in the universes doing it, changing. For the better? I don't know anymore, but we're changing anyway and usually for the better because we learn. We have to learn. Adapting to the world is really a cooperative transmutation because we're all coupled together, other species and their environments too. Look, a turtle evolves toward its optimum strategy embodied in a space, and a worm toward its, but the terrain surrounding them deforms as they do. See? Everything changes around them and every other thing all the time, continuously. It's as if everyone is walking on elastic."

What crap. I hope there's a dot of drugs left, any drug. I keep hitting the ultraviolet switch but the Sim freq won't change.

191

"And we learn too little, that's the problem. We forget. Autocatalytic sets co-evolved in symbiosis, not competition. Think about evolution, how we've been, or our consciousness and even our brains have been Everything. Everything. We've been Everything already. Minerals, vegetables, other animals and human animals. We should be able to remember all that. We should remember every existence and every experience in them that we've had as birds, coyotes, ants, trees, grass, tunas. But we don't, we don't. We should remember what it was like to live in those worlds. Our minds are adaptive and we've gone through those many universes in evolution and still go back to them sometimes when we're reborn just to learn about them, to work out some problems, or just for the experience, for fun, so we should remember these worlds. But when we're in the three dimensional reality we forget. It's only from here where I am for this flesh in the omnipresent state of energy, that we can see all of that, then we seek out another body and we come back into the small dimensioned world and we forget. There's a way around this, though."

While the simulated bare-breasted god strides around the steamy pyramids in a skirt, Schrödinger balances her way slowly up my leg and perches on my chest. Eyes opened like tunnels gleaming yellow from deep inside stare at me, draw me in.

"Last day, first day, it doesn't matter. Cross in and out of streams, it doesn't matter that they're the same or difference ones, whatever you want. It's all just whatever you want. Wow."

In his valuable work upon Egyptian magic, by far the most illuminating text-book on the subject, Dr. Budge says: 'The Egyptians believed that as the souls of the departed could assume the form of any living thing or plant, so the "gods," who in many respects closely resembled them, could and did take upon themselves the forms of birds and beasts. This was the fundamental idea of the so-called "Egyptian animal-worship," which provoked the merriment of the cultured Greek, and drew down upon Egyptians the ridicule and abuse of the early Christian writers.' He further states that the Egyptians paid honor to certain animal forms because they considered they possessed the characteristics of the gods, to whom they made them sacred.

Spence

TWENTY TWO

Timed Document Backup

Bruce Atman is a criminal. Not only did he flash data to me that can get us both in trouble, he's somehow locked my HoloSet system. I have to wait until his proselytizing Sim ends before I can change frequency to his coordinate address in the Net that lists him as Religious\Traveler Group. His interests come up as Galaxy Exploration and Translation of CEE's (chemo / electro / emotions) between life forms to Intereactive Recombinative experiences WOV. WOV (WithOut VirtReal) is reserved for people and things that avoid modern technology and cling to quaint life styles like transcendental religions, although Travelers aren't really religious. They are philosophers who pretend that twenty-three hundred years of technology hasn't made a positive difference in thinking. They want to get back the old ways of relating, all of us out on the streets again actually seeing each other and talking and going to workplaces, parks and SensSim theaters together.

It would never work. It didn't before. People together created violence so technology keeps everyone apart all the time. That's why crime is almost unheard of, and being inundated with totally involving entertainment from the diversion industry helps. That reminds me of my programs, where's the call from my agent? He said that my new VirtReal game would make me a Celeb.

I call him on the communer and get hi HoloMess. The auto message shows him in his mediator green skinsuit sitting in front of a rooftop panorama cluttered with domed single person swimming pools, smiling, looking directly into my eyes.

"Sorry we can't virt right now, Evet. You can tell me what's up on Augmented. OK?"

"I need to talk to you."

"OK," the image says. "If I can't respond from my pre-response deck, I'll get back to you. Go."

"I want a VirtReal meeting with you ASAP."

"I'll get back."

"No. Set the co-ords now. It's urgent."

"Sorry to hear about your trouble with the Police," the image frowns from its programmed data. "If there's anything I can do. Go."

"Set the coordinates right now for a virt meeting. Need to talk to you, really you."

"Sorry, not an option, Evet. Got to go."

"Hey!"

"Out."

His image fades with a preset wink and a smile. She watches him waving at her until the space around her is blank again. So close before, he had been negotiating a contract with a subsector of Nets for her work, and now it's obvious everyone knows she's been frequency confined. Without her agreeing to an in-person virtreal meeting she won't be able to access his message Augmenter again. One chance is all you get when you're freq confined.

"Call Kvino," she says.

195

Nothing appears in the room. Nothing. This isn't something I'm prepared for, being cut off totally from communicating. They can't do that, it's a basic right. But who knows what they're put out there about me. Bear B. said she'd authorize Kvino's freq but she's also elicited and recorded every reading she could that was once uniquely and exclusively mine. From terror to sex, every firing of every neuron can be replicated by the cops now. Who knows what they've found, or think they have, that changed her mind about my access ability. I don't know what I'm supposed to do about it without having the information Bruce Atman seems to be able to get to from his Travelers bootleg frequencies. And here comes my artificial love again, back arching, purring, she stalks closer.

"Kvino!"

It's no use. So I'm out the door and waiting for the vacuum tube to whoosh me to the street, but it doesn't come in response to the recognition of my hand against the identity panel for DOWN. I must be under magnetic house arrest and Bear B. didn't tell me. The stairs are somewhere on these curved corridors that branch but all of them look alike. I've never gone anywhere else on my floor, no reason to. The sealed doors to cubicles exactly like mine are silent when I pass and set off nothing on my wrist. Whenever I got out of the tube on this floor before the strand optic home-r always gently pulled me along the path to my door. Now I feel the resistance of trying to walk in a new unauthorized direction. The red glow warns I'm in territory I shouldn't be in and increases with a humming from deeper implants around my wrist, the connection to the central databank.

Finally, a door discreetly outlined by a beam's raised edge, and I slide down the dim EXIT chute as fast as I can, pumping my sympathetic nervous system implant behind my ear as I go. The induced adrenalin rush combines with the natural release already active and I grab for the thrust bars faster and faster to increase my plunge rate and my heart hammers and sweat flies out of my scalp, out from the skin along the midline of my back where extra holes for sweat escape were surgically punched long ago. I'm faster than a gravity drop now, and just go with my automatic reactions. Pushing off from the grab bars in rapid succession so my arms are a blur working to speed my hurl down the steep chute. I'm moving at a blinding rate.

I think my nose is bleeding from the pressure but I don't dare move my hands from the rhythm pushing off the grab bars to accelerate. Faster, faster and down, and suddenly the ground level slams under my boots and momentum ejects me forward into a padded wall I ricochet off. On my back, nose bleeding from the fall or the pressure, I hear myself groan. But no time for that, I've got to move fast to find the door before it's sealed against me so I scramble around and up and finally I'm out. Behind me the marked DISASTER door closes flush into one of the giant columns that supports the first floor five stories overhead.

Hushed grey normal day, grab a PedPad from the nearby stand and I'm off. They must not have expected this because I've gotten away. Weaving, lifting, dipping to varied altitudes through the streets the Pad's on max-fly speed I head downtown where there are fewer sensor stations to track me. Renegade now, they'll label me an Evanescent Citizen, too rare and distressing for more direct description.

"Where do you think you're going?"

"Bear B., why didn't you tell me you confined me?"

"What did you think? If you'd just stim-out like everyone else you would not be here now, would you. Look around and see how strange you've become, what a threat. You know there is something about the freeness of your emotions, the fact that somehow you need the Nets we all use less and less. Self-reliance? Really, you leave me no choice. You're going to be stopped. You should have done it yourself when I held you, when we were together. Don't you remember? You do, of course."

My knees buckle and I have to grab the vertical rod on the front of the pad I'm standing on, skimming over the streets. She's stimulating the sensory memory area of my cerebral cortex from the ultraviolet remote on the pad.

"Remember...?"

It's like she's whispering in my ear. All the sensations come back. Insistent motion over skin that seems peeled off so that she's touching me from the inside. The aftermath is like no other program or experience I've had.

"Stop it."

"You don't mean that."

Moist breath brushed my lips, and at my ear a tonguing insistence. My head lolls to the side.

"Take it. There's no hierarchy."

"What?"

Swerve and duck, the side of a building flares past only centimeters from my right arm. What did she say? I've heard it before but don't know what it means. All I know is that it frightens me because I think somehow the words came from me, created. But all there is, is hierarchy. One person, one network, one frequency over another. Was it Bear B.'s voice or someone else's? I've got to find out why I can't be certain of it.

~

Hail Mary, mother of us, discover all our enemies now, and make it the hour of their death. Amen.

The second chorus of the song has a lilting sweetness that echoes against the shuttered windows. Mary has taken over conducting the singers from Agnes to get this effect. The women respond better to her radiance than to Agnes' rationed movements and roving eyes that stalk perfection.

The last chorus is robust, almost raucous in the Beguines' throats and Sybelle has edged herself into a corner because of it. The smell of the words frightens her; the room reeks with effluvium of every sound. Sedition songs or songs of freedom, she can't understand why she can't separate the two and why she thinks that it should be hotter here, that this should be an island somewhere hot. Redemption songs. She doesn't know that coconut palms exist, yet she can taste the rough sweetness of their shape.

"That was good," Mary says. "We all know that we're going to do, right? The miracles I'm going to perform outside will be the same ones you've agreed to already."

"When are you going to use our babies?"

"You mean your dogs, Elley?" I'm not sure. The miracles where I have the dogs talking about how they were human once and hope to be human in their next lives is one that can only be done after the people respect me and trust what I'm doing. We don't want to be stoned or burned. It's been done and will be again, but not to me."

"They need to be afraid," Agnes says. "The people, not the dogs."

"A little, yes, that will help me get through it, and get to them."

"You won't hurt them?" Ellekindis says. "I'd stop you from doing that, we'd stop you, Petriss' and me."

"I know, I know. I won't hurt the dogs. It's only a trick, just another reality that I'll slip into, a device of the mind, my mind, that will let me talk to them and make them be heard out loud. Anyone who knows there's more to life than this that we're living can do it. I mean, that's the whole point of what Agnes and I have constructed, just a few peeks behind the curtain—"

"You mean like a look up the priests skirts."

"Exactly. Our Mary will expose the Marys."

"Sshhh, stop laughing! Until we have enough followers that joke is still profanity. Be careful."

"Very careful," Sybelle whispers and no one hears.

"They really need to be fought, those men. I'm tired of the way they treat me," Metza says. "Every time I see one in the street they ether simper and make the sign of the cross or ignore me like a dung ditch, like I'm less than them. They hide behind that girl they forced on everyone and elevated to being a Saint Mary because they murder everyone else who dares to call her a slut. Even after that story of hers..."

Everyone rolls their eyes. They poke each other in the ribs and laugh out loud.

"Immaculate Conception, hah!"

"Sshhh."

"Her son wasn't that bad, though. Always good to her, they say."

"So?" Mary arranges her hair. "He had to be, didn't he? She was always harping on him to be a success. Do this miracle, do that miracle, make sure people see you do it. A real nag, that's what the one who the priests will burn said. He was a good son when she was watching him, and she closed her eyes to the things he did with those men friends of his."

"Never mind. You're going to overshadow her and him too. They're not going to matter anymore," Agnes says. "You're the new prophet of the new truth, and I'm the first priest."

"And manager."

"That too. Now go on."

"All right," Mary takes a bow. "But I need the prop first, I can't find the prop."

"What?"

"You know."

"Is this it?" Petrissa points to something next to her.

"That's it," Mary struggles to lift it.

"What is it?"

"A brain in a vat."

"Whose?"

"All of ours, dear, all of ours."

"How the hell can that be true?"

"Because I say so."

~

Despair lives at the edges of my mind like a cat darting by, just caught in the corner of my eye in a quiet cottage late at night. That's how I feel when I see them plotting against me, talking with their mouths hidden behind their hands. I know they will torture me even more before they burn me. At least before when I was Isis—no, Osiris—then at least I wasn't tortured before I was lured to that coffin by my own greed and nailed into it. That was a kind of torture though, too, because I suffocated, and that wasn't an easy way to go.

Now I'll burn for other sins. Pride. Hatred. Anger. That's a fact, great universes, what rage I have, it's embarrassing. At cab drivers, at arrogant goddesses, at hunters, at children who pick their noses and, worse, at adults who do, at ignorant people with missing teeth, at people who don't speak properly, so many objects of my anger in every age over and over. Who do I think I am? Them. Yes, them. And hating myself is always my worst crime, most facile talent. See? I pay again and again for anger. Born time after time, learning in such miniscule increments, to think that I, at one time at least, was the mighty Osiris, but greedy.

"Listen to me!"

They never do. But do they not listen because they really don't want to or because I expect them not to? Do I really control more than I think if I could just remember to do it?

TWENTY THREE

Something Bypassed, Not Missed

"I don't know how you can help me."

"Yes you do," Bruce Atman says.

Travelers ON (<u>O</u>ff <u>N</u>et) *Center* is impressive. Across the sludge from the gargan-City's eastern shore it is a small complex of interconnected domes and towers each with its own weather, plants, animals. It's like something in VirtReal only it's real. An aroma of lush cleanness is overlaid with the fragrance of giant exotic flowers lacing the air with perfumes that lounge on my skin. All the crystal receptor nanopoints of my wrist glow mellow clearer than clear white. It looks like I've never felt this way before. I don't think so and my data precepts have stopped trying to match the sensation with anything already stored in me. No threat, the airy glow around my wrist indicates something approaching total calm.

"I guess this is a near death experience."

"Almost near," he says. "This is architected to release our own endorphins, a new kind of environmental psychology. Great, isn't it?"

"I smile back at him, amazed that I can't think of a smart remark. Who cares? I feel so good, is it only endorphins? Probably. Evidently Travelers participate in manufactured experience as much as anyone else does. Fine. That's fine with me. Right now everything is fine with me.

We are walking through arched transparent corridors that connect the buildings. A few normal looking people pass us but many more are blissed-out, grinning, or not smiling but appear to be in a deep meditation that makes them peaceful. They wear bodysuits whose pastel colors stretch over their movements, blur them. And the tints saturate everything, even the air they seem to float in. There are more people here than on the streets of the gargan-City across the way and I find it odd to not have suspected there were so many bliss-ninnies. Besides that, it makes me a little uncomfortable to have so many walking around who aren't plugged into SensSims so that their awareness isn't harnessed. Who knows what anyone might do without being occupied by perpetual entertainment? My wrist crystals flicker.

"Don't be afraid."

"You've got to be kidding. You think I'm afraid of these fanatics?"

"Obviously."

"Whatever. And where's Kvino anyway? Is he here?"

"See? When you get away from the endorphin freq you experience anger, the most destructive emotion you can feel, friend."

"So what? I can repair any sympathetic nervous system damage or ulceration abuse from adrenalin or anything else with a MedScan Renewer. We all know emotions affect our bodies, but can be fixed. So?"

"You've got no reason to be afraid of them," Atman says. "They're afraid of you."

"Why me?"

"You're a murderer. It's been on every freq for days. So you shouldn't be upset people stare at you, although I know you can't help it."

"What are you talking about? I haven't heard anything, there's been nothing on but the regular network stuff, no flashes."

"Yes there has, to everyone's decks except yours, Evet. You've been frequency-blocked. They're getting ready to try you and reformat your synaptic range and you haven't a clue. Your punishment has already begun. Information, data that is the only thing that's freedom, is being kept from you and the whole system knows it except you. The police are already controlling you by limiting you access to the Nets spaces. They think you're here only because we try to rehabilitate social misfits. The real reason, though, is much more important to you and to all of us."

"Why would my mess be important to you?"

"For some reason you know what we've been trying to attain for so long, the culmination of all our practice. You know about your lives."

"What are you talking about?"

"Your lives. You know about other existences in some way, in some form. The dreams the rest of us have you're living. Look, you are living, and living, and still living. Do you understand? Try to wake up and know the power that this is. Evet? Come on. Evet?"

I don't know why I'm crying like this but suddenly I am. Atman is crazy and I don't believe any of the repulsive things he's telling me. What is he talking about, weird things like my replicated 'Dinger really being alive? Crazy. Damn it, I want to go home, *please somebody take me home.* Kvino? I wish I believed in prayer or in anything except the new wiring at my

205

neck. I don't want to be tortured again. *Get me out of here.* A hologram, a simulation, that's it, wait. That's all it is.

"OK Bear B., you listening? Good try. Now get me out of here. Just make it go away, ok? Let's talk."

"You can't reach her from here," Atman says. "We've got a magnetic data shield protecting the entire complex. The police break our codes every few days and we reformulate new ones, scramble all communications here inside and send out fake ones, then we're safe for a while. We're safe now. The police can't hear you."

"Yeah right. Come on Bear B., change the freq. You're not fooling me."

"This is real, Evet, I'm really here. No one's controlling this reality except for you. Only you can change it if you want, if you really want to. But I'm here and I can give you information because I'm part of you as you are of me and I can give you what you know you already have. If you'll only let yourself know."

"That's funny," I wish I could laugh. "Don't you mean let yourself go, not 'know'? If I just let myself go then I'll think thoughts that the police can't account for in my genetic structure and Bear B. will zap me again, implant god knows what in my brain and monitor me every time I scratch or blink."

"That's not it and you know it. You have to let yourself know, know that what's happening in your life has happened before. Mat/leen was lost to you, and then your cat. But she's back, dead or alive? There's an equal chance for each, you choose, don't you see it yet? You're not just you. Your dreams are real—"

"Shut up! Goddamnit shut up and let me out of here."

"That's up to you. Let yourself know that you've evolved the way all of us want to, not just physically. Come on, you remember. You know what makes life happen is the balance between order and disorder, like the difference between solids and fluids where in-between is the transition place, an edge of chaos where things never quite lock into place and never quite disperse into turbulence either. Knowing what's there is up to you."

"Nothing is up to me! There's no control that's not Police control. The Nets are theirs and we're all caught in them. I don't believe you, I can't. There's some other reason the Police can't account for what they call my 'novel' thoughts. So leave me alone. I don't want to pretend I can fight the system that gives us images for every waking and sleeping minute, gives us dreams. I can't give myself dreams! That's crazy."

"Remember Mat/leen," Atman says. "She trusted you. And you trusted her enough to let her call you a snob. Remember? I told you the truth. We scan freqs, we know."

"Just like the cops."

"Not like them. You want to see Kvino?"

"Is he here?"

"Over there."

I turn and see him a good distance away. I wave toward where he's gliding out from quivering green ferns that are dense, visibly growing taller around him.

"Who's that with him?"

"Look closer. It's Mat/leen. Let me show you what we've scanned from you already..."

~

"I want to learn to make metal from the dirt and the air, maybe even with the water that is so gentle. If I change its form it will be stronger, it won't be hurt by people who destroy it by using it. If water were gold people wouldn't kill it by drinking it."

"They'll say you're mad, Sophia."

"And you?"

"I don't like to judge."

"I'm an artist."

"They'll especially say you're mad."

"But they don't say that about you, Magister. They wouldn't dare because they respect you. What's the difference?"

"I'm a scientist who practices alchemy, not an artist who accomplishes it. It's a difference in creative stance shown to people for a reason. You see if they only knew how creative I've been they'd do their worst."

"What do you mean?"

"Never mind. Practice your fluxes now, there, on the silver and gold alloy."

It's easy to distract Sophia back to her own products because the secret of making electrum is almost hers. Fabulous objects have been made with Church metals that were melted in the Magister's ovens, mixed in his crucibles and worked so they will never be traced to foreign religions' artifacts. Veneration cycling over and over again in the artist's hands. It is dangerous because this artist will add herself while the scientist-artist pretends not to. Sleight of hand, magic over materials, the Magister changes substance in secret and is venerated because he/she seems to produce only what was ordered, precious Church vessels or objects for function on the estate. But the apprentice is violent with emotion, chaotic, driven to the work like stinging sand catapulted by the force of a storm.

She wants her mother to be proud of her. As she bends over the crucible, squinting against the fumes, she sees her mother on the boulder with the other beautiful woman. They ignore her although she waves, occupied with themselves, doing something together she cannot determine. The water caresses her, rocks her, sings her to sleep in its billowy crests. Then it draws her down and kisses her deeply. And she knows by this that she is special, chosen. Her art will reflect this unique baptism, the extraordinariness of being able to commune with water and be taken by it. She will fight to keep this status, no one is as important as she is.

"I came to tell you," Sybelle's voice makes her flinch, her protective robes rustle. "They say that your brother is in Strasbourg. He's looking for you."

"Why?"

"Someone has died. His lover, they say. He has shaved off his eyebrows and doesn't care about anything, even cut off some fingers. They say he sleeps in the streets and he's looking for you, that's all I know and they wanted me to bring him here."

"No!"

"I knew that."

Sybelle watched Magister Ivo who didn't turn around while she spoke and she wondered why she accepted this parent's strangeness. She heard the emotion loud in her ears but she accepted being ignored by her father/mother and didn't know why. She acquiesced to the lie because the parent wanted it, like she/he was not her parent but a friend who elicits broad understanding and patience. Things you might not do for family you do for friends because they are farther from the heart of your injured emotions. Sybelle heard the tolerance in her ears although she did taste a little suffering at the same time.

~

If Atman's right about what I think are simply SensSims that seem familiar then why doesn't he go way? I mean I wish he was gone so why isn't he and why aren't Kvino and

Mat/leen still here with me instead? Just let myself know. Sure.

"You know, Evet."

"Shut up."

"You know the story already. There are mirrors in the cosmos, there must be. You recognize yourself too well, you know you do. What does it mean when the thought in your mind is spoken by someone you've never met? Huh? What about that? The words you write appear in a book you haven't read yet but someday you will and then you recognize them. You know already, you know now you've already done it. You'll recognize it later."

"But recognition means—"

"Yes!"

TWENTY FOUR

Scrolling Speed

Rudolphe carried his grief like a vast denial of the world, of anything that was real and could be held and tasted or that moved. Not being able to accept the loss he lived with his worst fear and this most hated adversary was always at his side. It was as if he loved what he said he loathed. There it was, always with him to torture him when all he had to do was drop the leash by which he clutched the sorrow of Death that gnashed and screamed against him. So he pulled out his hair and dismembered himself piece by piece until his hands held bloody stumps of fingers, his ears swirls of chopped-up flesh on each side of his cankered scalp, his feet bloodied from hacked off toes.

"You can't stay here," Sophia told him.

"But you're my life, how can you say that? You know we're meant to be together, always were."

"Now I'm alone."

"Without the cat, so am I. But I'm never without you. Don't you remember our great triumph even before we were born, the union?"

"I don't remember anything. Take this ring I made and trade it for food and things and go back to the cottage. Go live like a hermit if you want. Just go."

"But you're my wife, how can you say that?"

"Everything changes. Wives come and go, relations are impermanent but fame is forever."

"How can you say that? You know how we're joined."

"My work is me, that's all. Be quiet and go away. I have to go on and you have to accept change."

Rudolphe who was once so stunning is repulsive now, all bloodied and covered with sores. It made her angry, the mirror of her own soul had destroyed itself and it frightened her. There must be mirrors. She recognizes herself too well in him. But she will recognize something else later.

"I'll live anywhere, under a bench in the Magister's workshop, under any bench," he said. "You can throw me a few scraps when you think of it or else I can stand up with the dogs and run with them for castle refuse, I don't care."

"You can live that way, I can't. How could I concentrate on my work with the reminder of you around?"

A magnificence like Rudolphe sunk to this thoughtful disarray? He was glory ephemeral because he mourned too hard for what was gone because he had been her, too. Now Sophia needs another mirror. She can't concentrate."

"Go home to our father."

"You want me to die."

"Do what you want, only don't do it here. I'm busy."

"Our father's dead too."

"You tell me now? You've been here for days and now you tell me? Idiot. You really have changed. How did it happen?"

"I changed because—"

"No! How did he die?"

"I don't know."

"You wouldn't. Look at you, all you care about is yourself."

"Live with me, love me again."

"I'm busy," she said and ran away.

He wept while Sybelle watched from the other side of the street. Some of the traffic that passed tossed offerings at him, others spat. She watched it all.

~

Bruce Atman gave me a small statue of the Buddha to "work with" he said, but I couldn't help noticing it was a very bad one. Not only was the synthetic metal manufacture poorly done but the expression made it look like he was an old man, eyes closed, lips downturned, who smelled something rotten. This was supposed to be my icon, my connection to reflections, according to Atman. I didn't believe it but I had to try it. Kvino insisted.

"Look, I came back just for you, you know," he said. "You've got the key to all this and that's why the police want you although they don't get it, don't understand your story. They don't believe Travelers anymore than you or I did."

"And now you do?"

"You saw Mat/leen with me, you're the one who put her there and she'd be here right now if you wanted it. That's why Bear B.'s going to kill you, but first she's going to get your working brain if she can. That's why you haven't really been hurt yet, they wouldn't want you to retaliate and create something against them they don't have a defense for, that they can't control. You're not locked up somewhere because they don't want to risk you proving that you could escape."

"What are you on? They used to burn witches at the stake for that kind of thing. Come on, you know you don't believe it."

"I do, but you don't want to."

And I don't want to believe the stories he and Atman tell me either. Ancient fables. There was something about someone meeting a starving tiger with her cubs and lying down next to her to offer himself to eat so that she could live instead of him and, *zip*, instant Buddhahood. The point being that enlightenment means understanding that all living creatures are one. Give to a tiger, give to yourself. Sure. Give your life to another and save yourself. For what? Preservatives and death Holos can keep us around forever, but really, for what? I've got to know what that means because it's part of the control I always wanted. Save yourself for what?

Each moment unexpected, brand new. Never knowing what will happen next although you laid its foundation before. Exciting. Requires skill. Exciting, even if it's already charted by you. This was what life was, this was life. And this is living.

See? Listen to me.

The small image is enchanting, maybe because of its imperfections. The Buddha has one long ear higher than the other, the draped robe exposes half his chest, a nipple and the nipple on the other side is misplaced so it peeks around the edge of the robe that crosses over. The nipple, large for a man's, is getting larger. I blink. Somehow changed, the air around me evaporates and I'm there with that steely breast-point that stares at me, rotates, grows. It opens and invites me in.

If there are thoughts I don't want to think, I think them now. Words unknown to me like someone else's prepared speech swirl inside my ears like the hum I have never heard of electricity in copper wires. I want to know how to live, what to be. I want to know how to be better. *Is this all there is?*

This life, is this all there is? Atman told Kvino and me a story of someone who wanted to attain Buddhahood. I guess anybody can do it, it seems an egalitarian philosophy. Anyway, this person went and meditated on some mountaintop for five hears, decided he wasn't getting any closer to knowing what it's all about so chose to leave. On the way down the mountain he found someone rubbing a towering boulder with a feather.

Why are you doing that?

To make the rock into a pebble so it will not block the path anymore.

Hearing this kind of devotion to a task, the aspirant went back to the summit with renewed resolve for another five or six years. A feather wearing down a boulder? Christ. They can probably synthesize a polymer that could do it but I guess that's not the point, and I wish I could understand. Or is this what's going to get me into more trouble? Are they reading this unsanctioned wish from my implants right now? There's got to be something else.

"What it is you want? Kiss your lover's face with tonguing strokes."

"Who's there?" I say it and realize the image of my dead girl is gone.

"There is no hierarchy. Why don't you understand that?"

"Who are you? Bear B.?"

In the silence I sit down at the table in the windowed cell where Atman has hidden me, away from the databanks of CySpace, but it is just like my own place and now my Schrödinger is gone. It is my own cubicle, isn't it? I put the Buddha on the table. An anachronism, its *faux* bronze patina clashes with the whiteness all around. The few fixtures are standard like everyone else at my level is used to because furnishings like clothes, cars, apartment cubicles, none of it matters anymore because no one really lives here in the gargan-city or anywhere else. We're all in CySPace, we live in infoNets and in diversion worlds and it doesn't matter what we possess. Those with more credits like the MegaCelebs have access to more data space, grander alternatives to reality and therefore better possessions. But no one lives in this world, the real world, anymore. No one except the Marginals and, worse, the indigents who we don't know anything about because no one sees them. No one goes out much, we meet in our Holo and multiGraphic selves in the CySpace matrix and we space out.

"Not like it was with you, right?"

The odd sitting figure with one hand pointing toward the ground while the other holds a bowl, palm up, says nothing. I can make it come to life, give it an artificial vitality by getting into a sector and assigning data points for it. I can access a plot that would activate the thing as if it were real. Atman knows all this. Why does he keep insisting that there's another reality when in fact, there is? CySpace is another reality, the infoNets produce and interpret any realities we want. So?

Her thought is interrupted by a movement, a black speck that falls in front of the statue's downward pointing slender hand. It moves, crawling around in a tight circle. It's so small that her eyes can't really focus on it, not even with the mechanical parts. An insect, a tiny spider whose legs are so infinitesimal she can't see them? Or does it have wings? Whatever it is walks around, alive. She wonders if she should call a Squad. Maybe the thing is one of those cockroaches that she linked from an old chip were supposed to have inhabited all of the gargan-City in tremendous numbers up until the end of the 22nd Cent. Whatever it is it's alive and that makes it inexplicable. She watches it, fascinated, holding her breath so as not to disturb it. Her lasered lenses try to adjust, focusing on the image of the minuscule animal at different corneal points to magnify it. It's alive. She is struck by how precious this is, but at the same time a peculiar urge rises in her. She wants to crush it with her fingertip, can see it happening and the thought makes her sick. No, she wouldn't do that. Never.

"What?"

I don't know how the word escapes me but it does even though I don't really mean it. I mean there's nothing to ask, but it moved. The Buddha smiled. Now it's not doing it, but just a second ago its downturned lips grinned at me. Even now it doesn't seem as sour looking as it did before. It's laughing at me. No, it seems that way, that's all. It must be from the adjustment my eyes are going through trying to see the little animal. I wonder if I should feed it something, but what? Would it eat recombined molecular fuel?

"Evet?"

"Jesus, what!"

"Sorry, I startled you. But you are caught, this time. We've got you," Bear B.'s duplicate suddenly next to me says gently.

"No wait. I'm just—"

"Thinking, I know. That's the problem isn't it. Let's go."

"Where?"

"Where do you think? You're going to live the murders again so we can collect more data."

"But I didn't do it."

"You did. You thought them and they happened. That is the point. Wait. Don't run! Now see what you made me do? It's really all over for you, baby."

~

"Why have you denied your brother?"

217

"Who knows why we do things?"

"You do, you always know."

"I don't know what you mean, don't care. Just teach me about the art, Magister. That's all there is."

"It's all you want to see. Try to look over the edge instead into disorder, and beyond disorder."

"Just show me what I can make."

"You are chaos. You kiss the heated track that flames leave behind, you romance the water you take inside of you. But outside you order what you can control into perfect hierarchy, mastery over the material. For what? Some transient emptiness you don't even understand. Renown? Yearning for recognition from outside of you when what's important is recognizing who you are and what your real tasks are. But you are chaos. And you're mean."

"Mediocrity is worse, more difficult than being despised. I'm really sure of this, mediocrity is a monotone of life without failures and life without success. Maybe a little of each but the winning's never important enough, never bright enough to really shine and the pain never brings enough blackness to make you want to light a candle to overpower it. Little failures and forgettable successes. You see? Hate me, but teach me. I don't care as long as I get something that tips the scales, forces down one tray or the other of the balance. I don't care as long as the power of the movement creates a wind from the imbalance that caresses me with its force. Recognizes me.

"But recognitions mean you were known before, and then also will be again. Besides, you sound different already."

~

Why do they bother to torture me when I'm not worth it? My life is no example to anyone. Medium grade, medium rating. Why do they waste time terrifying me when no one cares enough to know about it? *Put me in a popular Sim! Make me an adventure hero. Monitor that, bastards!*

If they bother to read my thoughts they should at least act on some of them. But nobody listens to me. If I believe this does it make it true? Atman did, but if he knows so much why doesn't he get me out of this mess before the torture from the crystal dot they've put on my forehead starts to work?

"Your mother's here, Evet."

"Damn it, that's all I need. Bear B., this is really enough."

She just smiles in front of the thick light from the glass walls. Her magenta skin coating changes to somber white, unattractive. At the same time a SensSurround Sim emerges children playing in the room who shriek and run at play. Their sharp laughter is more than annoying to me and I focus instead on the plaintive cries of gulls circling overhead just outside the glass walls. I force myself to transform it, the children's shrieks are really gulls' calls, beautiful and calming as they glide overhead at Montauk, yes, and at Wellfleet on Cape Cod.

"You've never been there.

"In old Sims."

"No," Bear B. says. "We have a record of every Sim, every chip or dot you ever accessed. None are of those places, but you know them. How?"

"Leave me alone," I yearn to hear the gulls above those intolerable kids.

"But one of them is you. See? Over there by your mother. Why don't you look at her? At you."

"She's dead because I killed her, erased her from my data banks and I have a certificate for it too. Plenty of kids divorce their parents, it's only genetically engineered ties that are synthetic anyway. Some kill them, petition to have them deleted from their files if they're really disgusting to have around. I did it and I'm glad. Red and Obert are parents enough without the loathsome interference of the egg donor who tried to control my life. I saw that early on and that's why I did something about it. Everyone knows that mothering creates chemical skewing in the donor, traits of possessiveness, overbearing intervention, sermonizing and general control bias all go along with it and the reactionary *Back To Genetics* movement only lionizes these flaws."

"There, look out before you fall. I told you. Now she's going to hit you, see! Almost, almost... she would have if I weren't here. There, that one you like so much, *'friend'* my eye! She's nobody, not as good as us. Not as good," my mother's voice peaks. "You can't trust her, can't trust anybody. See what happens? See!"

The dark child doesn't answer. Pinned under a barrage of words like a butterfly still alive and stuck in a case, she looks around to see whether the others notice her humiliation.

"What are you with them for? They're no damn good. There's nobody like you. She would have hit you, that wasn't playing and I know you think it was. It wasn't. Hah? That's right. Hah?"

"I don't know," the child whispers and tries to leave.

"You're not going to play with her anymore, yes? You don't like her. She's too stupid, hah? What?"

"I don't know, ma."

Unanswerable questions, never a breath or hesitation breaking the torrent. The little girl could not whisper silently enough for her not to hear, not unless this prototype who demanded reverence in exchange for giving air to breathe needed time to think up a lie to tell and swear it was the truth. Her stinging aura cast a net wider than the police, strung with barbs.

"Get her out of here, Bear B."

"Talk to her."

"She never talks to anybody, she only talks at you. Lies, accusations. Nothing I ever do is right for her and I'm not going to bother to change. She'd dead."

"She's right there."

"She's dead."

And the shrieks of the children ebb away, encased by a gloom that is the funeral home where mother's body is laid out in a transparent casket. I've produced the scene and projected it into the room and I don't know who's more surprised, Bear B. or me. I've changed a Net produced HoloSim and I don't know how I did it but Bear B. is frantically coding something into one of her weapon wristlets and a data panel on a wall is sparkling and buzzing.

TWENTY FIVE

Good Thoughts Affirm Fairies, Buddhas, Unicorns, Dogs Who Smile

"I have trouble accepting the natural order," I say to Bear B. as she dabs her lips with white silk. "I have trouble accepting nature, death... maybe that's because it isn't natural. There's something else and I wish I knew, could understand it. But I don't even know if it's real, know what I mean?"

"I see that in you. But aren't you embarrassed to admit it?"

"You want to humiliate me because that's the way to talk me out of all this, whatever it is I remember."

"I wish you wouldn't do that. I'll have to erase that in you."

"More laser surgery, implants of those memories that aren't mine? Thanks a lot. Like the man with the sack, and what's in the sack?"

"Not at all," Bear B. says it with a kind of sadness. "For someone with too much history, we use history."

"Why? I haven't done anything. You must know that I haven't killed anything. You've got to know."

I feel the quiet horror of knowing that I've really done nothing, although maybe I should admit to it. A desperation that is becoming less silent. *Fame, Fame.* Like an insistent chant from iron train wheels on wear-polished tracks, the ancient subways. *Fame, fame.* The feeling of "medium" fills me with a kind of shame, as if there is someone standing above me who knows I should do something wonderful but I'm too stupid to figure it out. Or just smart enough to know it's there but not brilliant enough to make it come true. The recognition makes me appreciate the kind of surrender to *fait accompli* Oedipus must have felt and my fingers move toward my eyes. But I can't even do that, yank out my eyes. Real drama escapes me. I don't know what to do with my glimpses of excellence, my restlessness at knowing it's there and so I've done nothing. Do nothing.

"But you do kill. I'll have to change you."

The little girl I taught the coin trick to is in front of me again. See her there just like before, if there ever was a before. The old coin with the eagle on it rests flat on her palm and I scoop my hand under it and snatch it away. Magic. What is her name? –the daughter of those two professors when professors were still respected, I've learned about Then. The big stone lions from Egypt in front of the paper library. Strange times when producing no product was rewarded, thinking was rewarded. The little girl liked me and I felt her hair on my head, blond and stringy and very light although annoyingly present with a few strands clinging to my face. I like my hair short, when I have hair.

223

Are you listening?" Bear B. says.

Listen to me, I want to say. And I evidently have.

"Be quiet. I must change you so you won't mutate anymore transmissions without provocation, without cause like that."

Something changes in the room but I'm not sure of what. I feel differently but I don't know how. There's a distinct sound like a virgin aroma. Has someone come in?

"Something you're looking for," the masked person spoke in a synthesizer-disguised voice. "There's something I can get that'll give you and your friend... you know."

"Something," Evet repeated back to the smooth surface with two holes for eyes.

She had no idea what either the person or she herself meant but she erected an indifferent camouflage. She pretended she knew she was smart, advanced, not untrendy. What was 'something?'

The air and the plants, the stained sidewalks of the gargan-City before me, and all of it isn't real. I see it and it's not. It's all for me, and it's not. It's all from me, but not.

But if it isn't there then what am I? That's the question to dance to. The stained sidewalks with black abstract shapes permanently colored from leaking garbage or oil, food or corpses, urine and excrements, those cement walks beneath my feet are not there. But I am. There or somewhere. Where? And who is this 'I' anyway?

How do I know the oddities that are long gone from this place? Apparitions. Things gone from another century but I feel them, I know them. The young black man, prosperous in a trench coat and a fedora pulled down. He carrie(d)s a boombox in the blustery and sunny October Sunday morning, leaves and dirt swirling on Spring Street near the fenced cement playground. The radio is loud, plays "close to you" in

Karen Carpenter's voice. And he jives to it. While the stockbroker prototype in the subway car sat/sits next to me and begins to read a paperbacked book, Straight Tarot. He is engrossed, his briefcase rests between his feet on the ugly worn floor. Odd men, old New York City. Across from him was/is the young man going somewhere and going nowhere because his skin then was not fashionable, but his baggy clothes are and he slouches as is required by them. He wears the stupid look élan dictates. Obtuse, mean stare, it's a fashion statement. And then after that it's never Maria Callas in the cold loft with the screaming life outside, city life that's always beating.

"Evet! Where are you?"

"Jesus Christ, Bear B., right here. What do you want now?"

~

"There is no before or behind. We've known that since pretty early in the 20th, Gil, although they didn't admit it."

"You can't say that because 'since' indicates the linearity, the unidimensionality that does not really exist."

"Fine. So I say it now, here and in other places co-terminously. And it isn't known yet, but it's already old knowledge and forgotten. See, there's an illimitable quest for you."

"I know, the fantasy of time and space. It was what's his name who said that, or he was just one of those people then, and not then I suppose, who said that all activity is relative? What's his name?"

"Just wait a, what? —wait a unit of something, I'll think of it. Eisenstein. No, Einsteen."

"Right, Alfred Einsteen. He was me."

"He'll be me too. We know all this, for every action there are consequences although not necessarily in the same place or time, and intelligence changes form continually."

"That's right, Inquisitor so, \a: ^Evet:\ Kvino:\ Bear B.: \b: ^Sophia:\ Sybelle:\ Blessed Mary:\ Agnes:\ Metza:\ DiVitry:\ Rudolphe:\ Father/Mother: \c: ^Hag: \d: Osiris:\ Isis."

"Your fathers are women."

"Only sometimes."

"That's what you think, Gil."

"Yes well, then it's true isn't it."

~

"Bear B., where are you?" I say into ringing blackness.

"Time to realign," she says.

I almost say 'what' but I don't dare to invite the opportunity for her to explain it to me. Surrender like Oedipus and Osiris. There's nothing left to do but accept it. Don't take action like Medea, or Helen, or Isis. Let them do it, I can't fight. I'm dead, being programmed out little by little from the InfoNets so the points I occupy in CySpace are few. Try to relax. I'm going to die. I just wonder what it will feel like or if they'll really allow me to die. They might keep me around in some bottle, keep my brain hooked up and transmitting without my being able to do anything about it. A brain without a body. It's been done, *Donovan's Brain.* Thinking, feeling, desiring, and no body to do it with so Donovan reached out with will power to control who? —Orson Welles in the lab, no Lew Ayres. Will power? I linked this and I remember it made my hair stand on end it was so creepy. And oh my god that's why they're going to do it to me now because they know what frightens me. The Buddha, the sour-lipped, nipple-twirling Buddha, I have to think of him.

"And it's all the same... ooohhh ahhhh,
The same, the same, oh yeah...

Doooo-eee, doooo ahhhh, yah.
It's all the same, yeah yeah yeah!
A game, not a game. It's all the same. Wooo!"
"Redemption songs. They won't do you any good," Bear B. says from above me.
Yeah, yeah, wooo, wooo, wooo, it's all the same. The same. I'll keep thinking this, block them out. *Doo-ahh, doooo ahhh!* The beat, the beat like when I rayed-in to nouveau sounds when I wrote EroSims. Standing at my keyboard, infraHi-red connected to the magno-chip deck with the latest, and flying around, bounding in the air while I pounded text on the pad, on the air, and wrote the program. Yeah I wrote the reality, *baybee!*

"Transcendent potentia," my mother says. "Why did you write that trash? Stupid! Your fathers wouldn't like it if they knew. You don't even know it, dirty stuff like that. Somebody told you, hah? Who told you to? Who told you to do it, one of those friends? I know that's what they did.

—What? I didn't hear you. Hah? Evet!"

"What!"

"Who told you?"

"What are you talking about?"

"You didn't write it that way, dirty, those 'possibilities.' I know. See this, I'm going to beam-in for it. It'll look good on you. You'll wear it."

"That's awful," I say at the rotating image of a greenish striped body suit she's ordered from the shopping freqs.

"Just try it on."

"No."

"Here's a hat too. Stop doing that transcendent potential shit, it's not what you're like. Try this on."

"What the fuck are you doing?"

227

When I reach out to grab her away from my image space I discover I can't move. Like a Sim running on without my control, without attachment to any chip I've linked, my mother makes chaos out of my programs, erasing files, beaming data onto walls and out into the air, dispersing it. Everything that's mine scatters into streaming ionic trails that dissipate into vapors or particles that finally settle onto the floor, my input pad, and dusts the walls and windows with a fine ashy film of polymers.

"Goddamn you! What do you know about potentials and realities, you ignorant woman!"

"What do you know, is more the question," Bear B. says in my ear. "Why do you believe there are temporary things that can become real to you in harmonious unities? Show me how the coherent superposition of some entity, any entity, is just an abstraction of your manipulation of waves into particles, just like you think your cat exists both half-dead and half-alive there in what you call a transcendent potential. Parallel universes, adjacent realities. Tell me about it. Show me."

"You don't know this. No, I mean 'I' don't know this. Doo-ahh, doo-ahh."

The cat is half-dead and half-alive, that is, totally each way all of the time, fifty-fifty. It's because our thoughts are waves, no, it's that reality, the particles that make up everything are airwaves. Why do I know this? When we look at something, that's when it becomes particles we perceive. We create reality. Before that everything is simply a potential, a wave that exists in many places and in many ways at once, right at the same time. That's how my dear Schrödinger is now. Do I remember it was Bruce Atman who told me this? Transcendent potentia are potential states of "reality" that we think are real but are only one of an eternity of possible states that could be considered "real" depending on what we think.

Consciousness. Or on what we expect because we're so conditioned to anticipate a particular reality. What if there were no concept of gravity? Would we float?

"Ontogeny recapitulates phylogeny," I say. "The development of each individual repeats how everyone, how the entire species develops. There are fractals, what exists as the largest macrocosm, the universe, is replicated in each of us and in the most minute speck of matter, each microcosm."

"So?"

"Bear B., really?"

I know I roll my eyes. Was there a hint of embarrassment behind hers?

"No really," she says. "So what? What do you think it means?"

I know I have understood her. In fact I see a Holo of my brain, anybody's brain. Wernicke's area on the left temporal lobe just above and behind where my ear would be is illuminated in flashes. Neurons fire and send electrical impulses down their axons, the charge gets to the synaptic gap and serotonin sends it across that .02 to .05 micron chasm to the spidery arms of the dendrites to begin the process again. The strip of tissue on the cortex, the amygdal gyrus, glows. Broca's area, left rear frontal lobe, shines and the motor cortex that lies just in front of the central fissure of the brain at the crown of the head sends a signal through the neural net to the muscles of my mouth, tongue. Speech. But nothing happens, everything is working but no sound, no movement comes from me. What does this mean?

Neural net, InfoNets. Ontogeny recapitulates phylogeny and the other way around too. The DataNet is modeled on our brains. Have I been locked out of viable access to my neural network the same way I've been blocked from the InfoNets? Blocked in the macrocosm, blocked in the microcosm? I'm already a brain in a vat, comatose, and realities swirl around me.

"Evet! Where are you?"

"Right here, wherever. What do you mean? That you, Bear B.?"

"Not her. Look."

"How?"

"You can escape. Evet, see? You're doing it. Just keep listening to me, concentrate. Come to the domes. You can go wherever you want. Wherever. You can escape, you have escaped."

"I smell it, and feel the aroma lingering on my skin. Near death, I am calm. The world of Atman and Travelers surrounds me in rolling waves of halcyon wisdom that make me smile. Safe.

In control, nothing is a surprise, nothing threatening. The restlessness that always dances on my skin has faded. It's all mine. All me. And like dozens of HoloSims I see everything I've done in my life. I see me at my input pad, vaulting in the air and singing while I design a SensSim program that others will live in for a time and be diverted from their three dimensional lives. It's another three dimensions architected by me and added into the game. My Schrödinger is alive and playful, not half dead and half alive as I have learned in my confusion lately. And I see my mother drive me to madness with her domination, and know that I consented to it and that I learned from it. I smile, at ease, peaceful for the first time.

"See?" Atman says.

"How long will it last? Or is this it?"

"You know it must be. Really living, being. What you're doing is 'being.' You got there by yourself, it must be marvelous. Of course I don't know, can't feel it, but I see it on your readouts. And after all, you're here in the dome all of sudden, your corporeal body is here. Look at you. You've done what only the most advanced have done. I don't know what to think. I mean, why can you do this when so many of us have been practicing for years? I don't get it and I want to."

"Right."

"You're not listening.

"Right."

"Come on. Do you think you're capable to give me something at least? A *koan*, Zen riddle? You know, like the sound of one hand clapping? It's not the same, your answering 'right' to my saying you're not listening because of course you obviously heard me. Not the same, you don't know."

"Recognition," I find I'm saying. "I don't listen, I 'know.'"

He tries to touch me but he can't and his smooth face sets into a color of anguish that's uncomfortable to look at. It's the face of rejection that is unfair but with no anger or tears to fill up his eyes.

"It must be because of your karma and you don't even know it. You don't know it."

"We both made the choice, didn't we?" I say. "It's all choice. Relax. You wanted to experience this humiliation because you need to learn from it. Remember there is no competition. I'm not better than you, you know that's impossible, and we both agreed to be doing this, so don't feel badly. Not necessary."

Atman is crying. I know he will cry again. He can't stand to look at my bliss, the knowledge it seems I don't deserve to have. But it's all right. Everything is simply the way it's supposed to be. I'm totally at ease and satisfied with what I'm doing, learning lessons for reasons more measureless than what we think we're certain is going on here. Kind of like being on the oldfashion MDMA. Ecstasy.

But there is something pressing against me, soft prods pushing at me from the side. Something I have to remember, although I thought I know everything. I did just a second ago. What is that? What do I mean? Slipping away, slipping into coarse dimensions worn like a straitjacket, carried like scaly blemishes away from the stares of beauties.

"You're back," Atman says, touching me like I'm a saint or something. "Tell me about it, where you were."

"The Police?"

"Now you're here. Don't you remember?"

"No."

"No?"

"For crissakes, no! What's the matter with you, Atman? How'd you get me here from the Police Tower, away from where Bear B. took me, or where you had me hidden?"

"You did it yourself. All of a sudden you were just here. We were color frequency tracking you and recording output and of course we were meditating, focusing on you maybe it was us, maybe we brought you here. Maybe it was us! Finally real success from all our studies, we knew that they had you and what they were going to do because we got it off the secured freqs, that helped us focus on meditation. But here, we never expected to see you here like this."

I did it myself or he says Travelers did something to me. Did what? I felt something, but what? Some past forgetting abrades me from inside like hives in my throat. *What?*

"You really can't tell? You really can't get in touch with what it is, what allowed you to transcend? I mean, it's something theoretically that all of us can do because we're all the same, one, but you've done it. You're doing it and you don't even know. You aren't even aware."

"Maybe that's the trick."

I remember linking a chip that was the Sunday New York Times from eons ago in 1992 that reenacted the story of a Hispanic man stabbing a transvestite and then throwing himself out a window. How terrible the sudden exposure of our *selves*, the shame. Humiliation unworthy of me. How it hurts in an ache, not a burn. Ache. The defensiveness comes but I know I'm wrong. Denial. How much effort used to refuse what you've done even though it's a primitive tool to simply forget what happened. Guarding against shame, afraid to admit we commit horrors. My integrity is the philosophy I always forget which, if I exposed it and acted on it, is a philosophy shining with decency and with the flawless patina of being content and embedded in the universe that is me without any seams, no beginning and no ends. *Per omnia...*

~

...saecula saeculorum.

Sybelle smelled every word but didn't know where they were coming from. The meaning she knew, the subtext of it, was God residing in an individual. Sedition songs to the Church. And although the words were in Mary's thoughts she didn't know the scent of them like Sybelle did and that they had not come from where she was packing the colorful trunk under the tree in the yard.

"We'll construct eternity from the reality we build with the miracles of the brain in the vat."

"Just be careful those dogs don't eat it while you're performing."

"It wouldn't matter if they ate my brain. It's only a prop we all use anyway."

233

TWENTY SIX

"Socrates, Seeing A Great Quantity Of Riches, Jewels, And Furniture Carried In Pomp Through The City: 'How Many Things Are There,' Said He, 'That I Do Not Want.'"

Montaigne

Travelers Sims of reality are like nothing I've ever experienced before, at least not that I'm aware of now. Besides how substantial they are—but all Sims are that, you think you're really there—they make me wonder. Maybe it's their dreamy plasticity, the feeling of warm peacefulness that moans on your skin like a tropical sea, they make me wonder about being aware. The puzzlement about the consciousness of thinking this right now: Who is the "I" in "I think?" It's like they make you take another step back, farther removed. I'm thinking this, and I'm aware that there's this "I" who's thinking this, so it's like being aware of what's going on in this head and also looking down on this head from somewhere else. In standard reality entertainments you never worry about this grand regression to madness.

Everyone knows "self" is concretized with a node in the InfoNets that is the dimensional gleaming grid revealing how much data we have access to, so is that what I'm looking down on? My virtual body in virtreal data space? Data and its permutations are all there is that counts, that has effects. That's life. That's what they want us to believe.

What we do in CySpace is real enough because it makes those lines in the grid glitter with our interactions. Like Mat/leen riding the pitching prow of the pre-Viking ship. She glowed as a stinking barbarian approached. He had just left his faithless wife shackled and weighted down in the bog, left to slowly suffocate in the soggy tannic acid brown watery grave of the peat bog. The story offered the choice of becoming either the protagonist or victim and she started as the wife draped in roe skin, stone beads strung on gut thread for a necklace. But when she felt the blows from the cudgel she didn't choose the *a:\fight, b:\flight* or *c:\beg* modes but paused the game and tagged in as Vjal instead, the slow murderer of his wife. This was typical of the kind of adventures approved by her mixed-sex parents in place of acting in the "real" world that they forbade her.

So you see it's easy to ignore the authors of these Sims because what we write, and us authors, are destroyed by the decentering of that text. The people who plug into it can alter it, by choosing (programmed) possibilities, intereact. And they transform it into a network that way. Each of them*selves* becomes a focal point not through cognition but through action where you don't have to bother to think. Authors destroyed and text destroyed because the center of it, the actors of it, are malleable in the InfoNets, like mist. What sells isn't the most thoughtful Sim but the one most exciting one that rouses sensation to new titillations. They want to call anyone who gives them an adventure a designer—a real writer? Where does my *self* exist?

But Traveler reality changes the center of the node so there is only the self, your *self*, who acts. It's different from CySpace that supplants physical space so completely that we break free of bodily constraints and enjoy any virtual body we want, and any feeling of *self* that goes with it. There is no warmth, no closeness because without a body you can be whoever you want in the Nets and access whatever you want. It's the most complete seduction, the reason why everyone stays plugged in continuously on their hyper infraHi-red wavelengths. There are no limits in their artificial experiences except, that is, what the complexity of the amount of credit status allows you to access the Nets matrix, like Mat/leen's Sims that weren't intricate and didn't take up a lot of data space. No limits to experience, you are God.

I am part of the myth as I hear it, it's got a Traveler copyright. The SensSim begins, overwhelms each sense and becomes me.

I live the story in the secrecy of my thoughts now. I'm part of the group with a mother and somewhere there are fathers, but I don't remember them at the moment. I have sisters and brothers who are very odd, sometimes murderous, but beautiful. *Listen to me.* You can't get along without knowing this. Ageless, I can tell you. Listen for your part in the story. My dreams repeat the dreams of the species.

We sons and daughters of Nut are a powerful gang because mother is the one who gives air to the Dead in the netherworld and they depend on her. And me, Osiris, I'm revered as the patron of mummification. Part of the reason I got this position is because my brother Set murdered me. He invited me to a party where there was this fabulous jewel-encrusted trunk, coffin really. After everyone was very high he said whoever could fit into that case perfectly could take it home. What a party favor that was, all those jewels. Like everyone else I had to take a turn. Then *wham!* the lid slams shut and I hear it being nailed down. I suffocated slowly, I won't tell you the atrocity of it, and then Set scattered my bones all over the countryside and although I was re-collected and revived by my sister and wife Isis, I died again. *Find your part in the story.* I'm therefore as closely connected with death as mother is. By burning, plummeting from heights, gunshots, drugs, carbon monoxide, electrocution. I don't know how to break the cycle. Of course as I contemplate it I get closer to an answer, or I get better but I still end up dying every time I come back anyway. And everybody always seems to like Isis better. Even our sister Nephtys liked her better and had sex with her while she was still married to me.

One time when I was back I can smell and feel what it was like picking up a Sunday paper and reading about a man who is me. In the late 20th Cent he is doing right now what I want to do as a woman this time, you as a woman. Late thirties in age, dark hair, a thin Englishwoman, he has discovered spirituality and a more evolved consciousness but he's enamored of the famous and the rich, just like what I want to be or just like what is my curse of desire. See, I know what I must aspire to encompassing love in what was once the Tibetan Buddhist way in order to be better in other lives, I know this and am still beset with fury and longing for recognition and for things. How is this possible? That other man (not the one who killed the transvestite) I read about while the traffic roared and a bird fluttered on the fire escape, is me. Or I am there in him. *Find your place in the story.*

What makes this all so unbearable is that he has done what I want to be. What I imagined in my isolated dream of fame is already accomplished in someone else. Silly faggot I would like to say to him/me. And to me/him *self* he would say, what? Converse with yourself. It's wrong because there's no difference or it's right because of the same reason. Like reading a line in someone else's book that is the same one you wrote in your own journal the year before. Recognition.

Why does this happen to me so often? And it does. My HistSim adaptation of a classic novel long forgotten grew suddenly, when I have nearly completed it, it's issued on chip, produced by someone else who had the same idea. Is it true that we are all the same? So if I'm the Englishman A.H. who I read about and I understand so intimately what he writes about his quest for soul salvation in this idiocy of current existence, but doing it with style, if I'm him then why don't I share the fame? I have thought all this before. I recognize what he means.

I have the sensations of his mind in the 20th thinking as he drives into the country that he's struck by the inhumanness of it. How can there be any crowding everyone seems to worry about that is evident in the cities? Or is there really nothing there, or anywhere, and all this springs into life whenever I drive past? That is, when I link this Sim of it? The world is Potemkin villages. A quantum object appears in one place when we measure it and spreads out in a wave when we look away. We are brains in vats and we are the evil scientists who put us there.

"Listen to me."

Did I hear or say this before? Do I keep replaying it for a reason? Everything is for a reason. Was it from sometime before or after where I see I'm reading the Times and craving fame in its pages because the story of this A. H.'s commitment to Buddhism? Some other time, before or after, I know I must be worthy of more than this base desire. Is it base? I know the answer, let go of stupidity. The universe is here, the awesome stars are here in the droplets of my blood and the beauty is me and all of us. We are all the same and we are everything. So much magnificence. I must remember to lift my eyes from the mud, the small air holes in the wet mud at my feet. My webbed feet. But everything has its time.

"*Synchronicity,*" Mary sings to me. "*We're here, we're there, we're everywhere. I cause you and you cause me... And we do it far away, never even touching... you or meeeee.*"

The carnival trunk shines and changes colors in the dirty yard. Women in long robes who look like they've been walking a long way, dust clinging to their hems, stand or sit on crude wooden benches and watch her while they snack and talk among themselves. Some look bored. One of them is frightened.

"Did you hear the one," Mary says. "About Nasruddin?"

"Tell us.

"It's a Sufi story about what happened when the Mullah Nasruddin was walking on a secluded road when he saw a gang of horsemen coming toward him. The Mullah became apprehensive, started to run, and when the horsemen saw him running away they went after him. This of course made him really frightened and when, out of breath, he finally came to a graveyard he scuttled over the wall and ran around until he found an empty coffin where he lay down to hide. But after searching for a while they found him there.

'Is there anything wrong?' they asked him. 'What can we do to help you, and why are you here anyway?'

'To make a long story short,' he said. 'I am here because of you and I see that you're all here because of me.'

"Thank you, thank you. Your applause is generous." Mary says this in the silence as she takes her bows.

I feel like I know these women, this comedy of saints, as I stand among them smelling the odors of their bodies mingled on a warm breeze. The attractive storyteller who is now juggling a raw brain, a crucifix and a fiery torch has a halo around her head. Like an old icon, but more colorful, there's a rainbow halo on her and she's telling jokes and the other women are laughing. I can't figure out where I am in all this although I'm here. What is the perspective from which I'm seeing this? When I look down I can't see my feet although I see wet mud with air holes in it. A tiny bubble gurgles up every now and then.

"Stop it!"

I'm screaming when I yank out the chip behind my ear and run away from the VirtReal. *Fool! Imbecile! Asshole!* How can I have this revelation that all I should do is be happy and love myself and everything else and at the same time still want to be a slave to recognition? To fame? Ignorance of good is one thing but to know the good I must do to survive and to ignore it, that ignoring is real ignorance. Seeing and looking away is worse than never having seen at all.

I have good eyes but my heart is still bellowing with lust. There is something wrong with me, I murder the things I love with my mind and that's why the Police want me. And I know better, I know that I can do these great ills and I do them anyway. What a piece of work is man, how twisted in reason... Or is it just me?

You are what you dream.

"That doesn't sound right. Isn't it supposed to be you are what you do, what you eat, who you love?"

Yes. And it's all because of what you dream. It's all connected in the universal web. Step on it here, feel it there. Or dream it before and do it now, or vice versa. You know.

I know? And who the hell is this voice anyway?

"Evet! We can hide you again. We've rematrixed some codes and I think it'll keep them from finding you. But the choice is yours, always," Bruce Atman says.

"How much of what I just did was Traveler Sims?"

"You linked into the Osiris chip again and then you went somewhere else. The readings coming from you didn't correspond to the later part of the frequencies for that story. You were doing something else and blocked out our Sim. What was it?"

"Stories I seem to know. Scenes I walk into that seem familiar to me but can't be. I don't know."

"You've designed them, haven't you? They're your own SensSims. They're in you, from your head, your creativity."

"That's the problem. It's because of what Bear B. said they couldn't find coordinates for in me. You know that everything novel is just recombinations but she said they couldn't find the data points that correspond to things I know in any form. That's impossible, isn't it? I mean they've completely mapped the brain and neural operations, designated functions for what outside experience does at every synapse, right? So how is this possible in me?"

"Because it's not the brain but the mind that is us, our *selves*. Our mind is more than simple cause and effect from structures or magnetic forces or neural firing they think they can absolutely measure."

"Like what? Everyone says the mind, consciousness, is only an artifact of the hard wiring of the brain, the connections of neurons. That's why SensSims work so well, make us believe we're really there in artificial places. They've got the codes to produce experience, feelings, everything for christ's sake. We're aware of stuff because of the way neurons and their chemical balance work. So consciousness happens because of the way the brain functions, that's all."

"Please," Atman laughs like a crazy Santa with the sudden features of a Christ. "That is techno-crap of the simplest sort. Those brain scientists want us to believe the mind IS the brain just like those ancient philosophers wanted us to believe the 'soul' resided in the heart, or liver or whatever the hell they dreamed up it should be."

"Scientists hardly dream up data."

"You think not? That's exactly what they do. We all create our own reality. They create theirs and call it objective measurement that's all. They still don't want to admit that when you measure anything you change it because you put your own structure on it. When you look at a wave it could become anything, but by looking at it you make it the particle you expect, where you expect it! That's 'science' for you. Everything that's out there is in here," he taps his head with a finger.

"Fuck you."

"Whenever. But explain what's been happening to you. Explain it without using the working of nonlocal causality that would make 'scientists' blanche. Explain your dreams. Explain these stories that you know because you've designed them. Maybe you haven't sat at your screen and programmed them in, maybe you have, but you've written them. Get it? They're a reality that's from you and they live, my friend, they live."

"Well then, damn it, they're good. So why aren't they on the network sectors? Why am I not hot famous because of them?"

"Your motives are wrong and you're paying a karmic debt. You've got to understand yet what's real and what isn't."

"What in the hell are you talking about?"

"Form is only emptiness, emptiness only form. Remember hearing something like that?"

How would he know? I remember, and it scares me. I designed murder in a simulation and because that was in me it happened in the world. I killed my daughter, my cat. The evil that is in me lives because it is in me. It's there. It's here. That's the malevolence of me, what Bear B. has been trying to discover. I can make the secrets hidden in me happen. No wonder she wants to kill me. Whatever Travelers say, this can't be right. I mean, this weird power can't be right and Bear B. of course wants to eradicate it. She should. Evanescent citizen, that's me. Temporary and fading. They'll kill me when they find me. A blink in the dataNet.

Milarepa?

TWENTY SEVEN

Columns, Side-By-Side Display

Alone on a mountaintop within nature it's easier than in smooth cubicles where you always have to work to ignore something like the throb from an amputated limb that still seems a part of you. There's always something to distract you. I hate myself for not being able to get beyond it like Milarepa did. He became skeletal on Tibetan mountaintops, meditating, overcoming the self-righteous evil he did by causing a torrent of deadly hailstones to annihilate neighbors who had annoyed him. He ate nothing but pine needles for years and turned green from them. But he could *fly*!

The small Buddha with the twirling nipples tells me this. Sims that suddenly play in my head are activated by him. Or is that only what I think? Everything is what I think if Atman is right, and Bear B. too. There's something wrong with me although maybe that's not true or maybe it's only an artifact of what I've been doing, this designing of experiences. I have to look too closely at me and how I behave so I can program characters that people can relate to. I have to design many characters because they switch among themselves and can become each one of them. Give people thrills, some kind of truth based on my own need for rapture and it works. They get it. But I drew out murder from me, playing God by pulling creatures in and out of life. It was more than a mock-up, it was real somehow. Somehow? I did it. Why did I murder my daughter, my love, for a thrill whose origin in me I can't find and neither can those meticulous custodians of evanescent space? Bear B., the guardian of cerebral intervals in the same way oldfashion military exploits worked to maintain selfish realms. White men abducted America from Native Indian people, Nazi Germany stole Europe and the Japanese ferociously colonized the moon. From those landlocked victories to patrolling mindspace now.

I have to meet my stories, live the fantasies that are real somewhere. I'm afraid.

"Something you're looking for," someone says with a synthesized voice. "I can get what will give you something."

"Something."

I repeated it back to the smooth surface with three holes for eyes. But I have no idea what that person or I mean.

Travelers who dare to feel confidant of their mastery come to the meeting. At the edge of the rain forest whose fragrance is so dense it clings like sweat on a brow, they climb a green hillside from another climate's place. Silbury Hill, English countryside a short walk from lush Amazonia, rises with steep angled sides up to its flat summit. Travelers already there smile shyly at those whose heads glide into view over the rim and then look away, not wanting to interrupt with contact the magnificence of the vista they're sharing. The immense plane sweeps orchestrations of stone circles ever larger into view. The monoliths of Stonehenge glitter like a marching band moving by. And from Avebury the boulders slither in disdain with their faces turned away, accompanied by their ring of brooding trees and possessive ravines. Travelers reaching the peak become aware of the show and move out of the way of those who are engrossed, some with tears while others restrain the quiet laughter of the delight that escapes them.

The radiant blue sky is crossed by polished clouds so massive they reach the horizon but never interfere with the sun's purity. The light illuminates the stalk of an explosive weed where a brown and white snail climbs upward to reach the nectar in its wild corolla. A steady ascent, its little mucousy body works in billows of effort, tiny perceptive stalks waving on its head. Nectar. I can smell its wetness undiluted and precise as if I am clinging to that stalk and nothing else exists except the quest to do this right now. Nothing else but to carry the crusty swirl of my mobile home and move toward pungent confectionary that is nirvana. The effort deserves the reward, the reward earns the effort.

"This is the way it is. Or is it?"

"Of course it is. Stay with the feeling you had at first, don't doubt it. It should be the same for everyone."

I look at Kvino and his smile is not empty with drugs this time. He beams the contentment I can see is genuine and he sees that I see and recognizes it by nodding. Atman, who has had his hand on his shoulder, moves away and leaves Kvino and me alone in the soft air that sometimes moves as if it is a breeze.

"It shouldn't be," I say and know he remembers like I do something that makes all of this completely understandable.

"No. Yes."

"For a minute I really saw it. These petals from underneath like I was—"

"I know."

"They're going to kill us for this. This is no Sim, is it," I don't ask. "They've found all this, Travelers heaven, and I can't believe they're so good at it the Police haven't destroyed it yet."

"I know. We're in a space they'll never find because they don't believe it, don't look for it. It's slick. Atman over there does a job playing the bliss-idiot to make sure Travelers never get investigated too closely. He made sure the Police let them classify as a religion so no one thinks they've got any power. Just nuts. But this is it, Evet, look at all this. It's what they've made just by deciding to make it. No nanos, no nothing. All these people are the best of their Focusers and they've made their dreams real."

"Shouldn't be."

I look at the glorious sky and feel like I'm melded with it, peaceful and unweighted by anything else except for the awareness of being here, now. Everything should stop right now and allow this to continue forever and ever.

Per omnia saecula saeculorum...

It should be this way.

Amen.

The rustling chant whispered by the Travelers is something I can't make out although Kvino seems to be following whatever it is. I watch his gentled eyes and they remind me of my odd statue, radiant, and I love him even more for his new liveliness that is a connection to me and I feel bathed with him and perfectly peaceful. The thought seems to be spoken, loud, that we have to get everyone to evolve their minds to this point, believing that what they think can actually make a world and so only the finest passion is worthy of us because everything we give, we give to ourselves. Evolution of desire evolves to appreciate that it would be right to aspire to be one and the same with this air, these people, this luminosity all around and inside of me. The cataclysm should find me here.

That's why every day is important, should be lived as our last," Atman says. "When the end of this existence comes as it will to us think where you want to be stopped forever in a freeze-frame of eternity. I mean, with what thoughts about your sex acts or rage at who gossiped about your shoes, what kinds of things do you want on your mind? Would it be things like taking revenge or lying on your résumé? In other words, what kind of quality will there be to your soul? And whatever you don't get right you'll have to do over again."

"You're saying I was a bad designer in another life and I still can't get it right?"

"That's what you want to die worrying about? How to achieve to fame in other people's eyes?"

"No, but—"

"Recognition is important, but only of yourself. Whatever you're doing right now determines how your future will be, whatever you did in the past commands what you're doing now. See?"

Atman is smiling. So is everyone else.

"Basic Buddhism, Evet, *karma*. It's not what valuation can be put on what you're doing in your work now but what's important is that you're not succeeding because of something within you, not anything from outside, although you control it all. See, you decide to learn something from what you call your 'failure' here so there's no one to blame and what's important is only what your essence, your energy that will go on and on, has learned from experiencing it."

"You really believe that?"

"Don't you remember telling me this yourself? You understood it when you transcended for those few minutes when you escaped from the Police. You knew that we're all one and we decide to incarnate to experience lessons. Remember? That's why I couldn't be jealous of your transubstantiation—no, translocation. It was my choice a long time ago to watch you do it although I don't remember that decision or the reality in which I made it. We're all part of the same basic energy and go off to learn things before we meet again to compare notes, add them to the common file. You decided to live the life you're living."

I don't know what to say. Kvino laughs at me.

"You have to meet your stories, what you've planned," Atman says. "We think they're the key to your incarnations, the karma you've made and will make. We've never known anyone so close to really seeing before, but 'close' can be dangerous. You've got to learn to understand what you've created and getting inside the dreams that are real can be lethal. Do you want to learn from us? We can prepare you for the quest. If you go into your dreams you'll find out if you really murdered or if there's a reason for it, something else."

"Will I be able to be with her again? With what's really 'Dinger, not some hologram?"

"Why not?"

"I'll go with you as far as I can," Kvino says. "Come on, look at all this it takes them, what, a hundred Travelers to project this, make it real, and you can do it all alone?"

"It's dangerous," Atman says.

"Like what, dying? If you're right there isn't any real death anyway, so what?"

"You can get trapped, and so can you if you go with her," Atman touches us both with his finger, gently. "To a *bardo*, the place in-between where you have to wait for a body, a reality where you confront all the evil you've done and that exists in every heart in the worst of all of us. Wailing wolves struggling and bleeding in hunters' leg hold traps, shrieking infants raped and hurled off rooftops. The winds of hatred will choke you like molten fire rammed down your throat and it will blow from the stinking mouths of the rotting dead in their shrouds as they hound you, reaching out while you careen in tempest-blown blackness from the terror of their long-nailed hands grasping, grasping always just at your back."

Kvino looks like he wants to say something. His lips part but he can't seem to get out any words. And I feel paralyzed although I take a step and make some unproductive movement with my hand as if I have something to say.

"It's real, all those universal fears of humankind, real because we've been taught them and our eyes are conditioned to see them. They can damage you with their horror because you'll agree to live a life of ugly cruelty just to get away from the dread, just to put an end to your suffering in the *bardo*. And then where will you be? Set back on the karmic wheel because you will have chosen to live a life of evil to avoid the terrors of the void between lives, and on and on. See?"

Atman comes toward us. We step backward as if we had planned to do it together because the panic he's describing is real, a knife at our throats.

"Look at how easily this creation dissolves. And just from me, from my worry about you!"

The sky shatters into long cracks of crimson spilling over the clouds that used to be billowy. They deflate, are erased into dirty smudges on a paper that continues to rip. Suddenly there is no sky at all. Fetid heat clogs my nostrils and the hill is gone. The rain forest clamoring with sweet wetness fades away, disintegrates. We are in a basement under one of the Travelers domed environments, enclosed by grey walls. Everyone smiles with tender disappointment. Their show of the power of reality is gone.

"That was only a collective reality we all focused on. We used the power of meditation on our universal sameness and unity to produce it. None of us has any connection to our specific incarnations though. Not like you. You do, and that's more than a gift. That's what we need to know because then we can change ourselves and change the world. We have to stay aware in that chancy time between rebirths when we can be frightened into choosing a decadent path in a new life. We have to learn to be aware of our acts and thoughts because they all make a difference. It's their intent with take with us, good or bad. Awareness of this is the evolution of consciousness and you've started the last phase."

They decide Kvino will accompany me physically from time to time when he can be transmitted to me. The Travelers will provide focused meditation power that is continuous. I have to start running, hiding from the Police scanners that are set to my body frequencies and spectrometry and so the Travelers send me away. To meet what I have designed I run through a magnetic maze of strobing lights and sirens. Then there is deathly silence in a thick purple colloid that is air I can chew.

I have to meet my stories. Here in this subway tunnel where Atman has hidden me under the Travelers island in the East sludge that was abandoned in the 21st I have to greet those people I think I know. The funny women with the long dresses and others whose images glint at the back of my mind running along the platforms behind me, pictures I have seen in some album too long ago to remember clearly or I wasn't paying enough attention to, like when an aunt makes you view family icons when you're not interested. It's hard to remember they're there. Relatives? I have none. And yet there are images beyond some edge I can feel over there. From it comes a faint breeze I feel on my skin, the tingle that always presages in low swirling dirt and paper the roaring arrival of a train. This edge in the darkness looks as though it might begin to lighten, the fleeting memories have form and are gathered in the fulsome gloom that breathes and trembles. They are really there, just beyond the edge of, what? Subterranean tracks that run perpendicular to each other in a kind of mad design of capriciousness or necessity, I can't tell which.

Chaos in landscaped paths for speeding objects that will increase the probability of collisions and here I am on the edge. Will the impact suck me into it destructive vortex like the shock waves of some bomb? Drag me over the edge, implosion pulls me over the edge into what? There is that rustling sound in the darkness like rats or the scurry of dirt and scraps of paper whirlpooled by the gale of an approaching train. But beyond that there is nothing, no sound, an edge of the supreme unknown. Edge and chaos, and then nothing.

"It only seems that way, that there's nothing."

The person is standing a little way off down the platform under a burned out light. A brimmed hat pulled down, a raincoat wrapped tightly obscures the figure. He or she is holding up a newspaper and reading, head inclined to scrutinize something near its inner fold.

"There is, of course, something out there beyond the tracks, you just can't see it. Not from where you're standing."

"OK."

"That's all you can say?"

The person is amused, maybe annoyed. It's hard to tell without seeing the full communication, the body posture, the facial expression.

"So?" I say and move closer.

"You can move all you want, you're still on this platform. You can't see across the tracks. Why are you moving? There's

252

a wall between this set and those where the trains run in the opposite direction."

"But there are openings down there, arches in that ornate concrete divider, or maybe they're really just huge columns. I could see through."

"It's pitch black. How can you see?" The person says it while walking in a little circle under the darkened light.

"I can see where they cross, almost."

"You can just make out the crucifix where the traces going in different directions will meet and annihilate themselves."

"Could it happen?" I say, wondering why the person said 'traces' instead of 'trains'?

"It happens all the time."

"Wait a minute, I haven't heard about any. I mean, something terrible, collisions like that, everyone hears about them. It can't happen all the time. They must plan the running of trains through this junction very carefully."

"Of course everyone plans for everything but you can't control anything that happens, not here, not when everything's a particle at this level, or a wave. And when it's dark like this and you can't see well, then things seem mixed up. And across the cross where you can't see at all, well let me tell you, there are things from these explosions you can't even imagine. You have no idea. No idea at all, get it?"

"No."

"Good!" the woman says and lowers the paper so I can see her.

"What do you mean 'good'? I don't understand what you're talking about. Didn't mean that I did."

"I know. You have no idea and you're not supposed to. So, good. See what I mean? If you could see the structures out there across the tracks you would think differently, and if you thought differently you wouldn't be here. Get it?"

"I know you from somewhere, don't I?"

"Just ask me out. Don't use that old line."

"No, really."

"All right, they call me Mary. See? You don't know me," she smiles wonderfully and turns away. "You know, you shouldn't be such a reality snob."

"Mat/leen!"

TWENTY EIGHT

Beyond The Beyond

"Mat/leen? Milarepa could fly."

"Not in subways."

"Don't laugh. Believe in something for a change."

"Like you?"

"Please. We're all doing the best we can."

"What's the matter, not an experience snob anymore? Your feelings, your passions, your hurts were always more potent than anyone else's. You blamed your mother for all the faults in you that you couldn't control. Your judgmental nature, the hate you couldn't admit to. Whiner. So you murdered her, but in killing her you exterminated what you loved the most."

"My daughter. They say it was—"

"It's all the same, pinhead. If you kill your mother or anything you kill everything. And if you step on a spider you've squashed your mother. Dead is still dead in so many ways. You fool, you continue to insist to live in compartments even though you know better. What was it the Catholic church used to call that, culpable ignorance? You know how much you hate ignorance, ignorance and injustice."

"She was those things I hate the most."

"She's you."

"Mat/leen?"

But this person is now Blessed Mary and has been transformed into acrid cinders at the foot of where she was tightly tied to the steel girder. It's the proof that she's important. Sainthood solidified, locked in, a sure bet. The repetition of death, or is it repeating a life well spent? What a reward!

"I need the container for the ashes," Agnes says.

"You mean the reliquary with the jewels, the tangled scrollwork of gold filigree that Sophia made to such acclaim throughout the world?"

"Of course. Has it disappeared again? I told you we have to make a mark on it, dent it, something so that the imperfection will show up when the moonlight metal shimmers it beyond the edge of our vision."

"The vessel of the Holy Thorn isn't marred like that," Metza says. "And I won't tamper with another artist's work. Do it yourself."

"You stopped being her lover ages ago. Why do you care?"

"Agnes, you're an administrator and don't have the passion to understand. She's still my sister and my friend and she'll be my lover again. All those in-between are important for themselves, they don't taint her and there are sisters and daughters of mine, aunts and grandmothers. Passion is all around us. You have to express it even when it comes out wrong and then you have to learn from it. Forgive yourself."

"Be quiet. The bizarre one has been listening to us."

"You mean tasting us, tasting our words. Come out from behind that column, Sybelle! You and I haven't been intimate enough. I'm trying to learn from Mary's death instead of wallowing in it. Come on, look. I've been nice to Agnes so you can admit to me what you've been hiding. Come to my bed, girl."

"Slut." Agnes covers her face against the dirt and candy wrappers blown up by an unseen train speeding out of the gloom, and instantly gone again.

"Jealous?"

"Like Mary was, no more or less," Agnes spits. "She's no different than me, that's what you don't understand, the braid includes even me. Each of us, a strand. And what you can't talk about you don't try to see, that's what Wittgenstein's going to say. But what Mary and I did was exactly that, the truth. We gave them a reality they couldn't observe, not without us, not without Mary's miracles. Heisenberg's going to get the credit for it, though. He'll get it for the position of the cat who's half-dead and half-alive existing in a potential waviness that transcends us and it's only when we observe it that we collapse its duality into what we call our 'reality.'"

The young woman they call Sybelle holds her stomach, nauseous from the greasy words. Greasy? Why would I feel that? It looks like she might vomit onto the tracks. I wonder if she heard what Mat/leen and I said to each other when Mat/leen was here. What she said to me with that anger that is so unlike her. Unlike Mary, too. They seem similar to each other and dissimilar from themselves, what each of them was or is. And now I start to feel sick too from a bombardment of thoughts that are like inflamed whitecaps shot onto the Oakleyville shore by an approaching hurricane on Fire Island.

We played in the waves then, body surfed. The two tall men and me. Mimosa in silver goblets on the beach, the hot wind and noisy breakers. How we laughed. And now because I'm thinking of them, they're dead again. Mostly my rare Sam.

"Hello?"

"You were talking with Mary, she's a friend of mine. I'm Metza."

"You look familiar. Don't I know you?"

I don't know what I've just said. I'm still trying to figure out where is the beach I just saw. Where is it, because the dank shadows of the subway tunnel have not changed.

"Just ask me out, honey."

"No, wait a minute."

But time is up. Someone says that or I feel it in my head. Time is up and I'm in danger of being caught. I've stayed in one intersection too long, a particle.

Transcend.

"What?"

Go beyond your self.

The delicate scent of a giant flower lounges on my skin and lulls me to a recognition of bliss that makes that skin disappear. No boundaries. My body is nothing and the "I" that made me feel the sensation is gone. Nothing. There is no skin, no "me" to feel any edge that defines what that thing was. No objects. No past or future. The being that is consciousness is simply now and everywhere at once.

"I can't be doing this."

I said it and instantly became me again. The sensation of dissipation into space collapses into my body.

And there is heavy velvet material wound tightly around me like a shroud. I'm buried alive like the cataleptics of the 19th Century I have seen in history Sims. The coffin around me has only little air to breathe left inside. The weight of dirt on the lid and sides press in a creaking vulnerability now to make me feel as though bony fingers are reaching into the graves to get me. I worry about being *gotten*, someone sneaking up behind me and driving a knife deep into the thick fur of my back. Although my spine is pressed against the hard bottom of the coffin I still screech with a spasm of terror as a sound below makes me think they're reaching up for me from behind.

"Jesus!"

That's you. Rely on yourself, you're the God."

The earth around me rends and throws me up in a kind of projectile vomit that hurls me into neon-singing space. The interlocking matrices of the Nets open before me in informational splendor. But the shimmering data points veer away from my flight, moving themselves as they near as if I am repelling them. Dissimilar materials opposed at their core to having contact, data and spirit.

"But it's all the same. You created it. *We create everything, we create alllll...* Remember?"

"I remember that song, but I couldn't have been there when you sang it before, somewhere else and some other time."

"Of course you were. You knew me, and it's the same time and the same place as now."

"Mat/leen? Or, Mary?"

"Wrong again. It's me, Bear B., your worst enemy, and always a part of you."

I tear at my hair with my hands, running from death that runs next to me on a colorfully woven leash. Run from death over and over and over again. Howls gurgle from gargoyles' bloody throats that I slash with my fingernails as I whirl past them, overpowering them with my evil, the depth of my atrocity. I am consummate monstrosity.

Oh horror. Oh escape. Oh grasping hands of the Dead who walk. And the clothes they wear are terrible. Tasteless lines, vulgar fabrics. They try to engulf me, arms all outstretched. How I fought to leave this, my past. Spirit ebbs within me, ordinary stupidity waits to burst out, a vile pus in me. Within me. This is so bad...

And if I could believe there is some good in me what would I think then of my sordid dreams, the pictures?

...Where is there love and genius? In me? I don't live this badly, do I? *Stop trying, asshole!* Where is there love and genius except within me, no matter what. But I hate. I hate my family. Why? Hatred of family, this closeness.

But did I have any relatives, or only two fathers? I did, Sophia did. Really? I think maybe I see.

I don't help anyone I love. What good am I? Better not love them too much. Stay away. I fear the pain, the failure. I laugh at closeness, kill my mother or maybe it was my daughter.

Power? Look elsewhere for power. Control nothing because it doesn't matter. And like clouds or a gas that just reaches your senses, it always flies past. Control gone.

And if she would begin to believe there was good in her, what would she then think of all her vile dreams, the dirty pictures, the fetid relationships, in her mind? How could she be good in any way with such ugliness engraved inside of her? All we have to do is cut her open, cut into her by making a slicing motion and peel back a few centimeters of flesh. Inside are the images of corruption. There are contortions of cruelty people, ignorant drooling creatures she hates in the world. They are inside her. All the hatred of foreigners she never felt, all the loathing of tortures by bullies she never thought about, all the racist venom that disgusted her when she saw it in the world. It's all inside her, writing in her skin, all the worst of humankind is her.

I want to change it all. It can be done. The reality can't be all there is. How do I go beyond? I could die, I could do that. Will I gain control, will it make this terrible need, this awareness I feel that tortures me to make it all right? Torture in the world and what do I do? Nothing. *Asshole!*

"Come here to me, sweet one, to my bed."

"Bear B.?"

"Always with you," she says and the pulsating radiance of the universes shine from her mouth. "You know how it feels. Come on, forget with me. Relax."

"Is this a trick?"

"Come here."

"This is a trick, I know it."

Only if you want to be duped. It's all up to you. Try to hang on, remember what minds can produce. Remember that you're not you. You're nothing, everything.

Who's that? Who the hell is in my head? Atman, is that you? Or Kvino? Kvino?

"Kvino!"

"Right here. Or kind of here because you're not sure. Look over here."

When I rotate so I'm facing a glittering web of lavender and puce points of strobes I see him waving at me but he's very indistinct. Instead a robustly colored Bear B. streaks in front of him with a metallic *swoosh* and leans to kiss him with tonguing strokes that cover his face. Her body undulates into his while her tongue moves over him and makes him disappear. She erases him with her tongue. A glimpse, shards of shimmering images of her head thrown back in a convulsive reflex of fulfillment. And I want it to be me.

I know I am lost now.

TWENTY NINE

Forced Typeover

"Inquisitor? You fell asleep."

"Did I? Or was I dead to the world, as they say? Dead to this world but awake in another."

"What?"

"Some of us can do that and you know it. Be aware of our dreams.

Beautiful dreamer open your eyes...

You're really living, you wear a disguise.

Some of us can control where we are and what we do all the time, once you've reached a certain level. Don't you remember that all of a sudden? Have you slipped out of your awareness back into limitation, Gil?"

"I'm all right. I just forgot for a time."

"You were reborn?"

"A few words ago, and died quickly in a hut that swarmed with huge green flies before the body was put out into withering heat. I'm back now, content."

"And what did you learn?"

"Grief is terrible for us all even when we know, like those brief parents of mine did, that I was better off dead away from all they couldn't give me. At least this time I was better dead but that's because I'm so advanced. Someone else would have needed to go through those sufferings in a life. So I learned what I had to, wanted to. They learned anguish and I learned to give it, see its effects, and go away."

"Good for you."

"They had to understand the concept of giving up, that they can't possess another's existence, not even for love. Their love and need for the infant are not binders, and although I left them brutal emptiness my death is better than their love because it is change. They had to learn that."

"Guess so."

"What about you? Don't you need to go back?"

"Not right away. I haven't noticed any copulating pair yet that would mean something to what I need to know. No parents I could choose appeal to me."

"You might try anyway and then see what it's like to murder them."

"Do I need to learn about that? I've done it already you know."

"Plenty of killing in those Inquisitions, that's right. But maybe you want to interfere with the cat, the one she thinks she murdered."

"But she might still do it, Gil. It's both alive and dead now but in two places, at least two places. And so is she."

"Us more than her, for that matter."

"Matter it isn't, but you're right. That's why those machines they're using for their virtual this and virtual that only recapitulate eternal consciousness. In those artificial worlds there are no unsupervised areas, really, just like every being is always and everywhere supervised by the essence— our *selves*. When we call it religion it's like Buddhism but when we see it as parallel or simultaneous realities it's, let's see, it's Philip Dick, right?"

"And so many others."

"Aren't we all."

The black cat whose fur is luxurious walks away from the conversation because she's heard it all before. She just doesn't remember it now. Right now.

In the thin but solid blackness that enfolds glowing particles and streaking lights I see the being who I think I have murdered is alive and sitting in a graph-lined chair. I'm not afraid and I reach out to a node that is orangey-green where I wave in spatial coordinates directly to the Nets. It does not take long for two opaque capsules of light to glide up and surround each of us for transfers to where I have specified. Almost instantly we're both magnetically reorganized in my cell in the gargan-City. Home.

"Evet! NO!"

Kvino's voice screams off the transparent wall shields although I can't see him. The room fills with a stinging vapor and I take Schrödinger in my arms and hold her tightly. Sirens ping off the windows, Police Units screaming their lightning arrival. I back away and realize from what I can see through the stupefying vapor that the windows are different. They're not mine. This is Mary Sevenforty's cube. The cat shudders against me and I can hear Mary's daughter laughing from somewhere close by.

"Get out! Get out!"

I have been before. I've done this before. It seems I have walked on a rubbery web and everything has vibrated, reverberated me back here again before the daughter and the cat are found murdered.

The aroma of sex just completed with a woman clings to me. Was the one in the bedroom with me when all this started with the murders Bear B.? Or did she do it with me now only to recreate it? Somehow I don't think so and if it was her that other time that I'm reliving now then it was all planned. It had to have been planned. By me, like Atman says? It seems I was set-up instead. Like the plan came from somewhere and someone else, but who? And even if that's true Travelers would say that I allowed it, wanted it, needed to learn something from it.

"Why did you give them data points?" Kvino's voice sounds upset through the fog. "Why did you do it? They'll find you."

"I don't know, didn't think. I wanted to be with her. But I need to sleep."

"Get out! The hill, remember the hill. The snail! See it, Evet. Remember the flowers, the weed, the stem. Feel it now before the vapor takes you out. Feel the—"

Joyous air that moves lightly against mucousy eyes and does not even disturb the frail stalks beneath. The sky is infinite above me, around me. Nectar is an exhilarant whose scent electrifies my body and draws me closer, waves of endeavor toward attainment. Sweet reward.

Be aware you are dreaming. Right now. You are dreaming and you think it is real. Everything is equally a dream and there is no line between life and death.

When you learn how to control what you think are dreams and you dream lucidly then you will control what you think is real too. You'll see that all this is nothing. What you are doing right now, you, this, is nothing. Empty. And you are really something else than what you have believed all along.

Memories of no limbs. Feelings of being Lilliputian in the world. A weird nightmare of transmutation enfolds me and swirls sighing, sparkling portraits around me. Blades of grass blown up as large as buildings, the corolla of a flower is a damp bog under me that stretches in all directions and its heavy aroma wafts upward in bands of thick color I can see resounding in the air. Undulating over the screaming yellow field with these bizarre sensations I am content. Beauty of scent and sound and touch, immensity of satisfaction. Simply content. Nothing is anything except now. Content.

"Kvino?"

I think I call to him although I have no mouth to speak. No lips. And I remember what Osiris said about each of us being or having been so many things in the universe at different times or places and we should remember it all. We should remember what it's like to inhabit other existences. We are only vessels, containers drawn like outlines around the essence of everything. What's outside is the same as what's inside. Break the outline by dying and we become the essence again until we form a boundary that traps some of the energy within it. And on and on. I remember he or she said that.

Is that what the shamans mean by shape shifting? Reformulate yourself by changing your boundaries to enclose the essence in a new form, that's all. That's all.

You can do it.

"Atman, is that you?"

"You're almost there. Don't lose concentration now. Know what you're doing."

"Kvino!"

"Don't be afraid," I think he says as he reaches down.

I see diligent attention worn on every line in his face like giant crevices. His fingers gently close around this thing that feels like me. A softness I can't comprehend presses around me and then suddenly bears me upward with blinding speed that makes me sick. I shrivel, try to withdraw into my cool chambered darkness. Withdraw, sick and scared, squeeze inside my bony shell to protect myself against this nauseating

266

ascent and the booming vibrations of his voice that reverberate through me.

Help!

"Don't worry, I've got you."

That's what's killing me. Stop it! Put me down!

"Evet? Is it really you?"

Gigantic eyes surrounded by ponderous curved hairy cables waver before me, peer into my privacy. When he blinks the currents of air are cold and I feel my boneless carcass shudder.

"I'll put you down over here."

And now Schrödinger is in my arms and I'm curled around her like a fetus. *What a dream I had,* is my first thought. What an imagination, so real, but only imagination.

"That's what anything is. And you still have to run somewhere because they'll track you."

"Atman? Is that you?" I say at the image beginning to harden into shape next to Kvino.

"Are you all right?" he says.

"I dreamt about you, really odd things. Like I was a snail and you saved me. You were so huge, incredible."

Kvino and Atman look from me to each other and I realize they're holding hands. How long has this been going on?

"Don't you remember what happened? Your cat there, the Police ambushing you at your cube?"

"Wasn't that part of my dream?"

"It happened, I think," Kvino says.

"But it's still a dream only she doesn't want to know it all yet. Put together all the parts to save yourself, Evet, or else this leakage of other times and places and beings will kill you and you'll have to start at the beginning again and do it all over. You have to get control. Let yourself know and you'll be all right."

267

I remember now how Bear B. loved me then set a trap for me with a lush snare. She almost took me with her elusive love. She said ideas that can't be traced or accounted for is my crime. But if it's only my imagination, so what? The murders are a problem, though, deaths she says I wanted and I accomplished with my weird meditations on failure, retributions for my lack of success. The pain of failure always muttered in barely intelligible laughter in my ears and came from behind me. Pain of lack, pain of need, pain of jealousy, pain of greed...of course it would rhyme. It hinges full circle on itself like a demon so vain it devours its own tail. Retribution.

I am that fiend, a monstrosity. If I face my sins I will wither from them, disappear in a fume of shame. If in my *bardo* I see the blood torments I have heaped on envisioned enemies I will want to escape however I can. Rebirth as a deformed thing unable to see another of its kind without provoking revulsion. That would be my reimbursement for how I have lived. It is the restitution for seeking fame, a lifetime begging in the streets.

Change it.

I dreamed I was different. Something has changed. There was that beautiful woman they call Mary who I realize I saw in what I thought was a simulation from Bear B. Sweltering desert, acrid human smells and a carnival of miracles she presided over juggling brains and dogs and making someone who was dead jump down from where they had hung him amid applause from all those women in long dresses, dust covering their hems. But she resembles the one burned in the subway, too, the hag with too much power and a magnificent reliquary for her remains. I have dreamed all these things in recurrent cycles ever since I can remember. But I remember them only now after all these years, so many times of visiting and revisiting these people and the places where they live.

They are other worlds I live in because they can't be anything else. They're not dreams and if they are, then dreams are not simple anymore. I know too much. That's the crime, always has been, knowing too much.

The myth of Isis became so real to the people of Egypt that they came to regard her very intimately indeed, and fully believed that she had once been a veritable woman. In a more allegorical manner she was of course the great feminine fructifier of the soil. She was also a powerful enchantress, as it shown by the number of deities and human beings whom she rescued from death. Words of great and compelling power were hers... It is not necessary in this place to trace her worship into Greece, Rome, and Western Europe, where it became greatly degraded from its pristine purity. The dignified worship of the great mother took on under European auspices an orgiastic character which appealed to the false mystic of Greece, Rome, Gaul, and Britain just as it does to-day to his Transatlantic or Parisian prototype. But the strength of the cult in the country of its origin is evinced by the circumstances that it was not finally deserted until the middle of the fifth century A.D.

Spence

THIRTY

The Universe Begins To Look More Like A Great Thought Than A Great Machine.
Jeans

"When people remember me fondly or pray for me after I move into the *bardo* it really is immensely helpful. It comes like enchanting music that is at first barely hearable. Although you're considered dead to the world you catch portions now and then under the howling of your sores and the seething and raving of maniacal friends, family and enemies you trudge among. Terrifying. You're so panicked at their leaping onto your back and gnawing your brittle flimsy flesh. The pain of your mutilation is beyond comprehension. Ineffable. Every fright insignificant or profound rends at you and you have to try to move past them screaming and quaking as you go, your legs dead weights that will not move to your will like in a dream. Instead your will is all around you just like in a dream, the horrors that you smell and feel and taste are everything you have ever desired. Small decreases in the torment come from the luminescence of those few good acts you've done and are cool delicious air like the thoughts of those still living

270

that reach you in glorious music growing slightly louder. If there is enough of this hope, this noble *karma*, you have the strength to accept the misery of your existence and keep your eyes up."

"That's important. At those times of terror I try to recognize myself, although it's hard, and remember that I shouldn't fear the ferocity of the hateful ones because after all they're my own projections."

"Our own projections, Gil, true. And with our own will we can keep our gaze turned upward."

"But you've looked down."

"A few times. I made the choice. Remember once I was an Inquisitor and not even with intensity, a mediocre murderer is all I was. Luckily I can't feel the humiliation in its stupefying force anymore."

"You've gone beyond."

"Haven't we all, Gil?"

"Sometimes after I've passed the banked curve I look straight ahead through the atrocities and frenzied searchlights that blind me so I can come back as another animal. Because I've never hunted or hurt them it's always a pleasant existence for me. So unfettered and lavish with being able to fly or live an entire life slipping through cold fast streams. What pleasures. Well, sometimes. But usually I choose to replay the hag's soul with advancements I've learned."

Mary has heard it all before so she turns away and laughs radiantly with the crowd. She is so adept in her performance that they are hanging on her every word and are enchanted by the skills of her hands. Sybelle stands to one side tasting and smelling the mood of the people while Agnes supervises the collection of donations and makes sure the other Beguines are posted in strategic places. If Churchmen appear they must pretend that Mary isn't really as powerful as she has become or they have to pretend she is working her miracles as a saint within their Church so they think they're getting the credit for it. But she's beginning to find this tiresome and wants truthful publicity for her new order of reality. She's no magician. She can absolutely create anything she wants, from nothing.

"And now let's see whose heart it is I have here inside me, under my control."

She puts down the dogs she's been juggling while they're still singing, one of them not too gently who glares at her. Then Mary strides into the crowd.

"Is it yours? Or you, sir? How about this one?"

Mary stops in front of a girl with flawless skin and a shocking brightness in blue eyes that seem somehow uninhabited. She slowly caresses her face with her hands, lingering. The girl doesn't move, doesn't even blink while Mary serenades her in a loud voice and caresses her. Finally Mary breathes into her face.

"Tell me where you are."

"It's dark," the girl whispers into the hush of the crowd.

"What else?"

"I don't know."

"Cold or hot?"

When the girl does not answer Mary takes her in her arms. She begins to dance slowly, the girl's body flowing with hers although her face and eyes show nothing of the movement. There is still that look of beatific vacancy, blissful ignorance.

"Tell me what you feel," Mary's lips caress her ear. "Tell me."

"Cold," she whispers and the crowd rustles closer. "Cold and dark. Wet."

Everyone watches her shudder in Mary's arms. Then they are distracted by the sharp *CLACK CLACK* of a dowel striking against the side of the large crock Metza is hitting vehemently. She had taken it from where it was hidden in the back of the wagon that looks like it belongs to a circus. The girl spasms and shrinks, clutches her head every time the sound rings out. And when Metza takes the lid off the crude brightly colored pot the girl moans and buries her head in her arms to cover her eyes like she's being blinded by a bright light.

"See," Mary skips over to the frowning Metza. "She is not there where we danced but really here. Here!"

She takes the brain from the crock and flips it in the air. Catching it behind her back, she lifts her long dress to toss it under one leg and snatch it deftly with one hand. Everyone whistles and applauds. The girl spins and dips, her head bouncing in the air to mimic the acrobatics of the brain. Mary rolls it in both hands, rebounds it off her biceps and the girl arches and flips as if hauled by a chain fixed to the top of her head. A dancing doll manipulated by a force that is invisible. Finally, dizzy, she tumbles to the ground and vomits.

"Thank you, thank you."

Mary pirouettes to the gleefully painted wagon and drops the brain into the gaudy crock that Metza covers quickly. Then she goes back to take the girl by the hands and lift her to her feet. All this is amid wild appreciation by the audience, loudly expressed with nearly chaotic energy.

"I give you back to your own world now, dear. No more damp and dark vat. See the cosmos here constructed by all of us instead of my art alone? But isn't it amazing how I could limit your senses and all that you know through my will alone? Isn't it?"

"I guess..."

The girl is slow and dazed. It's like she's waking up from a dream.

"Tell your friends!"

273

Mary calls out as part of the crowd engulfs the girl to take her away and bombard her with a swarm of questions and gestures. The rest of the audience rushes Mary who is quickly protected by a circle of Beguines and the two dogs. People demand miracles. Blind, maimed, sick with moist sores of mysterious origin, all are thrust at her. They are pushed forward by the overwrought enthusiasm and the impatience of those far back in the pack. They have seen her change the world for one person, why not for them all?

"Holy saint among us!"

"Help me, Saint Mary, who are so blessed."

"Just talented really," Agnes says to no one as she takes donations for the new saint.

"Save us from our misery!"

"Haven't you seen what I did? There are other worlds and we create all of them ourselves. All that you see comes from our own awareness. We could change what we're doing right now if we wanted to. And if we believe we can."

Sybelle is trembling because this is blasphemy and she knows that sooner of later they're all gong to be burned alive for it. She inhabits a different reality every day of her life and it never saved her from abuse because no one else believed in what she heard and smelled and felt in her worlds. Intention is the key. Intention and confidence in it. These people will never change their minds about what they see because they see only with their eyes. If they could taste colors like she does, hear fragrance perforate their skin, maybe then they might know. Maybe then.

"We are the authors of awareness," Mary goes on. "You saw the heart of the girl in the container that lived only as I decided that it should. I am adept at what will be called 'nonlocality,' which is control from a distance, control from my mind. And I am all of us. I am the scientist who is really an

274

artist who keeps your interpreter of stimuli in a vat, giving it all sensations to decode. We are all like that. We are the brains kept in vats and we are the keepers as well."

"What did she say?" a man crosses himself and nudges a companion.

"It's not for us to understand saints."

"But it is!" Mary rushes the man and grabs him, drops him to his knees. "You can understand and you should, damn it. You have to try!"

Agnes smiles as spaciously as she's capable of while she pulls Mary's hands off the man's throat to keep her from strangling him. Still smiling, she leads the saint away. She thanks the crowd and tells them there will be more marvels at the next show. People are shouting for miracles now, though. When they don't get them they turn ugly. They clamor their doubts about the stories they've heard about her taking the dead man from a cross and making him live again. This is not good, so Agnes retreats from the crowd. She twists Mary's wrist behind her back to keep the saint from shouting back at them. Then Agnes says in a huge voice the crowd should nail someone up and Mary will return after lunch to take him down without touching him.

"Who should we hang?"

The crowd quiets. They focus on Agnes.

"Anyone, dear followers. Blessed Mary here can do it with anyone. Just another example of remote control without machines. There will be the new reality of dreams, this afternoon. Tell your friends. Thank you very much."

Dreaming is what I'm doing in all of this but I wonder if it is so simple, so dismissible as that. Nothing but a dream. *Merrily, merrily, merrily, merrily, life is but a dream! Row, row, row your boat gently down the stream...* Stream of life, stream of consciousness. Who is this "I" who's wondering what "I" am thinking? There has to be another level.

"Go and kiss her, use your tongue on the one who is dark and enchanting," Bear B.'s Holo double is partially filled with color that looks like static.

"How did you find me?"

I don't know why I say that to the wavering image. I have no idea where I am.

"I haven't. I'm beaming a wideband general freq continuously hoping you would scan it wherever you are. Bored? Kiss her."

"She's a nun."

"But there is no order. She doesn't have one that the Police of her place recognize. Beguines are tolerated because they pay their own way. Finances are always important. Then again," the image pauses to transmit a low voltage feeling that's like an embrace. "There is really no order like you think you know it. Whatever there is, you impose. See, now you're making me say it and you can't really believe someone like me would do that."

"It's a trick."

"Truth is stranger than, what? There is nothing but truth. Everything is the same, all one."

"You sound like Bruce Atman."

"Why not? You're changing your mind, aren't you? You perceive the world differently because of the compartments of you that are opening up, breaking down with all that has happened to you. You have to."

"This desert, these women with this carnival act of miracles and talking dogs. It's good VirtReal that comes from you Police, that's all. I told you before it means nothing to me."

"You did not tell me before. That's your explanation for trying to fit this into your existing pattern of the world so you call it a manufacture of CySpace, but it's part of you and you're part of it. It goes on because of you, all of this does. There is no fiction. Everything you think, everything you write is real."

"Very funny."

"That's how you committed murder."

"Shut up."

"Find your place in the myth as you see it here. Look at those women in the long dresses, dust on their hems. Which one is you? Your mother? She's there in the story because you're part of the myth as you hear it. The cat is there, your daughter, and when you are Isis she helps you to protect the dismembered parts of your brother who is your husband. We are all part of the myth. We play different roles over and over and over again."

"That's impossible."

"Can matter ever be created or destroyed? No, it only changes form. We just forget that it does. In CySpace nets we make with our machines we think are God because we can know every quark and boson. We think we can program every alternative that's possible to interact with. But in real consciousness we actually do know absolutely everything, but we forget it all for a while so that we can live again. Death means we're alive in our grander consciousness. Living means we're dead to our memory of that consciousness."

"Another *koan*? Death means life and living means we're dead? Leave me alone, will you."

"Do you know what living is? We live so that we can discover the joys of experience anew. Expectation. Be curious, discover love and hate and sex and chemistry and walking and flying and crying and learn again. Learn! Learn more each time

277

we live. Don't you get it, how fabulous that is? It's the great joy of the unknown, the ecstasy of surprise in experience each day. It's enlivening, it's exciting when we forget who we are like you've forgotten which one of those Beguines you are. Or are you the hag now, the one I'll burn at the stake in what we think is later on when I'm the Inquisitor?"

Let me die now. I wish I could say the words instead of thinking them but I'm so terrified that I'm paralyzed. This can't be the delight of experience this double of Bear B. is talking about.

"Go with those women and find out all over again," she smiles and fades away.

It must be the horrors of the *bardo* they told me about. The frenzy of demons and blinding lights in the gap when you die, the chaos between one life and the next.

"Look, here comes that famous artist."

"All the way from the Crusades. The silver and precious gems on the coach stun you with their luster."

"I wonder who they belonged to before?"

"Don't ask. Just shout *huzzahs* and maybe we'll get some coins thrown at us. After all, weren't you her brother?"

THIRTY ONE

Hard Return Display Character

"Look at that. You'd think the artist was an Essene come down from the caves."

"Why?"

"Didn't you see when they carried her past? She's asleep through all this commotion over her, and you know how Essenes feel about sleep."

"No," I say.

"But you're one of us," the woman is suspicious. "Everyone knows sleep is like a little death. It's very mysterious, anyone can see that. And who knows if you're going to come alive again? Those Essenes never go to sleep unless they're prepared to die so every day they tie up all their affairs, quarrels, settle their debts. If they wake up the next morning then what a miraculous surprise it is and everything is exciting to them."

"I guess it would be."

"It's supposed to be, don't you know that? You are one of us, aren't you? Everyone is lately. But I don't know you."

Cheers heave from a crowd around the artist and I see a hand raised. The shadow of a chain coils around fingers, slithers down a bronzed arm. Another hand is raised with a provocative jeweled box overdone with gold filigree. The sight of it silences the crowd. Everyone falls to their knees. I'm on my knees too although I don't remember how I got there. It's as if I'm attached to this horde by invisible threads, a marionette under distant control.

"It's like a fox's tail, intertwined," someone says.

"It reminds me of something."

"A foxtail, idiot."

"But something else... my life."

The Beguines in the long dusty dresses who I've overheard say these things start to punch one another. They scuffle like adolescent boys, yelling: *Tail! No, life!* It's interspersed with their blows. They jostle against me and seem to try to include me in the argument. One of them is one of the mothers of the dogs and the other is the attractive woman who beat on the vat that held the girl's brain. She's the one Bear B.'s duplicate urged me to fondle. I have to admit she possesses and earthy allure so organically seductive that to ignore her would be somehow like refusing nourishment. I imagine intimacy with her will be raw and lewd and something I will not want to acknowledge later. But it will be there somewhere in my memory and that will give it continued life. I'll recognize it even if I don't admit it.

"Let me help you," I say when she's pushed into my arms.

"How? The chain is my life no matter what she says. Petrissa and her will never understand the principles of Mary the Slut."

"What do you mean?"

"Ask her. Ask the artist," Metza says, rubbing against my leg with hers.

I feel her pushing at me, urging me toward the artist with hands that feel like paws and are hot as caressing embers. But at the same time her eyes make me want to stay. The throng parts as I move and I don't even think it's odd. Some people reach out to touch me, and although they act with respect I realize that I'm not wearing anything and I can feel their hands on my skin. Fingers probe at me, palms slide over my nakedness. I recognize the sensations. And recognizing means that—

"Hello again, my friend, my teacher."

The artist speaks to me, but she does it without moving her lips so I look for the mannequin through which she throws her voice. I think that almost-saint Mary taught her ventriloquism as part of this carnival act of hers.

"You don't remember me, do you? But how could you not? I'm famous. My works are famous like yours never could be. Aren't you envious? Look at all the attention for me, for what I can produce?"

She thrusts her hands I the air again and awe-struck murmurs rush through the crowd like a fire feeding parched beach grass. Everyone is on his or her knees again, or still, I can't tell which. I see Blessed Mary laughing and whispering behind her hands with her friends who shake their heads in a pitying way at the spectacle. Then they return to preparing her like a prizefighter for the next miracle. They rub the muscles of her arms and legs, towel her brow and neck of sweat, give her water to rinse her mouth and spit again. But this regimen of readying rouses the famous Sophia's anger.

"They waste my love, force its coolness to die in the sand."

She is seething under her breath so only I can hear her. Everyone else is bowing and murmuring, reaching out to try to steal the art, or else shading their eyes to see it better if they're too far back in the throng.

"It's only water," I say and she hits me hard in the face, "Hey!"

"You don't know what's good. You have no taste. And you're jealous, a nobody."

Look for your part in the story. You are part of the myth as you hear it. And you are your own mother, yes. Or are you more comfortable saying that you are your own author. Yes? Good.

"Wait a minute," I say. "You're not any different from me. I've wanted success like yours but look at you, you're narrow and obnoxious. I was that way too."

"But you have no excuse. Your products aren't revered. Your droppings stink, mine smell good."

"Who decided that?"

"They did, the public. And the Church that made me all I am today."

"You mean this Mary?"

"Kind of. But I got my start from the other Marys in the real Church so I owe them. I work for them both, they both pay me, spread my fame. That other one, little Sybelle the painter, she only works for this new reality of the new almost-saint Mary but she's very nervous about it. She and my brother think they're going to die any minute now so they're always ready for it. Never do a wrong thing, like every day is their last."

Now Sophia is smiling. She dangles the elegant chain above the heads of her admirers who gasp and grab for it but she yanks it away.

"You mean," I find I'm speaking without thinking now and I'm aware of the lack of preparation. Like remote control, but from where? "You mean what has made your fame is their thoughts, nothing but what they think of you. A giant advertising scheme that has succeeded is what makes all this real for you and it's the insubstance of thoughts that produces this tangible 'reality' of your products. But I'm here to say your dropping do stink and when enough people believe me the odor will be terrible."

"Cheater cheater, pumpkin eater!"

"I could wipe you out with my will because you're only my creation. Then again, I guess I'm part of yours because we're all interdependent. Equal. And somehow you're really me."

"Witch!"

The crowd goes silent at this. As I look around I see Sybelle running away with her hands clapped over her mouth. But I can't stop myself.

"Try to understand this. Listen to me. Consciousness moves actively in what we call the real world. It makes the world, for chrissakes. What we're aware of and how we're aware of it is inseparable from the physical universe."

"Burn her!"

"Would you listen? Just listen to me. Quantum physicists, or the field of quantum mechanics will show biogravitons are responsible for the structure of matter and we control these things with our awareness. Like magnets making shapes of iron filings with their fields, consciousness participates in making the shape of the universe we know.

I glance movement at the corner of my eye and I try to see where Mary has gone. The crowd rushes to one side and above their heads sways a bulky timber with a crossbeam. The festival atmosphere revives and the Beguines laugh and circle the group, skipping and clapping. More and more people throng to the place now and to get a better view some climb into the scraggly fig trees that hover on the heat. I have lived this simulation before.

"Another miracle," Agnes quells the din. "Done by Mary."

Everyone has been waiting for this. Cheers fly up like surprised pigeons and people fall back. The phenomenon that has been brewing froths over into shrieks of wonder. People run from all direction to get a look. In the deserted center of attention stands a bloodied man in front of a swirling cone of rainbow colors that are not unlike the garish paintings on the wagon that holds the crock with the brain. I can hear the crowd in a raucous clatter of sounds. I find I feel a puzzling affinity for this orangey-green and amethyst mélange.

"He lives again!"

"Because of her, the saint."

"But he lives! That's what's important."

"No, she is!"

The dogs begin to snarl, circling the crowd they snap at anyone who tries to escape from the commotion that turns ugly in an instant. The Beguines argue with people over what is more important, the agent of the miracle or the recipient of it. Unfortunately, that man with all the blood is actively lobbying on his own behalf, squeezing his wounds to make them worse and contending he's the one who has come back from being dead so many times that he should be the one who is the real miracle. That's not entirely true because, really, he's been brought back by her. It's an indecent scene for a saint to endure. But the almost saint Mary isn't here and I look around, laughing as if I'm her, suddenly confident and hardy the way she is.

Like a darting flame, laughing, I dare the impossible and survive but I survive because I choose to leave. And suddenly the shock waves of a speeding train just passed careen around me and paper and dirt from the subway eddy in filthy little tornadoes up and down the dark platform. But now I can almost see the other tracks through the arches of the cement columns, the ones that cross these at a perfect right angle.

"Why have you come back here?" I say to Mary who is smoking a cigarette, leaning against a steel girder.

"Why not? We can observe from here, the crossroads instead of the cross. Let him have it, the earthy control and all the politics that go with it."

"You're giving up our fame? Your new reality? What about the brain in the vat whose sensations you control?"

"Yes, so?"

"You're powerful, you can win. Don't give up now." I find I'm very upset.

"Observe, dear, be detached," she blows a smoke ring. "You're competitive in a race that's not being run. It's a dream even though it seems real to you. Let him have his day for a few centuries, it doesn't matter. The concept of him is already cemented in people's minds. Before we're born we carry the capabilities of the entire universe, of all our possibilities as energies. And also before we're born we begin to be conditioned in the womb. We hear words, begin to recognize sounds, movements, and all this teaches us what we should perceive the world to be once we pop into it. We recognize it when we first see it. See, our consciousness is already limited so we all need to evolve."

"You have. And you have power for chrissakes. You work miracles! Why don't you just change people's minds? Put an end to all this disgusting killing and maiming, this ugly human desire to hurt other beings and things in the world. My god, what's wrong with you? You have the talent to do good, to transform the horrific selfishness we all strive for. You can change how we think about the world and that means changing the world to a different construction from all these objects and puny people learning life after life how stupid they are so they can inch forward, inch forward, toward seeing we create everything. We create everything there is, all this absorption we have in ourselves and petty things. I mean look at it, that's what the awareness of the world produces now. Do something!"

"You're hyperventilating."

She has a rope in her hands and starts to tie me to the girder she's vacated. She's wearing a scuffed white motorcycle jacket I hadn't noticed before.

"You know I don't know why you're yelling at me, Evet, or whoever you are. You're no different than I. Remember? Remember in the crowd just now for a while they saw you as me, touched you. You recognized it. So why don't you change things, dear? After all, you have the power just like me. Start by changing yourself, because you know that phylogeny will recapitulate ontogeny. I guess I'm going to have to torture you to make you realize it," she sighs in a fake way. "A mind is a wonderful thing to change."

There is a blinking light that rises from behind her shoulder like a white-hot sun. Or is it moonrise, reflecting light from me? The rustle of her gown frightens me when she turns around, stands up and unfolds herself like a giant from where she has been bent, tying my feet to the pole. I am so afraid that I tremble and stretch the ropes tight into my flesh. Breathing is like drowning; my lungs expand with cement and not deflate. Then all is blackness and there is only a circle of radiance in the distance, white light that promises comfort, coolness. But it's so far away, the end of a tunnel where the screams that sound like my own voice cascade off the walls.

"It's your own projections, your own *karma*. It's all what you've learned through the conditioning of society. Come on, white light? Tunnel? Don't make me laugh."

"Kvino!"

286

"Yes, and Atman too. Don't be afraid, what you see is what you make. You can change it," two synchronous voices say.

"You can control this, like a dream. Remember? Like all those Sims you wrote. You are the author. You don't know you've been dreaming until you wake up. Some never know this is a dream until they wake in dying and death."

"Oh no, I'm already dead!"

"So? You know that. You saw it and thought it was a dream.

"NO!"

"Calm down. It's just transubstantiation, done by your friend Mary."

"But it's real."

"Real is what our neurons have competed for, the pathways that have been used over and over again and so they become the sensations that are commonly fired. It doesn't mean that's reality, it's what our conditioning leads us to see, feel, hear, trust, believe."

"Oh for chrissakes!"

"Him too. A reified concept accomplished by neurological connections. But we are capable of more than that. We are him and each other. We are all energy that is impermanent, not separate egos but a collection of elements."

I'm thinking, *I hate you.* But why should this flare in me in the face of goodness?

Hail Mary, mother of idiots...

Bear B. laughs and shatters the darkness. She melts the orb of pure light that was down that tunnel.

I wonder what advancements that witchy looking woman I see in the mirror is talking about and to whom. It seems as though I just got here to this arid place and I thought my Schrödinger was with me in my arms but she's not anymore.

I'm dreaming this, I think. And I'm going to have to do something over again.

And again.

THIRTY TWO

In Truth, There Exists Only The Perceptual Flow...Of Flashes Of Force.
David-Neel

"Some Travelers died during the meditation," Atman says. "Look at their smiles. Their decision to go beyond makes them content, omniscient."

"Did they die from burning out brain cells or something while they were keeping Evet safe?"

"They chose to transubstantiate and turn themselves into energy again. They learned from her and everything she lived that she thought were only dreams, but she dreamed with lucidity so that they could do it themselves. And because of it all of us have evolved a little, inched forward."

They watch the bodies, stiff and weightless, being passed from one Traveler to another to a receptacle where a rollicking flame consumes each one in an instantaneous *WHOOSH*. The black cat walks around and around singing a cheerful tune that may have Latin lyrics or those from some other language that is not quite comprehensible. She wears a handsome tuxedo and a gold locket around her neck that is magnificent and contains the picture of a dark woman. Now and then she walks away from the festival of the burning bodies and tends to what seems to be Rudolphe's corpse, curled in a doorway. She fusses over him, plumping a checked pillow under his head. He remains motionless except for blood that oozes now and then from the sores on his body, his stumps of fingers and toes, his ears. She tends to him because he is alive.

"His *bardo*," she might say now and then.

Every time this happens she helps to break the habit field, the force of conditioning to this unreal reality. Atman tells Kvino this as he caresses him. He repeats to him that everything comes from us, the world and our judgments of it.

"Do you know what the Buddha said, the one I gave to Evet?" Atman says. "He said, 'we are what we think. All that we are arises through our thoughts. With our thoughts we create the world.' It makes SensSims seem primitive by comparison. Technological toys."

"What happened to Evet? Where is she? What's happening to her while you Travelers burn your dead?"

"Our hero, Evet? She's here, dreaming and living at the same time like all of us. Only now she knows it most of the time."

"What does that mean?"

Listen to me!

"Did you hear that, Atman?"

"Smelled it. Didn't you?"

"You mean all those stories really made a difference to us? We didn't just experience them, they changed us," Kvino embraces Atman and turns away. "Where is she?"

Collect what will become my ashes. Make me an icon and then do not revere me. There is no me, only us.

"That's right, come here baby," Bear B. loops her arm in hers and walks like they are an oldfashion bride and groom

290

into the middle of the arena high above the gargan-City. There are multitudes watching from screens that can't be seen.

"You look fabulous. Good enough to execute. We're all glad you came back to take your punishment. Killing your daughter and intending to kill your mother are things you have to pay for because the rest of us, we all think so. Did I tell you that you're beautiful?"

Bear B. is radiant for her, quivers like a schoolgirl with first love. Gazing into those delicate eyes that could belong to a doe she feels everyone watching her, not in an intrusive way but glances on their way to somewhere else. She would make love to her there in the center of the neon coliseum but there is not time. Later, she thinks to herself, later she will replay those brazen things they have done already. And the thought triggers Bear B.'s artificial nervous system implants and she nearly swoons. The hero's arms stops her, caresses her with burning strokes so that she weeps from the joy of her touch.

"I wish I didn't have to kill you."

Laughter like chimes ringing far out at sea covers the thick light in the place. Bear B. shudders and would like to fall down but the weaponry on her wrists *whirs* into action. The gyroscopic effect keeps her upright. The only thing on which she leans heavily is the idea of a lover.

Incineration by electrocution accomplished by a magnetic chemical field. Bear B. waits for a signal to press the nanodot on her wristlet. There seems to be a murmur of excitement in the place, an aroma of charred flesh although nothing yet has happened. And although there is only a memory of her standing there, Evet the hero had submitted herself to die. Perhaps they have already taken her brain into a sleek chamber where they will try to discover what went wrong, what made her too unique. They will study it to uncover the neural connections that have made her inner world richer than the external one. It will not matter because they will not be able to understand anyway. Travelers have already taken her essence, ingested it and spread it among them. Each of them glows with it. They shimmer partway between this realm and the others that are so much more important. By this time Kvino and Atman have become one.

How?

How do you think, dummy? Pay attention.

The Sufis say that thought is inseparable from perception and it shapes the fabric of our lives. So how do you think it happened?

From sex? No wait, by recognizing the fusion of...them? They're the same. We're all the same. Right?

Whatever you think. See how it changes your life to think that all this is a dream and we are all the same, empty. Treat all things like they are appearances in a dream and you'll be happy.

"Where's Evet?"

Happy.

Novices who are training themselves according to the methods of the Secret Teachings, are sometimes advised to exercise themselves in creating mentally around themselves an environment completely different from that which is considered real. For example, seated in their room, they conjure up a forest. If the exercise is successful they will no longer be conscious of the objects around them which will have given place to trees, copses, and they will travel through the forest feeling all the sensations usual to those who move in the woods.

The usefulness of such exercises is to lead the novice to understand the superficial nature of our

292

sensations and perceptions, since they can be caused by things which we consider unreal...

The relative world is close to the imaginary world because, as has been said, error and illusion dominate it. That which appears to us as round may, in fact, be square, and so on...

The awakening from the dream in which we are involved and which we continue to live even while being more or less clearly conscious that we dream, will this awakening lead us to another world? Will it not rather consist in the perception of the underlying reality in the world in which we find ourselves?

David-Neel

THE END...

Sources

Chapter 3, p 16
WordPerfect, "Help File." Orem, Utah: WordPerfect Corp., 1989
p 25
L. Spence, Myths and Legends of Ancient Egypt (Limited 'Folklore edition) Boston: Nickerson & Co. 1914, p.5

Chapter 4, p 26
WordPerfect, *op. cit.*

Chapter 5, p 39
Michel de Montaigne, "Of the inconstancy of our actions," in The Essays of Michel de Montaigne (v.2) ed. W.C. Hazlitt. NY: A.L. Burt, 1892
p 48
Spence, *op. cit.*, pp 269-70

Chapter 6, p 49
WordPerfect, *op. cit.*

Chapter 7, p 55
Montaigne, "Of war horses, or destriers," *op. cit.* (v.1) p 319

p 61
Spence, *op. cit.*

Chapter 8, p 62
WordPerfect, *op. cit.*

Chapter 9, p 71
Pliny (in Montaigne), "That the mind hinders itself."
Montaigne, *op. cit.* (v.2) p 62
pp 79-80
Spence, *op. cit.*, p 273

Chapter 10, p 81
WordPerfect, *op. cit.*

Chapter 11, p 88
Montaigne, "Of judging of the death of another," *op. cit.*
(v 2) p 60
pp 96-97
Spence, *op. cit.*, p 283

Chapter 12, p 98
WordPerfect, *op. cit.*

Chapter 13, pp 116-117
Spence, *op. cit.*, pp 283-84, p 293

Chapter 14, p 118
WordPerfect, *op. cit.*

Chapter 15, p 129
Montaigne, "Of three good women," *op. cit.* (v 2) p 211

pp 133-134
Spence, *op. cit.*, pp 68-70

Chapter 16, p 135
WordPerfect, *op. cit.*
p 137
Bob Marley, "Song of Freedom," Uprising. NY: BMI Music, 1987

Chapter 17, pp 152-153
Spence, *op. cit.*, pp 174, 64, 80

Chapter 18, p 154
WordPerfect, *op. cit.*

Chapter 19, p 165
Montaigne, "That a man is soberly to judge of the divine ordinances," *op. cit.* (v 1) p 223
pp 173-174
Spence, *op. cit.*, pp 14-15

Chapter 20, p 175
WordPerfect, *op. cit.*
p 180
G. P. Landow, Hypertext: The convergence of contemporary theory and technology. Baltimore: Johns Hopkins University, 1992, p 58
M. Heim (in M. Benedikt), Cyberspace: First steps. Cambridge: MIT, 1992, p 72

Chapter 21, p 185
Montaigne, "Of experience," *op. cit.* (v 2) p 561

p 192

M. M. Waldrop, Complexity: The Emerging Science at the Edge of Order and Chaos. NY: Simon & Shuster, 1992, p 310

pp 192-193

Spence, *op. cit.*, p 271

Chapter 22, p 194

WordPerfect, *op. cit.*

Chapter 24, p 211

Ibid.

Chapter 25, p 228

A. Goswami, The Self-Aware Universe: How Consciousness Creates the Material World. NY: G.P. Putnam's, 1993

Chapter 26, p 234

Montaigne, "Of managing the will," op. cit., (v 2) p 500

p 235

J.F. Lyotard, The Postmodern Condition: A Report on Knowledge. Minneapolis: University of Minnesota, 1984, p 15. In G.P. Landow, op.cit., p 73

Chapter 27, p 244

WordPerfect, *op. cit.*

Chapter 28, pp 255 & 261

"The Heart Sutra"

Chapter 29, p 262

WordPerfect, *op. cit.*

p 269
Spence, *op. cit.*, p 230

Chapter 30, p 270
Sir James Jeans (1932), in M. Godwin, The Lucid Dreamer: A Waking Guide for the Traveler Between Worlds. NY: Simon & Shuster, 1994, p 186

Chapter 31, p 279
WordPerfect, *op. cit.*

Chapter 32, p 289
Alexandra David-Neel & Lama Yongden, The Secret Oral Teachings in Tibetan Buddhist Sects. San Francisco: City Lights, (1967) 1990, p 62
p 293
Ibid., pp 115, 122

Additional sources
W. Gibson, Mona Lisa Overdrive, NY: Random House, 1997 & Neuromancer, NY: Penguin,1986
A.R. Luria, The Mind of a Mnemonist (L. Solotaro, translator). NY: Ace Books (1911) 1968
Bertrand Russell, Mysticism and Logic. NY: Dover 2004